FATAL GAMES

Our nation's capitol reeks with the kingpins of politics and greasers of the corrupt system, but they could all take lessons from the new clients that Prich is asked to help. Rogers & Emory Development Company is a family-run computer game software enterprise which plays a real life game of financial intrigue wrapped within the enigma of murder and incest. Prich walks a tightrope as his father wishes to drop the inquiry while others are killing for fun and profit. Prich does a juggling act with his father, the dysfunctional family clients, a cop who is a good friend, and his sometime girl friend who is always justifiably suspicious and consistently jealous.

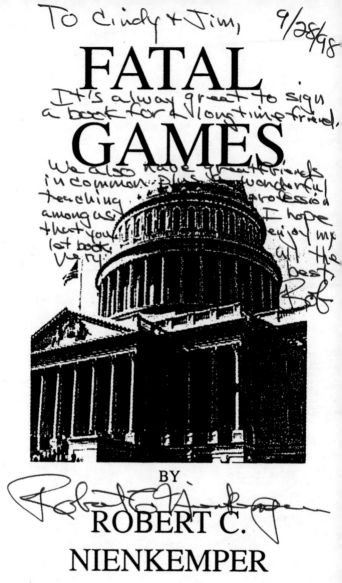

FATAL GAMES

To Cindy & Jim,   9/28/98

*It's alway great to sign
a book for a long time friend.*

*We also have great friends
in common. Plus a wonderful
teaching profession
among us. I hope
that you enjoy my
1st book. All the
Very best,*

BY

ROBERT C. NIENKEMPER

BRIARWOOD PUBLICATIONS INCORPORATED

Published by
Briarwood Publications
&
Sassy Cat Books, Incorporated
150 West College Street,
Rocky Mount, Virginia 24151

Sassy Cat Books is a trademark of Briarwood
Publications.

Manufactured in the United States of
America.

Printed by Briarwood Publications

ISBN 1-892614-00-6

This first novel and all that follow are dedicated to my life's partner, kind critic, big-hearted mentor, gentle soul, gifted editor, sailing first mate, unwavering supporter, most happy companion, cheerfully forgiving associate, extremely bright friend, wonderfully giving mother, warmly smiling face, love of my life, incredibly intelligent mate, count me lucky.....my beautiful wife, Mary Ann.

Chapter 1

Out in Left Field

Don't let anyone ever tell you, "What goes around doesn't come around." I can testify that you always seem to get repaid for your acts of brotherhood or dimwitted oversights. The recipient of my good will was Franky Angelino, a wickedly snickering good buddy of mine and a wonderfully incompetent stock picker. There's a story about our little burg that Franky, who was under the influence, went out walking in his neighborhood with his dog JD, which stands for Just Dog. The dog was sober and thought it was strange for his benefactor to be relieving himself on the same fire plug as he. The cop that brought them both home with this explanation completely failed to find any humor in the events. Neither did Franky's wife.

Truly, my yarn begins on a warm morning in early spring in the suburbs of Washington, DC...Bethesda-Chevy Chase, Maryland, to be exact. It's a wonderful hamlet tucked in among the snobs and the elite of this unique capitol metro. We haven't had too many of these sparkling days after a gloomy, damp winter. Ha, we aren't the murder capitol any longer. We're just the red ink and falling-bond-rating headquarters. Really now, that's some come down. We're only the junk bond metropolis now.

My name is Prich (for Prichard) Hale, and

I'm employed by my father to make covert and prudent inquiries for Hale & Son. My father, Winfred Hale, is an attorney, and I'm the son. I would prefer Hale & Hale as I'm also an attorney, but my father isn't very pleased with my legal prowess. My sister, Hattie, wasn't around when father started the firm so it became Hale & Son. Hattie was currently away in law school and already had begun questioning the firm's title. She also wasn't too fond of my saying, "well, little sister, those are just the breaks." No sense of humor would be my guess.

Father wanted me to graduate in the top third of my law class, and I was pleased just to graduate. This was accomplished with the help of the law school department head who was a personal friend of my father. Father also wished that I had passed the state bar examinations on the first attempt, but I was thrilled that I achieved success on the final opportunity. So what's the big deal? All I needed to do was to pass everything, and I did it with flying colors.

My examinations have been primarily concerned with the personal indiscretions of some of our wealthiest clients. Their prestigious positions in this social hierarchy were paramount. I cut off the official investigations before there was even a whisper. Things have a way of turning into a media circus very quickly in this town. One minute you're at the top of everyone's invitation list, and the next you're the source of everyone's chuckles.

I have trouble remembering if I took my vitamin supplement ten minutes ago, but I'll never

forget that delightful cherries jubilee of an evening
long past. Our household staff of two happily devoted
live-in and sometimes live-together staff, Romney and
Renate, invented glorious dishes as if it were black
magic. These two might have spent many hours in
Salem's stocks or dunking pools if they had existed
just several centuries previously.

Father always scowled at the two when he
thought Romney paid Renate a late night visit in her
distant bedroom at the other end of our second floor.
He had that righteously moral expression the
following morning, but Renate's blueberry waffles
with raspberry syrup mollified his spirits. I became
foolish after the second stack, and even mother could
not prevent father's lecture about waistlines and
longevity. After the lavish final delight of baked fruit
compote and vanilla coffee, I slid out of the kitchen
and started for my third floor petite apartment in the
massive structure. I was making plans to head over
to a favorite beachfront watering hole with my
sometimes faithful pal, Kate McCain.

Thus, it was not to be. Pops had other plans
for my time, and I guess he takes priority as he also
signs my paycheck. He was also wowed when he
saw my entire outfit while I was standing. He is
slightly north of conservative, and I am marginally
south of Pee Wee Herman. I got that one raised
eyebrow which told me to go back and try again.
Maybe it was the yellow ascot with the pink trousers?

"Prich," he asked in a commanding tone,
"are you planning anything special today that would

prevent you from being home at 8:30 this evening?"

"No, sir," I replied as my nose grew another millimeter, "can't think of anything special."

"That's timely. A client wishes to speak with us tonight and I want you present for your valued opinion."

Somewhat surprised but delighted with his compliment, I responded with all eloquence, "Oh?"

"Yes, Prich," came his quizzled reply, "his name is John Evans."

"Oh," I restated, "I don't believe I'm familiar with that name."

"He, I understand, is a widower who is now unmarried, but that is of no importance."

"It could be to him," I was happy to respond, "especially on some of these cold nights we have had lately."

"That's all well and good, Prichard," he gave me with one of his thin smiles. "He has been employed with Rogers and Emory Development Company for some time. They are one of our newest clients with an excellent retainer. I envision that we will likely have a substantial billable hour amount as they transition their entire business to us."

"Do you see us bringing in another new associate with this business?" I asked hopefully.

Already aware of my approaching questions, he tactfully stated, "Prich, you are my most trusted and reliable member in your current position. I couldn't possibly replace your skills and dedication."

I began to see where my genetic BS came

from. Mother was sweet and kind. The Lord of the Manor was also kind but ruefully diplomatic.

I tried to provide one of my most convincing sorrowful looks and play the victim to the hilt, but he was already accustomed to this approach from me.

"You wouldn't like that mundane, glued-to-the-desk type work anyway, Prich. You know people and those are valued talents. I know you will be in the office one day when you slow down, but you are having the best that life can afford you now. You don't want everyone watching every minute now, do you?"

"I guess you're right, father," I conceded with a whine. "The days do fly by when I'm involved with an investigation."

"An inquiry," father corrected.

"I understand this Rogers & whatever is really an upscale computer software development place," I stated after remembering the discussion I had recently with a fireman. "They started with some small games a few years back and have had a full parking lot ever since."

"Where did you get that information, Prich?" father asked with a puzzled look. "We have barely spoken to those people and you sound like you already have an in-depth knowledge of their financial statement. See how valuable you are to our firm!"

"Oh, wow, what a diplomat!" I thought to myself.

I knew his was just a rhetorical question so I remained silent. I didn't wish to tell him that I spent

5

more time than I should at the Gaithersburg firehouse playing chess and kibitzing. So what if I were on the official clock? I picked up some good info to help the firm and also sharpened my chess skills in the process.

"Mr. Evans called late last night and asked if we could meet this evening," father continued. "He wanted to see me as soon as possible, but he was concerned about being seen with me. At first I asked him to come to the office for a confidential meeting. He seemed very on-edge about being seen anywhere conferring with me. I then suggested he drop by here for a short time this evening. It is one thing to be involved with discreet inquiries, but it is another thing to hold anything confidentially from a client. I am not very comfortable with this, Prich. This might lead us away from our prime responsibility, thus causing a conflict of interest."

I nodded my agreement with a thoughtful expression, but I remained silent.

"I really appreciate your being here with me. You read people with the best of them, and I am relying on your instincts."

And that in good measure goes a long way to explain that on this otherwise lovely evening which would have been better spent at one of my beachfront haunts, I was positioned in an uncomfortable chair in my father's library. I was being gracious to afford the more comfortable furniture to the Squire and our guest, ready to hear John Evans present his mystery and the purpose of all this strange secrecy.

The wonderful evening didn't seem all that great to Mr. Evans at the time. He was obviously tense with sad eyes, and a tired look added to that frightened expression. As I led him into the library, he began pacing. I quickly seated him next to my waiting father who made a remarkably good effort to put Mr. Evans more at ease. This had little effect as our guest began squirming and shifting in his great overstuffed chair.

Despite this stressful time, John Evans was a reasonably handsome man in his middle thirties. His voice was surprisingly stable but this calm air was clearly betrayed by his body language. His palm was damp but his handshake was firm. Nervous, yes, but he certainly was on a determined mission.

His suit was an off-the-rack of a wool-worsted blend, and his shirt and shoes were of good but moderate price, all neat and crisp in appearance as almost having been just newly put on. I saw him park a Mercury Sable station wagon in front, rather than pull into the space we had been sure to make in our driveway. More comfortable on neutral ground, I guessed.

My father was grandly positioned in his massive blue leather wing back with ottoman, which was just a short step to his rich walnut judge's table. Our counsel never enjoyed a desk that hid whatever was needed. Why else would they build file cabinets? Having moved forward in his chair, father slightly gestured with his hand and said, "Well, Mr. Evans, can we assist you this evening?"

His nibs had already explained my role in this encounter, so I was dutifully ready to perform. Father began to enlighten John Evans of my importance at Hale & Son, which also pumped me up. I'm sometimes an easy sell, and my chest was really pushed out that night. I thought that I deserved a raise and promptly asked for it the next day but with negative results.

Father reminds everyone of our fiduciary responsibility and the fact that we are bound by client confidentiality. He just equivocated with the conflict-of-interest issue that was already troubling him. He needed more information and proceeded to that end. Evans seemed to understand the dictates of our being bound but passed over the issue of our conflict.

He told us that he had been employed at Rogers and Emory Development for a little under seven years, starting as a clerk in their shipping department. He then attended night school and finished the one remaining year of college to receive an accounting degree. He continued his accounting education while transferring to the accounting department where he made steady advances. Three years later, he had a CPA certification and was the chief of the accounting department, after his predecessor left for a larger company and better salary.

"It's a fine job," Evans volunteered. "I've got a good staff and I make enough to get by. I've been very pleased to advance to my current position. I haven't any hard feelings with anyone at all. I like my job but I have been changing it to come into the

8

modern age. You might think that because we are a software company, that we would be the most modern company at everything. Well, we aren't even fully automated with our accounting systems, and we are just getting close with our inventory management. We are probably still using the stubby pencil system as much as anybody."

Father nodded with an inquiring expression and said, "I don't see any cause for concern yet."

"What I'm trying to say here this evening is that I have no ax to grind and bear no grudges against my employer. I want to remain where I am because I need the stability in my life now. My wife died and my parents aren't in the best health. Dad is retired and may need to enter a nursing home because he had a stroke and can't function well. He really is helpless and requires complete attention. Mom is going nuts with this care giving and needs to have a life of her own. We pay a lady to come in one day a week and sit with dad so mom can have a day off. She needs that little time to get her head straight. I'm over there a lot too, since she helped me a great deal when my wife had cancer. I'm also thinking it's about time that I might feel better being married again as I miss the companionship."

He took a breath and surveyed our faces before continuing.

"It's just that the costs of a nursing home are outrageous, plus I still have some small amounts left to pay for my wife's hospitalization. Insurance is great until you find out what they don't pay. Her total

9

bills were over one hundred thousand, besides the twenty-seven thousand that I had to pick up. I've got the balance down to under five thousand now, and I 'm beginning to see some light."

He paused again as he still seemed to be trying to read us. He then straightened his posture. We remained silent and waited for him to continue. I could not totally relate what he was thinking then as his expression revealed nothing more. He seemed honest up to this point, and I had a twinge of heart-felt sorrow for his family. It was probably caused by a conflict between his honesty and something else perceived askew.

"The CEO of this family-held private company is Mr. Charles Rogers. He controls the company and Mr. Joseph Emory is kind of a silent partner. Mr. Emory is probably just an investor who wanted to see his name on something. He appears to be in his late seventies or early eighties. I don't even know if he gets any of the profits. My responsibility ends with accounting for the profit, not how it is distributed. Mr. Rogers is a fine fellow and a real gentleman to all of us. He's treated me swell ever since my first day there. I believe everyone there admires him and would do almost anything for him. He's very steady but doesn't kill himself. He steps out for the country club and plays a round of golf every Thursday."

"Here, here!" I found myself exclaiming, then seeing the squire with a disapproving look.

"Please continue," father said quietly with a

smile.

"Charles' son David handles the day-to-day operations while Charles' two daughters, Evelyn and Judith, are in marketing."

"Are they as generous as their father?" I asked.

He ignored my logical inquiry. I was beginning to wonder why I was there other than becoming a foil for the other two participants.

"Mr. Evans, you still have not related your purpose for this visit. I can see no difficulty in anything that you have brought before us," stated father with all the commanding pomposity I hope to gain one of these days. He then mellowed and softly stated, "Please continue."

Evans sighed, then raised his head. "It's been about nine months ago when I became aware that the income started to increase out of proportion to our sales. A lot more revenue, but the expenses seemed about the same. It's way beyond last year's revenue. At first I was extremely pleased and so was everyone else who took notice of it. We all thought that we might get some kind of bonus. Someone even suggested that we might be noticed by some of the big conglomerates and be snapped up into a larger company with bigger salaries and benefits."

Evans looked at father and then to me. Father and I then looked to each other and I finally verbalized what I believed we were both thinking. "So what's the problem?"

I thought this guy was probably over the

11

edge. Why would he become upset if the company were making more money? Why be bothered if maybe a larger company bought you out and you received a larger salary and grander benefits? Maybe this poor guy had really gone wawa with all his family problems — a dead spouse, a father who may go into a nursing home and a mother somewhat silly — not to mention that he's still in debt to the hospitals. He sure could use a few extra bucks!

"The income from all our products keeps increasing," he said. "I was confused but I like to think that I'm a reasonable person who is someone with a level head on his shoulders. This just doesn't seem very logical, and you know the reputation we bean counters have. I'm also somewhat nosey and that gets me into a little trouble now and again. I'm not one to look a gift horse in the mouth, but why this great increase?"

Father began moving aimlessly in his great wing chair. "There has to be some innocent story to make this appear appropriate. Surely it's the result of one of the daughters in marketing or a cost-cutting effort. You understand that profit margins are not only the result of increased revenues, but they can also come to the fore by trimming expenses. Are you aware of any newer downsizing efforts or possibly any referrals from any other part of the industry?"

Before Evans had a chance to answer father, I interjected, "Does your company have any goodwill with any competitors that are over capacity at the moment? I know that the principle of one hand washing another is always likely where there isn't any animosity."

Father gave me a stern look for interrupting and not letting Evans have enough time to digest mentally a limited number of ideas before mixing them with new ones. Good ideas but my bad timing as usual.

"No!" Evans stated decisively. "I've asked around a little and everyone seems just to be clawing by. I haven't heard anyone shoving anything our way. Christmas is past anyway, and that's about half of our business."

Evans reflected and then added, "This is a dog-eat-dog business anyway. It's cutthroat and everyone knows it. They'll all do anything to crush the other guy. Price wars, lies about computer viruses, media misinformation, or sabotage are just to name a few. Nobody gives anybody anything in the software business, especially the game business. We'll all steal something from each other though!"

Evans looked at the ceiling for a short slice of eternity, as if to continue, but he stopped his narrative. He rubbed his right cheek with the back of his fingers, but he did not reach to his eyes. That was where his attention was really needed as I could see the emotion beginning to well up in him.

"Prich," father said softly now. "We have been neglecting our guest." Then he turned to his visitor and stated, "Mr. Evans, would you care for any refreshment? I'm having a glass of good white Burgundy, but we also have coffee or juice."

Evans nodded slightly and stated, "Yes, a small glass of wine might help a little."

"Prich," father said again with a quick nod to me. "Would you please do the honors?"

I stood slowly and went over to the half refrigerator that was partially concealed on the short wall that contained the door. It was snugly but artfully pushed beneath the chair rail. If one didn't know it was there, it would never be suspected. I poured three small glasses from the bottle after I gracefully fumbled with the corkscrew. I finished my duty without one smack or lick of my lips. I would never have the nerve to tell the squire that many domestic vintners produce a much better product than this vinegary European version.

Evans sighed a thanks and stated, "That tastes good."

I thought that our guest was either a diplomat or hadn't much experience with the Napa Valley products.

"Mr. Evans," his nibs asked, "what do you believe we can do for you? From what you have told us, you are not a wealthy man. I have not heard you say anything that is illegal or unethical. It appears the company is only exhibiting some financial success and that is surely no reason for concern. What would you have us do?"

"I'm not sure what to tell you, Mr. Hale. I just know that something out of the ordinary is going on. It's strange that we are making more money in a somewhat down market. I'm a little scared. I can't go sticking my nose into things that shouldn't interest me. If I got caught, I would be blackballed in this town. I need to remain here in this career and not make any waves in the process. I have my obligation to my parents to think about. They are both elderly and can't leave. I'm stuck here with my obligation to my parents. You are our legal representation. As attorneys, you can poke and pry because that's your normal work. You are always wanting to see either this or that document."

Father moved his attention to me and said, "Prich?"

I understood what my father wished of me. He was asking me to come up with any enlightenment or query that would give some sense to what we had just heard. He also wanted me to comfort our guest and give some assurance that we would make his life less disturbing. Lastly, and above everything else, he wanted me to end this and dispatch our visitor on his way.

"We'll gladly look into this matter, Mr. Evans, to allay your concerns. I'll be at your company for several days anyway, so no one should become suspicious about my inquiries," I said with all the caring in my voice that I could muster. "What you just described does seem a bit odd, but there must be some plausible explanation. Let me ask you if you can provide us with a list of your customers, the products they purchase, your revenue and expenses, and anything else you might think of that will assist us with an initial audit."

"Surely, Mr. Hale," he said in a voice that sounded as if he were speaking to the elder Mr. Hale. " I'll probably be able to obtain most of what you will need. If there is a problem, I sure wish you could then take me out of the loop so I'm not directly involved. I don't want to jeopardize my position, and I also don't want to be nailed or be the fall guy if the authorities ever become involved. That may sound cowardly and something like I want it both ways, but I have to take care of number one first. If I don't, there are loved ones depending on me and I'll let them down."

"Great," I said. "Will you give us the computer printouts some time tomorrow? I can meet you at that little public park right down the street at lunch time."

"I guess so," Evans said hesitantly. "I really shouldn't be doing this, but I guess I'll take this small chance this one time. I don't think they are watching me now for any reason, so I'll be able to slip away. It is a little odd though, as I normally bring my lunch and don't go out."

"I understand your concerns and we certainly appreciate your position here," I stated in a lawyerly tone that even surprised pops. "It will provide us a starting point to our informal investigation." I gave Evans a gold and blue embossed business card and scribbled another couple numbers on the back with my cherished green and gold topped Pelican roller ball pen. It's those little extras that you can flash that make the difference. "I'm giving you my private at-home and cellular numbers where you can reach me anytime. Don't hesitate if you feel anything is important. I'm often not in our office, but I still can be reached."

He thanked us for our time and understanding and tucked my card in his wallet. He rose without finishing his wine and said, "Thank you both so much. This thing has been worrying me, and I just haven't been myself lately. It's wonderful to know that someone professional will be looking into this. I haven't been sleeping too well; maybe things will begin to change. I'll try to help you any way I can; I'll see you at 11:30 tomorrow morning."

My head was spinning at the mention of the appointed time. I was just thinking about breakfast on one of my good days at that AM hour. Now I was expected to be awake, dressed, and alert. What had I just gotten myself into?

We all moved to the door where father bade Evans farewell. He returned to his station wagon, and we watched him drive cautiously away. Father then turned to me with that inquiring gaze.

"Unusual?" father stated questioningly.

"Curious at least, sir," I remarked.

"Prich, why don't you give this only a peripheral effort to begin with, and don't spend too much time chasing phantoms. I worry the gentleman is given with an over-active imagination. I do not believe we have a major cause for concern here."

"I agree, sir."

Good heavens, were we ever way out in left field!

Chapter 2

Too Much Help

Father went into his study with a refill of the white Burgundy and the complete works of Poe. I never could understand his devout, undeviating loyalty to this master of hideous, grotesque macabre. Bobby Burns I could understand, but Poe for heavens sake! Well, I'll give Daddy-O one thing: at least Poe was someone from this side of the water, even though he was a demented deviant. We aren't all perfect.

I scampered up to my third floor loft and hastily freshened up. Our house was located in the old portion of Bethesda, Maryland, in the middle of the culturally rich, old money area. This section had many of the massively grand old Victorian houses often referred to as the "Grand Old Ladies." My parents assumed I acquired my foot to the rhythm. I've heard stories about when she was young and quite a fancy stepper in those days.

She looked up briefly as I poked my head in. She stopped tapping, smiled at me and started humming. I stepped over and gave her a peck on the cheek. "Still going out tonight, Prich?" she asked with her familiar caring tone.

I was in my mid-thirties but was still her little boy who probably needed protecting. "It's just too early to call it quits and I need a little air. I'll be back in a short time." She smiled again and went back to tapping with Lawrence.

I gingerly made my way to my old sixty-six restored red Mustang convertible with a bright white ragtop. I can't think of a more nondescript vehicle to blend in with the others when tailing another car. It was a beauty, and I should really have taken better care of it. Many of my tasteless acquaintances commented on my classy chariot while driving their sleek foreign wheels. Any wimp can throw money at the problem. I had a sometimes unreliable classic but I also got a big smile and wave from many others. I was also responsible for the education of my auto mechanic's children so I was always attempting to contribute my fair share.

I headed directly to the Chain Bridge Yacht and Country Club where I think I've been one of the charter members. I'm not entirely sure why they named my cozy refuge with the title of Yacht Club because there isn't even a canoe to be found within a mile. I believe I once heard they'd leased a couple of slips at a marina in Georgetown in the beginning. I think they discovered later all that the members were interested in was a watering hole with good food and socialization. The boat slips eventually went the way of the sinking enthusiasm.

The rustic, seasoned structure was in remarkable condition after the disastrous fifties "plastic is better" restyling efforts. There was a rich wooded patina found under several layers of white paint, while the bar was a priceless jewel of the Eastern seaboard. The sunken plaster ceiling had added depth with the ornate crown moldings surrounding the main room. The entrance was a splendid collection of wooden turnings that framed the wrought iron railings impaled in massive gray and red granite steps.

George Wilkinson, manager and bartender extraordinaire, spied me as I ambled sprightly through the door. "Hi ya, Prich," was his good natured welcome. "Starting a little late, are ya?"

"Yep, Georgey boy," I responded. "Someone told me it was happy hour for the night owls. Any truth to those rumors, big guy?"

"Sorry, Prich, I think you jumped the gun by a couple of weeks," came his smiling retort. "What'll it be tonight?"

"Have you got one of those sissy drinks with a prissy little umbrella? Something green with a red cherry would really set it off."

"Got just the thing for you, Bucko," said Georgey with a big grin. "I'll slide it over to your table in the corner. The folks that were there just left for the night."

"Looks like the great timing isn't going to stop for me today," I said with a flair and a toss of my head. "Can't wait to see what's going to happen next!"

I sauntered over and posted myself against the wall like Wild Bill should have a hundred or so years before. You can't be careful enough with all the bad sentiment out there with us legal gurus. Sue Quentin, the waitress, came over to my table with my drink and a puzzled look.

"Hi, Suzie Q," I called out with a laugh. "Cat finally got your tongue?"

"What on earth have you done now, Prich?" she somehow asked with lips not seeming to move and her mouth still open. I did a double take to see if a ventriloquist was behind her. "Have you lost it for good or is George just zinging you?"

"That umbrella's kind of cute, don't you think, sweetie? Where's my little sipping straw?"

Just as Suzie Q started to mumble something in return, Franky Angelino swaggered through the door and headed directly my way. I think I just said something about my timing today and this really ripped it. I wasn't sure if I were ready for Franky. He wasn't much better sober than he was blitzed.

Franky had too much time on his hands, as he'd retired early from the government with some sort of disability pension. His wife was well off, and he indulged himself at the bar to have something to do rather than to satisfy his past addiction.

"Hey, fellow, where's your big pup, JD?"

Ignoring my question, Franky's eyes fixed on my drink, and then he began shaking his head as he sat down.

"Why don't you pull up a chair?" I asked trying to restore Franky into the conscious world.

"Have you switched sides, Prich?" Franky finally mumbled.

I thought I'd actually detected a sober Franky Angelino. Boy, this was really going to be a night. Maybe the stars were crossed, or perhaps I had offended some Egyptian god. I didn't really do anything bad like disturbing Tut's tomb, really I didn't!

"Buy you a drink, big guy?" I said with my best straight face.

"Not one of those," stammered Franky. "I wouldn't be caught dead with that in front of me! I'll just have a seltzer with a twist of lime, Suzie."

Suzie Q nodded and headed back toward the bar. I could see Georgey Wilkinson chuckling as she returned.

"How are things going with the Italian stallion?" I said. "Your drink is crazier than mine. Seltzer water, what's this world coming to?"

"Okay, sport," came Franky's retort. "I'm off the sauce, now what's your excuse?"

"I haven't got a good one, buddy," I replied as honestly as I could. "I just see all those gals drinking the hard stuff straight up now, so why can't I have it both ways too?"

Franky just laughed and shook his head. The guy didn't really look too bad sober. This was a real revelation. Franky had been on the other side so long that it was just hard to think of him any other way. I wondered what his wife and his faithful dog would think of him.

"Does JD growl at you when you come home now?" I said with a joke and half real curiosity. "Guess you know what you're doing, so you don't need to explain."

"I realized it was about time for this after I

22

almost went home a week ago. I left here at closing and thought I'd gone home. That's where I always go, anyway. Well, the next thing I know a cop has his gun out, poking me in the ribs. Guess I made a mistake and walked in the widow's house next door. The blasted door was open; the places are laid out the same. She had an empty guest bedroom where we have our regular bedroom. Well, I just laid down in the bed, and the next thing I remember, this cop starts poking me."

"That doesn't sound too bad, Franky," I said, really laying on the sympathy. "You didn't do anything to the widow, did you?"

"Gee, Prich!" exclaimed Franky. "Have you seen her? Don't think I've ever been that drunk. My former mother-in-law looked better two days dead at the funeral than she looks alive."

"This looks like a wonderful time tonight," I complained. "I'm stuck here with a dirty old man who's drying out and not a female in sight." Franky gave me one of those questioning looks and then swirled the seltzer in his glass. "If things get too bad, maybe we could go out and hustle a couple of old biddies."

"Oh, wow, Prich!" wailed Franky. "Don't even joke about things like that. I'm having enough trouble trying to live this thing down, and I'm afraid someone might take this seriously. My wife can hardly raise her head when she's at the grocery store. She says she can hear the chuckles and whispers in the aisle she just left."

"Well, what's going on with your life other than your midnight raids?" I queried just to make conversation with a complete stranger, a sober Franky Angelino. "Got any hot stock picks?"

"You always bet the opposite way I say and make money off me!" growled Franky. "Just isn't fair, Prich."

"I don't make that much, Franky," I consoled the old friend.

"It's the principle of the thing. I feel like the point man in my old squad. I go out and draw fire while the rest of the guys ambush the opposition." He paused, then said, "I've got a good idea; why don't you pick up an option on a block of Mexican pesos."

"Thin skinned tonight or just grumpy?"

"Just sober for a change. Hey, what are you working on now?"

"Nothing all that exciting. I sure miss a good run for the money."

"Got anything that I could help you with?" Franky said, as he looked at me with his big sad eyes. "Need something to keep me busy."

"Pops would flip his top if we put anyone else on the payroll," I said with a frown. "I can't believe that he still signs *my* paycheck."

"I'm not looking for a paying job, Prich," came Franky's response. "That would mess up my disability pension. We don't need the extra piddley few bucks that you cheapies would pay anyway. Sandy has more family money than I could ever spend.

I just got a case of the nerves and need to have something to keep me busy. Helped you with a favor last year the time you were involved with those bait-and-switch insurance brokers."

"Right, but you almost blew the whole thing!"

"I was drunk then. It all worked out okay anyway."

"Well," I articulated with great fanfare. "I don't know what to tell you, buddy. There's not much going on now. We're going to check out one of our clients just a little, but it really doesn't seem very important. I don't see any problem with them and it'll probably only take a day or two." I was pleased with my ability to shrug him off.

"What-do-ya want me to do, and I'll be there?" He changed my mind. Some great backbone I had.

"Okay. Just be at that small Gaithersburg city park right down the street from the industrial park row that's right off the interstate around 11:30 tomorrow morning," I said reluctantly. "I'd like to see if anyone is following our guy or me after I meet him."

"Great, I'll be the sober drunk lying on the park bench."

"You don't need to be that dramatic, big guy. Just be your self and that'll be fine."

My attention had been with Franky until I saw two lovely young things whisk through the door and look our way. As they slid up to a couple of bar stools, they both smiled directly at me. I shyly returned their smiles while Franky kept talking.

"Hey, am I talking to myself?" growled Franky.

"You're cute, my little pretty, but they still got you beat," I replied with a grin. "What say we cure some of our loneliness right over there at the bar?"

Franky turned toward the gals and remarked that he hadn't seen them here before. I felt the membership committee had certainly been earning their dues with the new arrivals. I began to get up as Kate McCain came through the door. Some people measure their lives with opportunities lost. I was about to join that little clique.

"Evening, sweetie," I greeted Kate when she arrived at our table after waving to Georgey and Suzie Q as she passed. "Didn't think I would be seeing you this grand evening. You look great."

"It's a wonder you even noticed, you two timer!" Kate scolded. "I just was on the line over here and spoke to Suzie. She told me you were here with Franky behaving yourself for a change. Now I walk in and find you leering at those two floozies at the bar. Doesn't take you any time at all, does it?"

"I'm always faithful, love," I protested. "Franky just told me a joke about his going on the wagon, and all I was doing was laughing."

"Why were you getting up, bozo?"

"There are some things we cultured gentlemen simply don't discuss with our lady friends.

But, if you must know, I was psychic and remembered I should always rise when a lovely lady approaches."

"That's baloney, sport," Kate nipped again.

"Well, I guess I'll just need to fess up then," I said and then promptly stood up and walked to the men's room. Always have to stay a step or two ahead of them. When I returned, I found Kate grilling Franky, and the two gals at the bar didn't even return my nod. They were fickle too.

"It's a good thing I got here when I did," she continued.

"You don't let up, do you? I don't understand your attitude tonight."

"Well," Kate said with a long drawl. "Let's start with an accounting of tonight's events. First, I'm asked to accompany a not-so-faithful ding-a-ling to the Chesapeake Beach for a fun evening of a good dinner, dancing, beach walking, and maybe a hug or two. I foolishly accept and am told at the last minute that he can't make it. Work is what I'm told is the sad reason, so I also feel bad for you. Then, Suzie calls me and says she's surprised that I'm not here with you. I tell her I'm also surprised, but I want to come over here and see for myself."

"So, what do you see that's all so terrible, my love?" I countered.

"Don't start with me, fella," Kate continued. "I get a call all right, but it has to be from a friend rather than you. Why didn't you call me to say you were coming here?"

"Well, pops had me tied up with a new client,

which was a surprise, as I'd mentioned on the phone. We finished too late to head for the beach but a little too early to lay my weary head down. I didn't think you'd want to do anything on the very last minute without any notice. So, here I am talking with my good buddy and having a drink."

"Ha, you call that side-saddle umbrella glass a drink?" Kate answered. "And, what's all the leering you were doing when I arrived?"

"Don't let me interrupt your lover's quarrel, folks!" Franky interjected.

"Butt out!" Kate snarled and flipped Franky a glare.

"Now you're growling at my friends," I said, coming to my buddy's defense.

"You'll shut your trap, if you know what's good for you," Kate added.

"She's right, Prich," stated Franky.

"Let's get the devil out of here, sweetie," I declared with an authority that surprised everyone including me. I told Franky that I'd see him on the job tomorrow morning and congratulated him for his liquid abstinence. As Kate and I headed for the door, I received a smile from the cutest of the two gals as we passed. I shot back a quick wink on the sly. There was always tomorrow.

Kate was still growling as we left the Chain Bridge Club. I could plainly see that I needed to use a little finesse if I didn't want to head directly home without passing GO.

I quickly changed the subject and asked Kate

how her job as the Gaithersburg hospital administrator was developing. She indicated that the downsizing fad was also a part of her world.

"I don't like what happens to the people after they are cheerfully restructured," Kate indicated with a frown. "Too many people have to leave areas where they're the experts and displace someone with a completely different job. That person then does the same to the next person, and so on."

"Seems like everyone is stressed out, and the jobs get done slower if at all," I enthusiastically agreed.

Kate smiled and squeezed my hand. I drove behind her to make sure she arrived home safely. She invited me in for a nightcap to make up for leaving my umbrella drink prematurely. Oh, well, I thought I could usually sneak into the house at sunrise without waking mom and pop. I believe Kate planned to make sure that I wouldn't need to look for those two gals for some time to come. Kate usually did accomplish any task when she fully dedicated herself. The night did end well, indeed!

Chapter 3

Cold as a Dead Fish

I sincerely hoped that I hadn't become a misanthrope, but I simply didn't feel well enough to enjoy anyone so early in the day. It seemed as if I'd barely sneaked into my loft when the alarm on my clock radio screeched something the Federal Communications Commission hadn't licensed. The station selector had been moved slightly off the correct frequency, which produced a sound akin to stepping on a soprano cat's tail. That's a wonderful start to anyone's day!

The phone rang with a shrill scream. I'd forgotten to turn down the ringer from the previous day. Holding my head as if I had a one umbrella drink hangover, I quickly picked up the receiver, "Yes, for goodness sakes, what is it?"

"Something wrong, love?" came Kate's inquisitive voice. "You surely seemed in a sparky mood the last time I saw you. I usually don't wear off so quickly."

"You usually don't call in the dead of night, either," I whined in return. "I believe I've gotten my days and nights mixed up. Maybe breakfast will help. I normally only eat brunch so this will be an experience. I just don't want to make it a habit!"

"Well, I didn't think that I'd reach you, love," continued Kate with an amused voice. "I was only intending to leave a message on your answering machine. I thought you'd have been long gone by this time. It would have been sort of a non visual E-Mail love tap."

"Thanks for the thought — I'll call you tonight," I said.

"You'd better, sport!"

I struggled off to the wonderfully hot shower, which always seemed to revive my poor body after a night of abuse. I count sleep deprivation in that category. All body parts responded but didn't jump back to my rousing teens. I felt every moment of my age.

While I was sitting on my bed with my feet propped up, letting my hair air dry, I picked up my diary of events that I religiously kept current. The old memory, or gray cells as Poirot would say, often needed jogging and sometimes it helped to write things down. If it became more involved, I took it one step farther. I believed it's something like talking things out with a friend, but who in the world would be silly enough to listen to my tales.

An interesting smell was coming from downstairs and I noticed a hunger pang or two. Maybe, I thought, it might be worth the effort to investigate. Renate had been busy with her own concoction of French toast with a dash of vanilla and several grinds of fresh nutmeg. I thought the dusting of confectionery sugar was the most satisfying of the lighter topping alternatives. Naturally, I had to have my banana, even though I didn't have my corn flakes for the accompaniment. There are only so many deviations one can make in a single day. The cinnamon coffee was just what the doctor ordered. I needed that caffeine for a kick start. Everyone should have one dependency and caffeine was mine.

Renate packed a few goodies as a take-along to give a little more realism at the park for lunch time. Sometimes a little planning helped make up for my other deficiencies.

Father already had left for the office over an hour ago, but mom was still shuffling about. She had an intense devotion to her floral collection that she kept alive in her solarium through the winter months. It was about time for her to be involved heavily with ground preparation and spring planting. Romney did most of the heavy work; however, nothing escaped her gentle but critical review. I believe that she may have that special aura that only mystics or technicians can detect. All living things flourish in that environment. She had a remarkable talent with orchids, which are noted problems even for professionals. She once tried to help me start a horticultural interest, but my black thumb proved too big an obstacle to overcome. Some of her sensitive and artistic nature was passed along to this generation, as she paints landscapes in oils while I draw super stick figures in the sand.

I thought that I had better get on the road with some time to spare. The metro area is renowned for traffic surprises and I didn't wish this to be one of those moments. The day was a glorious event, and I was beginning to appreciate the morning hour a little more. I even thought about putting the top down, but vanity quickly won out. I didn't like to be seen with wind blown hair after taking all that trouble primping a short time before. We men spend a great amount of time before mirrors, but I believe gals still end up with better results.

The Gaithersburg park was much busier than I'd anticipated, which made a meeting much less conspicuous. Since I had fifteen minutes to kill, I was happy that I'd brought the cookies with the brown bag stuffed with a little newspaper to make it appear like I had a whopping appetite. I knew that I would receive some counseling about the waistline, but a soul should enjoy the sin or what's the purpose? I didn't spot Franky anywhere, so I thought the abstinence probably didn't last long.

Evans was prompt, but he continued walking past me. I thought his paranoia had won. It was his dime so I let him play it as he saw it. I scanned the area and didn't spot anyone of notice. He could feel better about his adventure, but it was up to us to explain his uncomfortable perceptions and untidy bottom line.

I watched Evans eat a sandwich while sitting on a bench across the walkway. He had his windbreaker lying beside him and a package concealed inside. As he finished with the sandwich wrapping, he easily reached into the jacket and added the package to the wrapping and discarded them both in the wire waste-can. I continued scanning the location where Evans entered the park, but everything looked natural. I didn't see any new faces in the few minutes Evans spent at this placid setting.

He finished quickly and left the park by the same path he used when entering. I carefully looked around one last time before walking over to the trash bin. It was then that I noticed someone move on the bench located on the crosswalk, about thirty yards on my right. Franky was slumped over in a street person's garb and appeared inebriated. I thought no one would spot him if I couldn't detect him until the end. He probably had spent a great deal of time in that appearance and was an expert character actor.

I casually walked back to the Mustang with Evans' package and drove directly to the office. Our suite of offices was located in a seven-story building, of which father was one-third owner with one other law firm and a pediatrician. Hale & Son had the two top floors and father naturally had what easily could be termed a penthouse. There were eleven associate attorneys with over twenty-five paralegals. There weren't any full partners, except for me. I had my name on the marquee, but I wondered where the big salary had disappeared. I knew that was stretching it a bit, but one likes to hope. Maybe I could have been called a minor partner if one wanted to use partner at all, given my paltry income. Father was the sole founder of this firm, and he wasn't generous with a buck. All of the lawyers and about half of the paralegals were also on the top floor. The sixth floor held the accounting department, the balance of the newer paralegals, and almost a dozen other clerks and supporting staff. We still could have used more room, and I'm sure that if the fifth floor ever became available, we would surely have snapped it up, too. We were really in a tight spot for some essential storage space.

If my expense vouchers ever saw the light of reality, I knew where my next office would be. I thought automation was supposed to eliminate much of the file-drawer clutter. Well, no one told this to our firm. It was one of those nondescript boxes of a building that was built in the early sixties when everything built looked very similar. Luckily, our building didn't have some of the problems that many other buildings of that era experienced. Father assured us that we wouldn't shiver in the winter, but he was only partially correct about the plumbing. We were all happy that the Environmental Protection Agency didn't stick tape across our main entrance as they did with several other sick buildings in this sprawling Washington, D.C., metropolis. Pops was just thrilled, I'm sure, that there wasn't a huge lease payment every month like many other law firms enjoyed. They had to build those hefty costs into their billable hourly rates. Come to think of it, our rate was higher than most. I just wished our walls had something better than beige paint. I supposed it was still better than that shiny plastic paneling. I just thought that if I ever became the Big Bwana of this legal retail store, I would certainly make some changes. Posh is the word that popped to mind.

I was greeted by pops' secretary, Mildred

McCarthy, as I entered from the side door. Mildred, a fifty-five year old grandmother, with not one blond hair in that beautiful auburn pageboy hairdo, always made everyone smile. She had been with the firm for all but the first five years and none of us was sure who was really the boss. She certainly made us question who really was the professional in these professional offices. I hated to think of this place without her.

"Is the Grand Pooh Bah available, love?" I said lightly. "I just need to see him for about ten short ones at the most."

"He's reviewing a brief, sweets," Mildred replied. "I'll buzz you when I see an opening."

I retreated through the door and into the large room where my small cubicle sat in the windowless corner. I believe everyone thought I should have a grand office with a window. They also probably thought I would likely be watching the squirrels play in the trees and lovely females walking by. They didn't realize that I could daydream with my eyes open or shut. I had my own window to the world, even though I only had a small interior work space.

Again, I don't really wish to appear to be a perpetual pain in the posterior, but I believe my position among other street vagrants deserved something considerably better. My small cubicle sat next to the noisy copy machine on our floor. It seemed as if that grinding, whiny, clunky thing would continue without any reprieve. Then, there was the wonderful impact printer that was hooked to the local area network (LAN). It was used for pounding through multi-layer forms that have something akin to carbon paper between the sheets. This cruel apparatus buzzed and grinded and then thumped and whizzed. It almost made the LAN laser printer with the ahhhhhhh and then the ummmmmm sound benign. All of these irritants were welcome, though, if I could have exchanged for another office mate. The fellow with the extra red bulbous nose, who sits in the cubicle across from me, ran up the volume on his hic-a-billy radio station. He also had a window cubicle to show for it! Oh, did I tell you; he's a lawyer too...go figure.

Just as I arrived, the phone buzzed. I thought pops was ready to see me but was told that Frank Angelino was asking to speak to me.

"Hey, Franky, glad you called right away. See any problems or anything suspicious?"

"Not a thing, Prich," Franky stated matter-of-factly. "I did get a little hassled by a cop right after you left, but I simply walked away which made him happy. I followed you from some distance because I wasn't afraid of losing you. I knew where you were going, but wanted to lag back and see if anybody was a little curious."

"Can't blame that cop, fella," I replied after visualizing Franky's appearance. "I didn't even spot you for the longest time and thought you had forgotten. You could've fooled anyone!"

"Thanks, buddy," Franky responded, and I could hear the pride swell up in his voice. "I had lots of practice."

Franky asked if I needed him anymore, and I gave him an uncertain answer. We planned to meet later in the week at the club. I asked if he knew any more about those two gals we saw the night before.

"Hey, you're the hot shot detective!" Franky jibbed. "I'm just a drying out old cripple."

"Sure, fella," I retorted. "Sounds like you don't know much more than I do. If you want a new mission, start working on their bios."

Franky and I said our good-byes, and I settled back to daydreaming about my weekly expense voucher. You haven't seen any creativity until you have read one of my concoctions. I found a way to list a round for the house at the club last night and to add a full dinner for Kate. I don't think anyone has ever caught on to any of my charades. I was working on my projected lavish expenses for this coming weekend when the intercom buzzed again. I gathered my parcel from the park, along with a notebook and pencil, and headed directly for the king's lair.

If anyone would ever like to see a study in contrast, they should walk into my daddyo's shop after visiting mine. Visitors almost lost their balance when they sank into that deep lush pile carpeting or the exquisitely expensive Persian area rug with its origins from the Caucasian looms. I should have such a pedigree. There was no LAN printer anywhere to be seen. The paintings on the walls were expensive originals. The rich walnut period furniture didn't match anything I usually saw around my circles. I wondered how many cows had to shed their unneeded winter hides to add all that leather to his humble abode. I also wondered if cows really had that expensive looking blue leather skin?

A small fridge with a variety of mixers and a whopping silver service sat on an inlaid walnut and hickory sideboard. The opposite and side walls were filled with books. Probably a third were law books, but the rest belonged to my father's cherished collection. There were even a couple first editions to be found. However, pops did not flaunt them. What was the point in having them, right?

Now we came to pops' private privy. I mean really private. I worked with the big guy for over an hour once in that land of Oz and had several cups of coffee before I went in to his office... bad move! My eyes were about crossed as I held my bladder for an eternity. He used the privy twice while I sat there making strange faces. I don't even think mom was allowed in that holy sanctuary when she came to visit several times. Maybe that explained why we didn't see her around the office very much.

I told father what had just transpired and handed him the packet of financial documents. I also indicated that I was not followed and that was confirmed by a friend. He quickly asked if this friend could be trusted, and I had no trouble vouching for Franky's faithfulness. Father was always true to the client's confidentiality. That was one conviction that we completely shared. He then asked if this friend was going to need a check for his help, and I replied that I'd merely given Franky a quick cash advance. I would just add this meager deduction to my next expense voucher and who would be the wiser? Father indicated that I should ask our small Accounting Department to review Evans' documents. He also indicated that I should probably start an interview with Charles Rogers at his office to begin our investigation. This would merely be a standard course for our complete transition to a full representation of the firm. That task would be in addition to Evans' request for a covert audit.

True to my word, I was out of the big guy's office in ten minutes. It didn't take me long in accounting either, which was only one floor down. I picked out Joe Lindsey by the water cooler and interrupted an inter-office flirtation with a buxom brunette who was happy to display her endowment to Joe's smiling wonderment.

"I know that I'm a poor substitute, but I surely wouldn't do this if it weren't strictly business," I pleaded to Joe's pounding good heart. "Could I get a minute or two, and then I promise to flee this confinement?"

"Anyone ever tell you about your wonderful sense of timing, Prich?" Joe grumbled good naturedly. "Only because you're the boss's singular son!"

I explained what needed to be done, but didn't tell him anything about Evans' suspicion. All we needed was our own evaluation of how we wanted to proceed with our transition to full legal representation. If there were any questions, they should be directed to me. I would be the intermediary to the accounting office at Rogers & Emory. I exited by apologizing again. I really did feel like someone with a proverbial cold bucket of water, happening upon two love mates. I sure hoped that I wouldn't be repaid in kind in this lifetime.

I bounced back up the stairs and asked our secretary, Joan Compton, to call Rogers & Emory to make an initial appointment for me to meet with Charles Rogers. Joan returned ten minutes later with the news that a three o'clock meeting was set at his office. She seemed a little too proud of herself. Maybe she was in that select group of folks who liked to see others deeply involved with drudgery. Guess she didn't understand how well adjusted I became with some distance.

It was about lunchtime and I had a couple of hours to kill. The Mustang was on autopilot all the way to the Chain Bridge Club. When I swaggered through the door, George Wilkinson was in his normal happy mood with a big grin to match. I waved and headed directly to my table in the corner. Suzie Quentin slid over my way after delivering a tray full of drinks to a table full of slick suited businessmen. It was easy to see who was selling whom. I just was happy that I wasn't on either one of those sides.

"What'll it be, laddie boy?" Suzie asked with a grin. "Got fried Whiting with slaw and fries or there's a great turkey salad on honey wheat."

"I'll take the fried cholesterol special with slaw and an explanation of your spy network, sugar britches," I needled our happy waitress with a snicker.

41

"I wasn't here more than ten minutes and the next thing I know, you've got Kate on a rampage with her scalping knife out. I'll bet you could teach those CIA folks over at Langley a quick graduate course."

"We gals need to stick together," she snickered in return. "You guys don't stand a chance!"

As Suzie Q scampered off to place my order, my attention returned to the table of businessmen. It appeared that all wasn't wonderful even after the sales pitch had been well lubricated with several cocktails. Their voices had become elevated an octave with hand gestures as an accompaniment. I thought, "Just keep the hands open, fellows, and let Suzie Q and me do the squabbling." The only thing at stake with us was her tip or maybe a fish full of bones for me.

I dipped my napkin in the glass of water and made an admirable attempt at wiping the tarter sauce off my tie. If you looked really hard at my three or four ties, you could probably tell exactly what I had for lunch in previous weeks. They never looked the same after having been to the cleaners.

The brightly gleaming Mustang was the poor victim of several pigeons with a severe case of the stomach flu. I wondered if those foreign car manufacturers imported those birds too. The service station two blocks away had a nice window squeegee that worked like a wonder tool on their deposits. I just couldn't get that tool cleaned afterward. I hoped the next motorists didn't get too upset when they noticed a strange film on their windshields.

I arrived at Rogers & Emory with five

minutes to spare, owing this common practice to having set my watch fifteen minutes fast. Walking up to the front door, I noticed Amos Freyer's old Jeep Wagoneer parked right out front. Amos was with the Montgomery County Police Department; I'd worked with him before. I couldn't imagine why he was right out front like he owned the place. He knew something about automation, so I reasoned that maybe he was looking for future prospects. It was also about the time of year when we all got hit-up for some kind of benefit.

I saw Amos through a glass partition after entering the building. I quickly spoke to the receptionist while I handed her another business card and pushed on over to Amos.

"Circus time again, buddy?" I quipped as he looked to see me for the first time. "I'll take two down close to those clowns and super-smelling animals."

"What the devil are you doing here, Prich?" stumbled Amos and then stood there looking odd with his mouth opened.

"Our firm is transitioning to represent this company. We already have the personal side with the owners, and they wanted to wrap all their legal work together," I shot back just as quickly. "Now, how about answering my question."

"Makes sense that you'd be involved with something like this," complained Freyer with a frown.

"Like what, sport?" I complained in return.

"Old man Emory was killed late last night,

and we were just touching base here," Freyer stated as if he were reading the sports scores from the evening paper.

"Ah, come on, Amos," I stammered back. "You're not telling me that nice old man is dead?"

"Yep, cold as a fish by this time," answered Freyer.

"How?"

"Well, now there's the rub, sonny boy," replied the homicide detective. "I believe someone thought he'd make it look like a mugging. No pro or even a dumb street kid did this. I'll bet a month's pay on it. He only took the cash and left the credit cards."

"Sure doesn't sound right to me either," I firmly agreed. "Even I know you can sell credit cards anywhere on the streets."

"They also left an expensive Masonic diamond ring on his finger," added Freyer. "That's the first to be stripped in a street heist."

"Uh, huh," I moaned in agreement. "And what gives with you out here? Got anything yet?"

"Just getting started and then I see your mug. Now, I'm really becoming concerned! Anything else you haven't told me, sport?"

"Hey, we worked together a couple of times before," I said. "Everything always worked out well, as I remember it."

"Yeah, I remember you sandbagging me," returned the cop with a groan. "Seems like you've got a very short memory."

"All that I remember is you got all the

publicity and credit while I quietly walked away," I reminded my friend.

"Sure, you did!" exclaimed Freyer with an incredulous yelp. "Some walk that was. You skipped away with a big fat commission check!"

"Ever see one of my salary check stubs, Amos?"

"Still looks better than mine, Prich."

"That's your fault, friend," I was happy to state. "You're the one who wants to remain an honest cop."

Freyer shook his head and started to walk away, but stopped and turned. He asked if I knew about any will or financial motive. I tactfully reminded him of our client confidentiality and then told him that I truly hadn't seen any of the wills.

I left Freyer with his problems and sought our remaining client. Charles Rogers seemed genuinely distraught about losing his long-time friend and business partner. He volunteered that Emory had unselfishly helped him start the business, and there would have been no business without Emory's friendship. Rogers was clearly agitated and wasn't in any emotional state to conduct any business discussions. The only function that I could perform was a support role for a client. The authorities would need the initial deal involving the personal aspects with our firm before any additional formalities with our clients.

I excused myself for a moment and made my way into an adjacent, unoccupied office. I was immediately on the phone to my office. Mildred said father was in a short staff meeting, but it was just ending. I asked her to interrupt on my behalf, but she told me everyone was leaving the conference, and she connected me with him soon after.

I quickly communicated the events as I'd learned them in the past several minutes. Father was both shocked and saddened by this knowledge as he evidently was somewhat closer to the late Joseph Emory than I'd realized. He instructed me to continue as I had with my legal support and condolences. He also requested that I add his own words of sympathy. I asked about Emory's heirs, and father indicated that he had no living blood relatives. I asked if pops remembered anything about the will, but he was evasive. If father didn't want to share any information, he simply wouldn't respond to the question. I often wondered about how much he knew when I didn't even have enough information to be aware of a question.

I plodded through the balance of that traumatic afternoon until I decided that I was more of a hindrance than an asset. I spread around nearly a dozen more of my business cards after sitting through Freyer's short session with Rogers. All was very polite as Freyer was only at the information gathering mode. He indicated that he would likely be returning as information was developed.

I left shortly after Freyer and made my way directly home. This certainly wasn't normal for an early Friday evening, but it hadn't been a usual day.

Father cornered me after dinner with an additional inquiry as I related the balance of my experiences with Freyer and the Rogers & Emory staff. All I could get out of pops was that Emory had the standard business clause of survivorship to the remaining partner in case of his death. That small piece of information spoke volumes.

After retreating to my small enclave, I entered everything new into my diary. This time I went the extra step of organizing the thoughts. I found a half used package of index cards and began transferring all data to them, no matter how trivial at the time. I then took the completed cards and pinned them to the cork sideboard on the wall beside my bed. I could now rearrange these thoughts and events in any order that would facilitate my non-rational analysis. This didn't go very smoothly as I was very weary from the day's activities. I wasn't accustomed to stress and I didn't look forward to any more. The last several late nights and early mornings didn't add to my luster, so I packed it in and was happy to know I would sleep late on a peaceful Saturday morning.

Chapter 4

We're Here to Help You

At seven o'clock in the morning on a marvelous beginning to another spring weekend, that loud screeching phone did it again. I sat up straight and thought if I could kill an inanimate object, that instrument of irritation would be the first on my hit list. I shook my head and picked up the blasted receiver to stop its infernal noise. That worked for a moment, but then I heard another screeching of a female's voice coming out of that technological wonder that I now had in my hand.

"Yes, hello," I mumbled into the mouthpiece just to stop this new clamor.

"So, you promised to call, did you?" Kate half growled. "What in the devil do you take me for? Do you think that's all I have to do is wait around this place for some floozy chasing bum?

"Kate, is that you, Kate?"

"Who did you expect, ding-dong?" came Kate's angry quip.

"Kate, please stop the racket," I pleaded with a throbbing head. "I'm just trying to get in gear. I've been wiped out, and I'm trying to get caught up with some rest. I crashed right here after dinner last night. I guess the poor bod just buckled under too much stress."

"You're telling me that you haven't been out

on the town?"

"I swear!"

"I'm coming right over there now and get this straightened out," came Kate's reply.

"No wait a...," I said, but the line went click, and then the dial tone hummed.

I shook my head as I set the phone gently down on the nightstand. I shaved, showered, and brushed the old ivory to a polished gleam. Throwing on my robe, I slowly descended into the cheery sunlit kitchen where Romney was helping Renate prepare the family breakfast. They were both surprised to see me so early on a Saturday morning. I'm sure that I didn't look very together after putting my pajamas back on with my robe over and not combing my hair after showering. Renate offered me some orange juice while Romney pushed a Danish towards me to start on. I accepted the juice, but thankfully declined the Danish. A toasted bagel with cream cheese and strawberry jam sounded much better.

After Renate helped me find the bag of frozen bagels in our auxiliary freezer, I located a large serrated bread knife with a pistol grip handle. The bagel that I pried loose from the frosty plastic bag was extremely cold. I thought that if I wanted this prize for breakfast, I had two choices. I could either slap it in the microwave for a minute or so, or I could just slice it as it was and the toaster would solve the rest. As I began slicing, the doorbell clanged and I jumped.

"Holy cow!" I wailed and then began yelping

and hopping in terrible pain.

Renate looked over my way and her face went white. She rushed over with a clean dishtowel. Thanking her, I quickly wrapped my injured hand and trudged to the front door as the doorbell clanged on. I opened the door to find an angry Kate ready to continue her verbal blasting: then she gasped.

"Oh, my God, Prich, I came here to straighten out our arrangement, and I find you bleeding to death."

There I was, standing before Kate bleeding profusely, a bloody knife in one hand and a towel around the other. Kate's face went as pale as mine. She grabbed my one remaining good arm and pulled me directly to her car that was parked in the middle of our driveway. We headed for the hospital with my mumbling an unintelligible explanation.

Ten minutes later we were in the emergency room with a young physician smiling and working over my injury.

"Oh, a bagel injury, I guess," the doctor happily put to me.

"What!" I yelped in surprise and pain.

"Not a weekend goes by where I don't see at least one bagel injury," the young man proudly said. "You're right on time, mister. I usually see bunches of these every Saturday morning. Sunday must be French toast day because Saturday is my big bagel day."

"You've got to be kidding us. I don't feel this is the time or place for your humor! You're very lucky that I don't work here!" yipped Kate as the hair on the back of her short cropped hairstyle bristled.

"It's the bane of my culture, and I sincerely apologize for all the trauma it has caused," joked the young Jewish physician. "I'm atoning for our shameful contribution with my service to the medical profession."

"We're out of here!" Kate curtly stated after the weird doctor promptly finished his repairs.

We found our way back to the house in better spirits than a short time before. My hand throbbed, but the Doc had otherwise bandaged my poor paw so I could utilize my appendage reasonably well. I ate that bagel as soon we returned. This may have been my final act of accomplishment that weekend, but I can barely begin to describe the satisfaction I felt with the last yummy gulp. Revenge is sweet and a little crusty, as well!

I knew Kate might be angry enough to slice off my entire arm if she didn't get her beach excursion sometime soon but that was on hold. It was just as well with the new problems consuming me. I surely knew that I would find a way to stick my poor wounded paw in that Atlantic salt water if I got anywhere near the beach. I never suffered in silence in my entire life so can you imagine what it would sound like if I had salt water in that wound? I planned to baby this little puppy for some time to come. I didn't even believe that I wanted to get this poor hand wet under any circumstances. The water-proof bandage didn't guarantee me anything. It might have looked silly to hold one arm outside the shower with the door open, but I reasoned that was why they invented mops.

I received a call from Amos Freyer Sunday evening. We discussed our lack of anything certain that would firmly suggest an involvement with Rogers and Emory. The confusing demise of Joseph Emory wasn't consistent with the average mugging. However, this didn't lead anyone anywhere. The missing cash and nothing else being disturbed was certainly puzzling. There were many young dumb dope heads that would do almost anything for an instant ecstasy, but would they leave all the other obvious items?

Forensics hadn't even been able to provide any conclusive evidence that Emory was killed where he was found. There were two head wounds, though. The front wound was just barely above the left eyebrow. This was definitely the fatal wound. The other injury was on the back of his head. What seemed strange and potentially challenged the lab boys was that the back of the head wound appeared to have been caused at a somewhat earlier time than the front injury. The frontal bleeding was little-to-none compared with the rear wound, suggesting that the rear wound was created prior to the front wound. That differential would normally have been nil, if caused by a fall right after receiving the fatal front blow.

There was also no weapon or object found that caused the death. Perpetrators usually don't leave the scene of the crime carrying a bloody pipe or baseball bat in their hands for all to see. The less display, the better for any killer. There would normally have been some evidence at the scene of a struggle. Scuffed shoe residue such as shoe polish or leather scrapings might be found on the pavement. One would also have expected to find fiber evidence consistent with the victim's clothing and hopefully, the perpetrator's. The most obvious indication we had was the lack of any large blood splatters. Blood should have sprayed in a very wide arch upon impact with the weapon. Any kid knows that if he hits a ripe watermelon with his baseball bat, he would be wiping up the mess all afternoon. One can clean a crime scene of that mess but, the forensics folks can come in years later and tell there was blood spattered all over. It's almost impossible to get rid of blood indoors. With all its life- giving benefits, blood also benefits us much later than we would think.

The place where Emory's body was found was definitely not the place where he was killed. That conclusion shouted at us. It was more the lack of anything physical or logical, rather than finding solid evidence. Someone was playing games and whoever that someone was didn't appear to be a professional killer. I also didn't believe the killer was a mugger, looking for funds for a quick drug buy. What mugger takes all the care and effort to move a body? Things were becoming more curious by the second hand on my watch which didn't keep the correct time, anyway. The perps may have been pros in their own fields, but they had just stepped into Amos Freyer's world where he was the pro with access to all those forensics assets.

Joseph Emory had a considerable fortune. Even though the portion invested with the computer enterprise was sizable, it wasn't a significant percentage of the Emory estate. The largest share of Emory's assets went to an individual named Cassandra Johnson and a select variety of charities. One of the larger recipients was the Salvation Army which was one of my favorite charities as well. I wasn't sure if it was the name of the Salvation Army or if the specific area designated with the unwed mothers which caught my eye. It just occurred to me that this wealthy man may have also had a soft spot in his heart. The community may have felt his wound, but maybe it would also be somewhat healed by his bequests.

Early Monday morning was a real chore for me trying to shave and get dressed with one hand. I was fumble-fingered even when I was endowed with all my appendages, so that morning was an experience I hoped not to repeat. I was wishing for French toast, but the old standard of corn flakes with a sliced banana worked well enough.

Father and I left the house at the same time, which seemed to unnerve him slightly. I had gotten somewhat used to this healthy life schedule with getting a fast start in the morning and retiring at a reasonable time, though I didn't plan to make that a habit. I had found a sling that father had used several years earlier when he'd sprained his wing with a fall on the ice. That made my ensemble.

My arrival at Rogers & Emory was somewhat under-whelming. God bless automatic transmissions, even on this classic pony car. They might have had someone like me in mind when they invented that wonderful thing. I couldn't possibly have driven safely that morning with a stick shift and one game paw. I was certainly happy that I was right handed as many tasks might have been hopeless otherwise. However, it was darn near impossible for a one-handed fellow to keep his dignity after visiting the privy and then trying to zip up. The last thing in the world that I would want to do is to ask another fellow to help me hold one end while I pulled up the zipper. I would have rather died first!

No one rushed to my aid to help me open the doors while I was holding a briefcase or to assist me with my coat. I began to appreciate the everyday problems of the handicapped even more with each unthinking or unhelpful event. I did, though, receive a smiling sympathetic gaze from a real dazzler who walked by and then looked back to see if I were watching her. I was caught again.

Charles Rogers could have given me a little more time on that visit. He introduced me to his son David, the president and chief operating officer. It was this younger Rogers that made things go after the senior had opted for the semi involved figure-head. While Charles was pleasant and smiling, David was strictly business. The father wore the sport coat while the son had the $800 Hinkley pin-striped suit. Dad had the slip-on-loafers while the kid had the wingtips tied so tightly his eyes bugged out a little. I won't even mention who wore the gaudy palm tree neck tie and who wore the maroon paisley version.

"I thought that I would only be assisting you folks with a simple transition to our firm," I began with a lead-in exploratory statement. "Now the entire question is open. I'm so sorry to hear about Mr. Emory's death, and my father asked me also to convey his sympathy."

"Where do you think we should go?" came the pleasant inquiry from the elder Mr. Rogers. "I'm still in a daze about my dear friend, and he'll be forever in my thoughts. It's a shock, and I'm unclear about our proper course now."

David Rogers was sitting across from me in an upright position, following me as a cobra would his prey. I felt uncomfortable in a position where my every twitch was cataloged and later could be used against me. We humans don't like to feel inferior or have our Maslo's safety base of the pyramid threatened. When I sat at any table, I preferred to experience some pleasure rather than forbearance. When I looked at a yummy piece of lettuce, I didn't expect that wonderful piece of greenery to lick its chops back in my direction. I much preferred to be at the top of the food chain rather than the main course on someone's menu.

"I believe that is entirely your call," I responded as I moved uncomfortably under David Rogers' gaze. "Certainly, we need to begin the transition with Mr. Emory's estate and whatever effects that will have on the business. Beyond that, you pay the bills and I feel that makes you the boss. We'll analyze your business operations to a limited degree to find the best legal approach for you. Then we'll make a recommendation which could take any number of directions."

"Can you do anything beyond that scope?" came the ice man's first utterance. "We may also have some wider needs."

"If you can be just a tad more specific?" I said.

"We may wish to expand or alter our operations," came a somewhat cryptic answer.

"I'll tell you whatever I believe is economically better for you, if that's what you mean," I indicated rather forthrightly.

"How so?" asked Charles Rogers with his pleasant voice still resonating very slowly.

"I can tell you that we can tailor our services to any need you feel is in your best interest," I continued. "Our firm also has a business consulting division. We have a staff that will perform a complete management analysis and financial analysis if you wish. I've seen our people go into a struggling business and have it turned around in one quarter."

"What about our vulnerability?" asked the younger man with a slightly better intonation in his voice.

"We can certainly look at all your legal obligations," I said confidently. "Our best attribute is found in our basic package. That being, to what lengths can any business operate without going to jail. If a viable operation plays it too safe, it won't need to advertise its failure. We'll all know it soon enough."

"Operating on the edge might be more stress than I want to endure," stated the elder man as he appeared to be thinking more out loud.

"Yes, father," answered the younger Rogers. "But, that is where the larger margin of profits are found."

Seeing that I was in the middle of a policy dispute, I decided to keep my big mouth shut. I might come back after there was some accord, but I didn't want to take sides and make an enemy of either man. That was Management 101 and the differences of opinion about the general direction of the business needed to be resolved by management first. I liked papa's general posture, but I knew the son's statement made better business sense. What I didn't have a chance to say before the disagreement started concerned the opposite side of the business coin. Sure the business needed to take some chances even with the knowledge that it may fail a time or two. They needed to minimize those failures, stopping before the business was driven over the edge.

I left their office with the understanding that I would do some general looking around and get back to them with my recommendation in a day or two. This would give them a chance to get their act together and give me a chance to snoop into Evans' dilemma. They made that an easy start by calling Evans to the area as my initial contact and indicated that he should assist me with this get acquainted routine. Evans played his role better than an Oscar award winner. The introduction by the elder Rogers was a glowing report on Evans' aptitude and loyalty. I was a fairly good performer too, as I didn't break out in laughter about that loyalty statement...not even a tiny snicker.

We continued to play our roles well for the balance of our time together. However, he did mention that there were some additional documents already in the mail, but no one could hear the statement. Even so, they wouldn't glean anything unusual from an innocuous statement in a casually delivered tone. Evans might be the guy I needed to assist me with my expense vouchers if he could be that creative. Maybe a little quid pro quo was in order here.

John Evans made the best appearance with his subordinates by pretending only to give me a very cursory explanation of his function, but then asked everyone else to be very helpful. When one lady asked what exactly helpful meant, I softened the process by just adding the word "forthright." Evans then amplified my responses by indicating that I was an attorney with the firm representing Rogers & Emory. They began to come around when I stated that I was being paid, so their firm might as well get their money's worth. If I were working for them, why snooker one of their own?

The work was about as interesting as a wild-eyed liberal reading *The New Republic*. Evans and I previously agreed that he should indicate with a scratch to his anatomy if he felt any document was possibly relevant to his inquiry. One time he would scratch his head and the next time, the back of his hand. After about twenty documents from the three subordinates, I was wondering what he would scratch or rub next. He'd run out of all the decent or sanitary places, and I was sure that I didn't want to continue watching.

I had made copies of the documents, but couldn't force myself to continue acting like they were interesting. I simply put my copies in my case and stated that I needed to see the marketing department after lunch. On the way back to the Mustang, I told Evans that we should have some answer to his quandary in several days. I wasn't stretching the truth about his process being worked, as I had started that ball this morning at the water-cooler.

Pops was right about my being uncomfortable in an office all day. I put the top down on the warmer-than-usual spring midday. It was still somewhat chilly, but I needed the sunlight. When I reached our office, I was shivering but still smiling. I was in our accounting department in a flash, hoping to be out in the same fashion, after adding the new data sheets to the ones I provided earlier. I had my fill of that kind of environment for one day. Joe Lindsey had probably recovered from my poorly timed faux pas earlier, as I saw him give me the high sign with a motion to wait a moment. I was walking over to his modest digs when he put down the phone and stepped out to meet me with a big smile plastered all over his ruddy face.

"Didn't expect to see you back here so soon, Prich," Lindsey said with an ever widening grin.

I was wondering what could cheer up a soul so much in this environment. Maybe he'd made a wonderful find with those documents or had gotten lucky with the buxom young gal after my clumsy bungle earlier that morning. I hadn't heard anything about a big local lottery winner.

"I've got a few more cryptic puzzles to pass along with the other that I gave you this morning, old buddy," I responded as I happily handed off the mystery sheets. I believe the cliché goes something like, "An action passed is an action completed!"

"What's this, 'Old Buddy,' stuff you're dishing out so freely, Prich? Do I detect a little twinge of remorse?"

"Me thinks you're psychic," I snickered with a devilish intonation.

I prided myself that I'd handed the new accounting forms to Lindsey before anything in our conversation could deteriorate to the point where he would refuse to accept this new lovely tasking. The last thing in the universe that I could imagine myself doing was poring over a stack of folded strange paper with light green lines across and those tiny holes along both sides. God bless computers, but I would have drawn the line at anything that deals with number crunching on that wide accounting computer paper used on those extra wide carriage impact printers. The one near my own cubicle upstairs that buzzed and whined had made an enemy of me for life.

"Some of what you gave me this morning made sense and some is incomplete," began the green eye-shade type with his good natured inflection. "I was hoping that you could expand this information to show specific accounts and maybe the general ledger sheets for this particular time in question."

"I'm not sure what we have here, Joe," I responded. "There might be some of that info in those sheets that I just gave you. Our contact also stated that he'd put some other info in the mail to us this weekend. With our luck and post office efficiency, we'll probably see them around the Christmas holiday."

"Right!" agreed Lindsey with an emphatic tone. "What decade do you want this analysis?"

"What questions do you have so far?" I asked without adding any other information about Evans' suspicion. I hoped to get an independent evaluation without any bias. "Is there any problem that leads you to think you need more information?"

"Only the preliminary questions we nosey folks always ask," answered the accountant. "How do they make all that great income?"

"So you can do the same?" I promptly said.

"You bet," came the short answer. "I'm always willing to learn from the bright ones that have made it already. However, I really need more information from the other accounts. One account feeds another account. I wanted to see the source documents like the journal and ledger entries for a specific period that supports some of the wrap-up sheets that I have here."

"That is certainly some interesting information," I offered with a yawn and then a pat on my mouth. "Could you please jot down those ideas on a short list, and I'll pick them up in a few minutes?"

I escaped that entanglement and headed back to my humble hovel one floor above. It didn't look too bad after the accounting department.

Robert C. Nienkemper

Chapter 5

Stunned by the Headlights

I had a post-it note message attached to my chair back and the approved version of my expense voucher lying on the chair seat as I arrived at the place where I "worked." Naturally, the seat version of a message was much more welcome than the chair back version. I had a direct deposit process for my funds at the same bank where the Hale & Son firm had their business account. It seemed to function much better that way, as I had overcome some accounting problems of my own in the not too distant past.

Mildred buzzed and asked if it would be convenient for me to see her boss for a short explanation. Thinking that I might be facing a great inquisition about my last expense voucher, I asked if she knew what type of explanation he wanted. When she indicated something about accounting, my heart skipped a beat, but then she mentioned the name of Rogers and Emory. I told her that I would be right in. I was standing before the big guy with a renewed heart but still a guilty conscience.

"Prich, you look somewhat worn," stated his nibs. "I hope all is well with you, son."

"Just on the run, but the challenge is worth all the hassle," I said with an upbeat voice.

"We were so worried about you with that terrible wound. Is there anything I can do to help

64

you along?"

I appreciated father's concern, and I was wondering why it didn't occur to me to play it for more than I had. I almost forgot that I still had one wing in a sling and looked like a poster boy for the downtown homeless shelter. What a wonderful opportunity I was letting slip away so easily.

"Thank you, father, for your concern," I started with my best sad soldier face. "Sure wish that I wasn't so blamed clumsy."

"I was surprised that you made it in today. You would've been perfectly correct to remain home until you felt better."

"Well, sir, I'm not one that would want to be thought of as a shirker. I suppose that I inherited your work ethic."

I could almost see a tear well up in the old guy's eye, and I nearly became mushy about that time. I had to hold on and not allow my emotions to run away. There wasn't a better time in the world to press my advantage.

I wanted to get that expense voucher closed out as I knew how the accounting system needed to have these things resolved. I also needed to assure our new clients that we were not neglecting them.

"What if anything is happening with your inquiry? Is there any news about Mr. Emory's mishap?"

"I just started with the analysis of Mr. Evans' documentation, and we're getting it in dribbles."

"Can anyone here give you any assistance?"

asked father while displaying a parental caring expression.

"Joe Lindsey in accounting has started to help," I confessed after some artful prodding by the senior.

"Good. He's a sharp young man, and we are fortunate to have him."

"Right," I stated, thinking it was about time to change the subject. "This thing with Emory just doesn't feel kosher. I got a funny feeling when I talked to Amos Freyer."

"He is the homicide officer you worked with before?" Father stated with a questioning intonation.

"That's the guy."

"What does he think?"

"Well, it's early, but I know he'll do just fine," I assured the grand master.

"What's your opinion, son?"

"About the same as Freyer's, I guess," I indicated, thinking, "Why spill everything in the first inning?" I could pull out the heavy stuff when I needed to, but restraint was always the wisest path at the outset.

"Well, just be extremely careful with this, son. I certainly don't want you to be endangered," Father cautioned with some additional emphasis. "That police officer gets paid for that line of work."

"I understand, father," I answered with sincerity. "I'll be the pillar of conservatism."

I left pops with a warm feeling of closeness and family which was accompanied by a seeping manifestation of hunger. I had to begin thinking like a female with child as I also needed sustenance for more than the single individual. I required nourishment to replenish the damaged cells and facilitate the healing process. It appeared the trauma didn't disturb my rationalization skills.

I thought that I would start the new expense account with a legitimate charge for a novel change. Settling in at my desk, I flipped through the Rolodex file and called Amos Freyer with no success. I left a message for Freyer and went back down to accounting to search for the person who handled our benefits. I was directed to the opposite side of the area where I was normally accustomed with my endeavors. Two inquiries later, I was standing at the cubicle with the smiling buxom clerk that previously had all of Joe Lindsey's attention at the water-cooler. She was endowed with something more than the obvious, and my opinion of Joe's taste was improving steadily. She knew exactly how to filter through the morass of complex forms and get to the pertinent aspects of a medical claim. It amounted to little more than a "staple this" and "sign that" and the task was completed. I can say that I was relieved, but also somewhat disappointed that my reason for being there ended so efficiently.

I was certainly reassured to find that the shocking hospital invoice for the few minutes of emergency treatment was fully covered. I'd thought that our firm's billing was often obscene, but we could take lessons from those folks. At least, everyone who came through our front door in the lobby in a warm and vertical mode left in the same fashion. They might be somewhat lighter in the wallet with their exit with us, but we didn't kick any of them out the back door in that cold, stiff and horizontal manner. I believe that our technique was certainly a little more gentle.

I trudged back to my desk to find a phone message from Amos Freyer waiting. I called Freyer's office again and was told that he'd just left about a quarter of an hour before. I started for the club to replenish my withering frame. A couple of blocks down the road, I dialed information on my cellular phone for the number of our local Denny's. I put through the call and got a twangy waitress that I could hear yelling Freyer's name. Then I heard a loud clunk in my ear as she dropped the phone on the counter. A few seconds later, the detective's growling voice, muffled with a mouth full of food, came my way with a side-order of scratchy static.

"We've been playing telephone tag, and I thought you might be as hungry as me," I started. "Been there long?"

"Is that you, Prich?" scratched and whirred the response.

"Right-O, big guy."

"Guess I don't have any secrets from you," Freyer stated. "Just got here and took my first bite. Want to join me?"

"Sure, I'll be there in five," I said quickly. "Why don't you order that $1.99 Grand Slam special breakfast and over easy on the eggs."

"Gotcha."

I pulled into the Denny's parking lot in five minutes on the dot. I would probably hear about the extra minute that it took me to get out of the car and walk into the 24 hour restaurant. I spotted the cop as soon as I cleared the door and walked right over to the window booth. Our waitress seemed to be right on cue, as she appeared with my chow and a steaming pot of very black coffee. Freyer was in a good mood after disposing with half of his triple stacked burger. After filling both of our coffee cups and pulling a bottle of ketchup from her pocket, she bade a happy "enjoy" and quickly peddled back behind the counter. I was lucky Freyer had this booth as the place was filling up fast.

"Hey, you get around pretty good with that one wing flapping in the breeze," started the cop. "Hope you don't feel as bad as it looks."

I was reasonably proud of my effect. First father and then this hard-nosed guy. I thought to myself, "Good show!"

"I'll make it okay," I stated with that British type of stiff upper lip. "It'll just take a while to get through this. I'm having the most difficulty in the shower and the john."

Well, I knew it as soon as I said it and saw his eyes light right up. If I could have pulled back that final statement, I wouldn't need to put up with that abuse. I hated playing straight man to the cops.

"Ha, I've heard that you've always had problems in the john!" said the cop with the satisfaction spilling all over his face. In fact, he almost choked as he was so anxious to make his digging point. He just sat there in a dead silence, smiling with a piece of lettuce sticking between his teeth.

"Okay, ha, ha," I finally said with a mock laugh. "You and I could start a road show, but I'm not sure if I'd want to set you up all the time."

I began sloshing ketchup over my cut-up eggs as Freyer groaned. The pancakes were the target of choice after I asked the waitress to bring another half beaker of maple syrup. The better they're saturated with butter and syrup, the better they are. I was also looking for a refill of that wickedly black high test java. I listened to Freyer discuss the strange occurrences that presented themselves at the Bethesda constabulary this morning. Nothing sounded as odd as the purpose of our meeting at this restaurant.

"Found anything interesting with your work at that Rogers & Emory Company?"

"Only what you would normally expect," I said with an uncertain tone. "People are still stand-offish as I'm a new face that they aren't familiar with yet. It's still get acquainted time for all of us."

"I know what you said about your purpose there the other day, but I'm not sure if I'm buying it," the clever dick indicated. "I always seem to remember your being around some sort of trouble."

"I'll keep an eye open for you, but you need to tell me what to look for when I meet with those folks," I responded. "They're our clients, and my first responsibility is to them."

"Does that mean you won't help me?" said Freyer with a frown.

"Of course, it doesn't," I told him quickly. "You know I always try to help the officials, especially when you're involved."

"Sounds like we're back to where we were the other day, so I'm just putting you on notice," stated the cop strongly.

"Well, let's get started right now," I countered.

"Okay, you first, my man," smiled Freyer.

"You can plainly see what I've been up to with this wonderful injury," I answered with a similar smile. "You also have all those resources that I don't. We both probably have some questions with what was found, but where do we go from here? I'm at the company for a specific task, and it's not the reason that you were brought there. How about your keeping the faith, amigo, and pony-up some of your results?"

"Okay, Prich, I'll give you the first of our debate club matches just because I feel sorry for all cripples, but I'll be waiting for something in return real soon."

"If I get it, you'll be the first to know," I happily told him.

"Sure you will," the homicide detective dragged out slowly.

"Oh, ye of little faith," I thought, but kept my big trap shut. Amos Freyer confirmed all my suspicions about the impossibility of the murder scene being the same place as where the body was discovered. He indicated that he was in the process of interviews with company personnel and anyone who even had a remote connection. I wondered if that much effort would be put forth if the victim hadn't been the wealthy individual that he was.

I grabbed Amos' check and he didn't protest in the slightest. I indicated that he could leave the tip and added that it should reflect the great service and extra coffee refills. I smiled as I saw one eyebrow raise ever so slightly. Cops sure have me beaten in the cheap skate category. However, I didn't tell him those checks would hit my expense voucher with a little inflation and would also include his tip.

My return to Rogers & Emory went without any difficulty, and I was beginning to feel like a one armed Grand Prix racer. The thought of the automatic transmission brought me back to reality. Happily, I'd slowed down just before I passed through a radar trap that already had several victims nabbed on the shoulder of the road. I quietly mouthed, "Shame on you," as I cruised right by thinking of my last hassle in traffic court. You would think they would be more understanding of some poor lawyer in the very place where they practice their profession.

John Evans welcomed me back with an attitude like I was his exclusive ethics police. We had a short and amiable discussion about my spreading myself around to accomplish the task that this company was paying our firm to do. He made a brief call to verify that the chief of marketing was available, and then we headed towards the back corner of the office building. Boy, was the chief of marketing ever a pleasant departure from the chief of accounting.

We walked over to marketing in a serpentine route so Evans could introduce me to several other key individuals that he thought I might need to see with my official get-acquainted process. He was being very helpful and didn't pester me for some immediate results to his allegations. Ten minutes later, I was deposited on a new doorstep facing a perky brunette who acted more like the president than the boss of marketing.

I was welcomed like a friend of the company who might be able to assist them. I wasn't an adversary, which made our time much more pleasant and productive. When I asked a question, a direct answer quickly followed. Big brother could take a lesson or two from his sister. Judith Rogers was about five foot five, fresh as a new spring breeze. She was open and happy with a genuine smile. Her clothier probably was smiling too as nothing she wore was inexpensive or off the rack. Although pricey, her tastes were conservative and muted. She looked as if she preferred fitting in rather than standing out. Her under-statement was her charm.

"So, Mr. Hale, you think I might need a lawyer," she said with a trifle portion of mischief and a twinkle of a grin. "If I confess now, can't I just throw myself on the mercy of the court?"

"I've tried that same ploy several times and look where that's gotten me," I cracked with similar trickery leaking through.

We got along famously for the first meeting between any two humans, and I was amused that I was actually communicating with a female. Some days were better than others, and I would have just settled for a great half day. We'd finished most of the preliminaries about my purpose at Rogers and Emory, and now she was interested in particulars.

"Things have been very unsettled here, and I'm running as the point person with all the inquiries," she said with more intensity. "We don't know what happened to Uncle Joe, and everyone has been calling for some news. I even have to break it to many of them. It's a tragedy, but they all want to talk to me and won't accept what the staff tells them."

"Uncle Joe?" I asked, thinking I already knew the answer.

"We all called him that because that's how he behaved," she volunteered. "He was such a kind old man and was always asking people about their families. I remember once when he even went to the hospital when one of our staff was having a miscarriage."

"But he didn't actually perform any function here?" I asked as I thought I saw some sadness creep into that cheery face. "I thought that he came by to check on his investment."

"This investment wasn't that much to him," she countered without hesitation. "He was a very crafty old gentleman, though. He was hoping to expand the operation and eventually go public. He thought we could make it on the NASDAQ some day and become one of those emerging companies they advertise on TV."

"Like when they show Microsoft and say something like 'where do those wonder companies come from,' and then they show the over-the-counter growth on the NASDAQ."

"Looks like you saw the same ad," she chuckled as the joy came back to her face. She then paused and looked at me with a reflective stare, but she shook her head.

"Something you wanted to say?" I said in a puzzled tone.

"Well," she started with some thought. "I didn't see any rings on your finger, and I was just stood-up by this jerk who I was happy to hear couldn't make it tonight."

"Could this be true," I thought. "was there really a Santa Claus?" I had a suspicion that this day was getting better, but I had no inkling of how good. Opportunities like this didn't appear everyday, so I thought that I had better do that right.

"No attachments at all," I quickly stammered while feeling just a little teensy weensy twinge of guilt. "I can't understand anyone standing you up."

"Thanks for your kind support," she shyly grinned. "The National Symphony has a wonderful soloist tonight that's doing Beethoven's violin concerto and several Brahms' violin works including his own concerto. I'd been waiting for this for some time and then here's this last minute pullout."

I guess she saw my face go from euphoria to bewilderment as she was in mid-sentence. She almost began laughing at me, but the thought of losing another escort stabilized her behavior. She had me hooked, and she wasn't going to throw this one back. She set that hook deep when she reached across to hold my hand for a very short moment.

"I'm not really a classical aficionado, but I might learn something," I advanced with some reservation. "Who knows, I could even enjoy this event, and I certainly know I'll enjoy being with a lady of your quality."

She beamed at my mention of her and added a short laugh. I thought that anything looked good after she had been dumped by some jerk, but I hadn't been fibbing about being happy to be with her. As we set the time and place, we talked about the appropriate dress for the evening. I thought tuxedo, but I was very subtly educated about many new things that I would be facing this evening. With the logistics solved, I began easing my way out of her office and onto new adventures. Her final warning was to watch out for her sister who was just coming back from a business trip. I wasn't exactly sure what she meant, and she didn't see any need to elaborate.

I was then introduced to Judith's assistant, Cassy Lewis, who gave me a concise run through on the top ten percent of their customers which accounted for over half of their revenue. I got the low down on what gets kids' attention with computer games and where they thought the industry was headed. They were making it big right now with a new version of Galaxy Mega Thunderbolts on compact disk. Cassy was even nice enough to give me that CD and one named Hot Rod Speed Demons which had just about run its course. Then someone came strolling through the door, and I knew at once what Judith had meant by her warning.

Evelyn Rogers was a stunner, to say it quietly. I preferred to have it shouted at me, though. She was blessed in every curve and angle that I saw and a few others that I only imagined. Her eyes shined, her lips were wet, her flaxen hair glistened, and my heart pounded. She glided to meet Cassy and me with a regal motion. The chic, slinky, two-piece expensive ensemble must have been conceived with a form like hers in mind. I couldn't think of a more appropriate position for her in any company. She could sell me anything. If you believe that she didn't know that too, you've got another think coming.

She greeted me with a firm, smooth voice which intoxicated us male mortals. Her command of this controlled situation was clearly noticeable. She let us know this was her territory, but we were her guests. She was gracious now in her own neighborhood, but I wondered if she were different in foreign territory.

She pirouetted effortlessly and led me into her glass walled office with barely any notice of the other females she left in her wake. I wouldn't have ever wanted to be on her bad side. She could cut you like a razor-blade, and you wouldn't feel it or bleed until you walked away. I thought it was fortunate for me that I could be monitored by others. It certainly prevented me from making a silly fool of myself. She smiled as my knees buckled when she offered me a seat on the colorfully upholstered couch by the glassed wall. She sat beside me at the opposite end and then offered me a drink. I accepted and was happy that I did when she rose and turned to flick on the intercom button to her secretary. My, my, what a piece of work!

"I've heard you're here to get an overview of our operations?" she said. "Is there some process that I can help you with?"

"There probably is," I found myself saying with some shock to hear my voice. "First I'd like to see how your organization is structured, and we can go on from there. I've already spoken with Judith, and we're somewhat settled on procedure."

"What would be the likely next step?" she asked.

"Our staff needs to see if your office interacts efficiently with the rest of your organization."

"That's a significant study in itself, Mr. Hale," she continued. "I would think you wouldn't be involved with the entire inquiry."

"You're correct."

"That's a shame," she started with a warm smile. "I was hoping to see more of you."

Gulp was what I heard next from down deep in my throat. I thought that I'd just stumbled into paradise and was beginning to find out what it was like on the other side of the fence in heaven.

Chapter 6

Not an Elliot Ness

After getting everything straight with who did what in marketing, I penciled a few notes. It appeared that my date of that evening, Judith, had the in-house responsibility to keep the day-to-day functions running smoothly. The vixen sibling was the individual who worked on a one-on-one basis with their customers. Evelyn could spin her web around most of us poor mortals, except for just a very few that I knew. Naturally, other females and some guys who swung the other way had that genetic immunity.

After making my farewells for the day, I skipped to the Mustang with glee. It was a wonder that I even touched the ground after that experience. A date with a beauty without even trying and then a subtle flirtation with a Venus. This would surely require a big star in my diary.

I glided to the house with a sixth sense. It was remarkable that I didn't get a traffic ticket in the process. Luck continued to be with me, for sure. I stopped at the local car wash to be sure no feathered bombardier had found its mark. I put out a ton of effort as I even raised the top for the wash and got out with a towel to wipe off the water spots. I was really getting into the teenage mode again. I could see all the signs and recognize those testosterone levels rising. I hoped I wouldn't see those acne blemishes again.

Renate had dinner prepared on the dot, which fit my tight schedule. After appearing with dark tan slacks and my all time favorite camel hair sports coat, several at the table counseled me about the more appropriate garb for the Kennedy Center Symphony Hall. So what if I didn't step right off the cover of *Gentlemen's Quarterly*, I had other redeeming qualities.

My favorite meal changed with increased frequency, but authentic German sauerbraten with ginger brown gravy, potato pancakes with cinnamon apple sauce, and sweet and sour red cabbage hold their place right near the pinnacle. Then there was Renate's apple strudel with ice cream. There went the waist line out one more notch in the old belt for just thinking about all those wonderful calories.

I raced back upstairs in a jiffy and started scrounging around for something more suitable for the evening among the more cultured group. I found something even pops would be proud of: black slacks with a deep blue ultra-suede coat and maroon tie. It was boring, but acceptable, I guessed. I zipped through the shower with remarkable time and set about to shine the old choppers with a little brushing. That also did wonders for my breath after the luscious dinner I finished. My face was somewhat scratchy so I quickly pasted a handful of shave-cream on my mug and took a couple fast swipes with a disposable razor. I paid for that haste with three pieces of TP stuck to my chin and cheeks to stem the flow of blood.

I looked at the diary, but knew I probably already was going to be late and hoped that I would still be in some good graces. Maybe she had me figured out and programmed some float time with me. The light was getting low in the sky, so I thought the cops were probably off the radar mode, and maybe all I had to do was watch the rear view mirror.

Luck was still with me as I pulled up to their residence only four minutes late. My last hope was maybe her watch was a couple of minutes slow, and I could convince her that the watch was actually a couple of minutes fast. I didn't know why I began worrying about time as I never seemed to do that before.

I used the term residence earlier because I didn't see a moat so the term castle might not have been appropriate. I looked up just in case as I pulled the door chime, hoping that some serf wasn't going to dump a vat of hot oil on me. I reached to feel if my tie were reasonably straight and then remembered the TP sticking to my face. With two hands flailing to grab the small pieces of tissue, I just about had the task completed when the door opened. I was greeted by a houseman named Walter who made no attempt to hide what he'd just witnessed. I was given that one raised eyebrow and a snobby welcome. Walter's name seemed to fit him just right. Some people looked like a Walter or a George, and you feel comfortable calling them that. It simply wouldn't seem right to call them Walt or Georgey Boy. I was led to the study where a TV was displaying the game show *Jeopardy* with the audio muted. Walter indicated that Ms. Judith was almost ready and would be down shortly. I couldn't imagine someone treating a fellow like that after I'd gotten there so early. The table had turned.

I kicked back in an over-stuffed chair and began surveying the palatial surroundings. Someone had hit the good times to afford these digs. I saw only the limited portion of the residence and was very impressed with the structure as well as the furnishings. I could clearly see the hand of a talented decorator here. The eclectic use of fashionable period pieces with more modern upholstered items blended well in the room designed for comfort. The warm earth tone wall covering was in fact a small floral print wallpaper that seemed to blend away. The windows looked as if they went from floor to ceiling. For individuals who were fond of low window sills with very tall windows, this was their mecca. The tall doorway with a gorgeous transom was a treasure. This great room actually had a full size pool table. Add the wonderful wooded library table and gun case next to the pool cue rack and maybe this was heaven. I thought this would be a wonderful final resting place for any male.

Judith walked through the door with a bright smile and a faint scent of an expensive perfume. Her pale blue, low cut back chiffon evening dress probably cost more than my current checking account balance. Her hair, pulled to left side, flowed in larger soft waves that dipped over the side of her forehead. The style reminded me of my late grand aunt that I saw in our family album. The jade earrings complimented the color of her eye-shade and dress. The dress highlighted her thin waist and made her ample bust line seem better endowed.

"Sorry to keep you waiting, but we still have plenty of time," she said as she walked over to hold my arm. "I see you're a *Jeopardy* fan."

"Always trying to improve my mind," I quipped with a smile. "Guess it's just our lot in life to wait for you lovely ladies."

"Have you really been waiting that long?"

"This is the second game show I've had to endure!" I joked and then gave a big grin.

"Oh, you!" she said with a slight dig into my rib-cage with her thumb.

She took my arm and was leading me out of the study when Evelyn turned slowing down the gentle spiral staircase, and our eyes met in the doorway.

"So big sister beat me to the prize, I see," Evelyn said with a mock air of hurt in her voice. "I'm forever playing the poor second fiddle."

"I thought you always played first chair?" I laughed.

"Boo," laughed Judith. "That's a terrible pun!"

Seeing the bewilderment in her sister's eyes, Judith explained that we were heading for the symphony, and I was referring to the concert master. That didn't make sister Evelyn any too happy to have her less than million dollar glamorous sister teach her anything. All of this in front of me made those gastric juices just a tad more caustic. Evelyn did her famous

83

pirouette, almost as if a bullfighter had just let the great beast make his pass and left us to ourselves.

"It's been a long day for her," Judith began to apologize. "She had a difficult flight in today and had to confront the fact of Joe Emory at the same time."

"She already knew, didn't she?"

"Yes, but it really hits home when you're back here, I guess. This thing hasn't been easy on any of us, and Evelyn doesn't like to admit that she's vulnerable too."

Her apology sounded good, but I had a different feeling about dear sister. She was a sizzling temptress and a sexy vixen; however, she was also very self centered. I could imagine a conscious reality of turmoil with her as a life's partner. She would continually be pulling some string or making someone's existence troublesome, except for those few moments of bliss.

Judith asked what I was driving this evening, and I proudly answered that she had the rare opportunity to ride in a Mustang classic. That went over like a kiss before taking a breath mint. This wasn't a *Happy Days* rerun, and she wouldn't consider being seen in anything that ever needed restoring. She gave me one of those pained expressions and then indicated that her car was in the garage being serviced. When she said it was in the garage, I thought, *"What's the problem? Lets go get it."* Then it hit me that her vernacular was somewhat different than mine. Okay, I wondered, what do we do? Call a cab? While I was pondering this earth shaking dilemma, she was already taking corrective action. She picked up her father's Mercedes keys, and we headed for the real garage this time.

She insisted that I drive, which took some getting used to as I was unaccustomed to large luxury gunboats. I was fiddling around with the dashboard switches, trying to find the lights and important gauges. Judith turned on the overhead light and gave me a fast run through. It seemed the lights came on automatically with an internal sensor. The next chore was the garage door which was solved with the small opener switch hanging on the ignition key-ring. The electronic marvel was just too much for my poor soul, and I longed for the old reliable Mustang.

Evidently, Judith had noticed some remnant of TP on my chin when she turned the light on in the car while we were still in the garage. She made a kind remark about my grievous injuries as we were just pulling onto the street, and she gently rubbed my face.

"Seems like I'm always scarred up and pieced together," I apologized with a mock frown. "I've been that way since I was a little tyke."

"You certainly don't need to apologize, Prich. You should see my legs after I shave."

"I thought you gals just came that way. Weren't you really a perfect creation that didn't need any alterations?"

"You should see all the effort I go through every day."

"I'm told that I was one of those kids that never fell over backwards or on my side," I admitted with a chuckle. "Every time I toppled over, it was straight down on my face. It's a wonder that my nose isn't splattered all over my puss."

I became somewhat self conscious, so I stopped at the curb and turned to see my face in the rear view mirror. As I found that last piece of telltale evidence of my shaving prowess, I caught just a slight movement of a vehicle at the curb start out with its lights turned off and then stop. As I continued to joke around with Judith and hide the scraps of the TP from my face, I kept a sharp eye on that rear view mirror. I pulled away slowly from the curb, glancing short peeks at the mirror. Sure enough, the same car repeated the previous process, but continued to follow. I turned slowly at the corner and Judith gave me a strange look. She started to express some concern about my new route. I used my hand to signal her to wait a second.

The car continued around the corner with the headlights switched on. It began allowing the distance between us to stretch to several more car lengths. I asked Judith to pretend to argue with me with exaggerated arm motions for an instant when I gave the cue. Seeing the concern in my eyes, she did as asked.   As I slowed at the four way stop at the next corner, I gave Judith the signal by moving my right arm in an awkward movement first. Judith dutifully picked right up on our "off Broadway" play with a performance that should have received an award. I moved my head back and forth so I could get several quick looks into the mirror as the car approached the rear of the Mercedes. The first thing that I paid attention to was the positioning of my feet on the pedals. I had my left foot on the brake and my right on the gas. If we needed to move quickly, all I needed to do was mash on the gas and let go the brake instantaneously. Thus, we would lose no time with my switching one foot from the brake pedal to the accelerator.

The first thing I concentrated on was the license plate and the action of the vehicle. For instance, was the car going to hit us or were the doors remaining closed. The last thing I wanted to see was some big ugly bent nosed lug with a weapon come running our way. I got a good look at the plate as the light at the corner was very bright. It was a Maryland plate stylized with a nature scene of a big brown Heron and the JIB 819 showing clearly. The car stopped easily behind us and remained there waiting patiently as Judith and I flailed about the Mercedes with our performance. Judith was a real trooper throughout the entire event.

I continued at the ready with my feet, but the dark blue Chevy Impala didn't do anything out of the ordinary other than show more patience than was common for these parts. The windows were extra dark, and I suspected they were tinted very heavily. I had hoped to see what the driver and anyone else in the vehicle looked like. No such luck other than I thought that I only saw one individual in the car.

I was beginning to wonder if I were being paranoid, so I told Judith that we would play it straight for a short time. I started away from the stop sign and continued for three more blocks before signaling one way, but turning the other. Sure enough, the Chevy which was following at a distance, turned with us. The old gastric juices got my tummy going again. I turned onto a main thoroughfare and watched. Still back there, Damn! I slowed the pace and the Chevy kept the same pace. Okay, folks, I might be a little slow on the up-take, but whoever this guy was, he had my full attention.

The Mercedes wasn't a dragster, and I didn't feel like a Grand Prix driver at that moment either. I knew that it was super safe, and if I had to use it as a weapon, I thought we could walk away from it. I reached down on the console and picked up the cellular phone. I had Amos Freyer's work and home phone committed to memory and asked Judith to dial the instrument at the work number first. She was familiar with the phone, so she quickly handed it back to me after she heard a voice on the other end. I asked for Freyer, but was told that he hadn't been on night duty since last week. Judith dialed Freyer at his house, and she just about hung up when he growled on the other end. I grabbed the phone and rapidly related the events of the past several minutes. His attitude changed immediately.

"Where in the devil are you now, Prich?" he asked excitedly with an air of tension.

"We're just entering the GW Parkway in a

couple of blocks and heading downtown to the Kennedy Center," I stated matter of factly. "I'm still not sure what this guy is up to, Amos. He hasn't made any overt move yet."

"Doesn't matter," Freyer said in a clipped tone to say just the essentials. "Stay on the line and I'm calling for backup on my cellular right now. You in the Mustang now, Prich?"

I quickly related the current situation and car change, but Judith didn't know the license number of her father's Mercedes. I told Freyer the approximate year, model number, and color and hoped that would be enough.

"Don't hang up, Prich!"

"I'm glued to you, good buddy," I rattled off nervously. "Just make sure your compadres completely understand that the folks they see in the Mercedes are the good guys. The last thing in the world that I want on my tombstone is 'Here lies another poor soul taken out by friendly fire.'"

The phone went silent for a time, and I held it down so it wouldn't be unnecessarily displayed. Judith was still calm and she asked me what I was going to do when things began to happen. I didn't have any answers to the million and one possible scenarios so I told her the truth. I simply didn't know and would need to see how the other guy continued to play out the events. Freyer came back on the line as I could hear him from the phone lying on the seat. I picked it up and heard him loudly asking if I were still there.

"Okay, Amos, we're still with you," I recited to get his attention.

"Prich, I've got some great backup heading your way so hang on," the cop said stated with emphasis. "I want you to head directly toward the police station, and there'll be at least two patrol cars coming right at you. I'm out of here right now, and I'll be with my cellular phone as soon as we disconnect here. Do you still remember my cellular number?"

"Sure, I call enough times, don't I?"

"Yeah, and I have to pay all those charges, don't I?" came the rhetorical question from the cop. "Ask Judith to call me on it and I'll be back with you. I'll also have the police radio in my car. Hang in there, buddy, and call me as I hang-up."

"Gotcha!"

I had the hang-up procedure right, but then I hit the redial and that got Amos Freyer right back on the house line. He started cursing and I found a way to laugh, even in this rotten three act tragedy. I hung-up again and then handed the cellular phone to Judith to dial correctly as I fed the new number to her. That blasted little thing sure had me buffaloed. I felt as if I were technologically inept. Sure was a fine time for those sorts of revelations. She had Freyer back on his cellular phone and we were cooking fine.

Judith began speaking with Freyer and relaying messages to me so I could handle the car better. I'd been trying to steer the car with my bandaged hand and handle the phone with the good right hand. I would have been encountering difficulty with both hands serviceable and free. My driving was somewhat sloppy under normal circumstances, so the guy following us might have thought he was following a drunk.

I averted the entrance to the GW Parkway and looped around after several blocks to head back to the police station. Judith kept passing Freyer's reassuring instructions to me, and she continually passed along the series of events as they unreeled.

I kept glancing at the rear view and side mirrors for just an instant without moving my head. I didn't wish to tip off anything to the guy until we had some heavy support on our side. If I forced his hand prematurely, I didn't know what he might try. I didn't even know what his purpose was or what method he intended to use with us. He could be a car jacker or someone preying on wealthy people for quick and easy drug money. He might be a part on some investigation, legal or illegal. He might even be a part of Emory's death. He could have already shot at us or could have rammed us with his car. The possibilities were limitless, and I was anxious to find out what the devil all this meant.

The Chevy maintained the same pace with us for several more blocks until it suddenly swerved at the corner immediately behind us and squealed the tires. The Chevy was trying to avoid us all of a sudden and I didn't know why. We relayed this information to Freyer on the cellular phone the instant we were sure what was happening. Judith passed the phone to me after she knew our pursuer had broken off the chase.

"Which way is the Chevy going now, Prich?"

"He made a left hand turn."

"Which way is that?"

"You're asking me directions? You know that I can't find my way around my own house without a floor plan. I've got to be the worst person in the world to ask that."

"You've got to have some idea," stated the frustrated cop.

"Call AAA!"

"Damn, Prich!"

Judith spun around in her seat and was peering out the rear window. She'd heard enough of our mixed up conversation to realize what Freyer had been asking. She told me that it was probably northwest, but she wasn't certain. She also indicated that the Chevy was nowhere to be seen. I related this new information to Freyer, but he just seemed to grumble.

"You sound disappointed that we didn't get our heads blown off," I yipped at the cop.

"You see the patrol cars?" Freyer asked as if ignoring my previous statement.

I started to tell him no, but then I saw one and then the other. I stopped the Mercedes in the middle of the street and was relieved to see the cops get out of their vehicles without any weapons in their hands. The first patrol car had two police officers, and the second had one. I went through the introductions fairly rapidly and then pointed to the corner where we'd last seen the Chevy. The first patrol car had one cop transmitting on the radio while the other continued to question us. The cop in the second patrol car decided we were wasting time and started returning to his car to pursue the missing Chevy.

The cop almost reached his patrol car when Freyer came skidding around the corner and screeched to a stop. Freyer's Jeep Wagoneer barely missed my right foot. Wouldn't I have been a laughable sight with one arm in a sling and the opposite foot in a cast?

Freyer began giving orders as if he were the watch captain of the entire county. I imagined that was just great because he was trying to assist me in this strange set of circumstances. I tended to believe that I was the Arch Duke of Prussia after a couple of highballs and then having been told that I'd been out in the street directing traffic later. The cops were told to start searching in the opposite direction as the Chevy could have just as easily doubled back to confuse any pursuit. I congratulated Freyer on some smart thinking. He was so busy that I didn't really know if he'd heard me. He was back on the radio issuing advice and instructions. After the melee quieted down somewhat, we began to make some sense of it all.

"I was just told that the plates were reported stolen yesterday," Freyer said as he sounded a little winded. "This is beginning to have the feel of a pro. Either of you folks got any ideas?"

"Not a single one," volunteered Judith first,

who gave a shrug of her shoulders. She looked pretty with the early evening wind in her hair and the light shining across her face.

"I don't have any explanation either, Amos," I started slowly. "Nothing has been making any sense."

"Either of you have any enemies or know of any reason someone might wish to follow you?" Freyer asked another way.

"Got any jealous boy friends?" I asked, looking at Judith with a smile.

"Don't I wish!" she quickly replied with a laugh.

"I don't know if the guy was intending to harm us or just follow us for some reason," I said.

""What do you think spooked him?" asked the cop as he began pacing and looking the Mercedes over at the same time.

"Might have been anything," I answered with some thought. "Maybe he saw me groping around with the cellular phone. I was pretty darn clumsy in there with the steering wheel and the phone at the same time."

"Were you that obvious?" Freyer asked with some annoyance in his tone.

"I may have been, bunkie," I snapped back. "You try it some time with a messed up hand like this and your pulse going twice as fast as normal. I'm a lawyer, not an Elliot Ness, remember?"

"Okay, don't get your feathers ruffled," Freyer said somewhat apologetically.

"I'm getting a little cold," stated Judith as she wrapped her arms around herself. "Is it okay if I sit in the car?"

"Sure," Freyer said immediately. "Sorry, I wasn't thinking."

I began walking back to Freyer's Wagoneer with him so we could speak out of ear-shot of Judith. He got back on his police radio and found that the Chevy hadn't been detected. Freyer shook his head in an annoyed fashion.

"Damn, I thought that we were going to get a break and tie this thing to the Emory killing," the cop said, shaking his head.

"You know, Amos," I started with a very light sound. "I'm not even sure this was meant for us."

"Yeah, I was thinking the same thing, but I didn't want to scare her any more tonight," the cop said with a very earnest expression. "I do think, though, that you should caution her, Prich."

"Right," I answered. "We could easily have been mistaken for the owner of the Mercedes, and when he saw that I wasn't Rogers, he simply broke off the chase."

"We may never find out."

Chapter 7

In for a Penny

I'd continually watched for dark Chevys or any vehicle that appeared to be tailing our car. I even pulled over right after we exited the GW Parkway to verify that we were being left alone. I waited for several minutes, but all appeared normal. I left the temporary parking place and continued on while watching very closely. Regretfully, I thought, we managed to find our way to the Kennedy Center before the performance was concluded. My capacity for the arts left a considerable amount to be desired. After an extremely stressful initial journey, I thought that I needed the time for quiet contemplation and a slow wind-down.

What I found first was a downtown traffic jam with rude drivers. One lane fed into a traffic circle that seemed like a trip to nowhere. I went around that thing twice and discovered I was in the wrong lane when I exited. That gave another driver the opportunity to relieve his stress level by venting something my way. I wasn't exactly sure what he said, but his expression appeared somewhat pained, and the hand gestures seemed a bit overdone.

After running that gauntlet, we finally appeared at the basement parking garage of the Kennedy Center. I rolled down the window to find a smiling attendant very happy to tell me the garage was filled to capacity. He also was more than happy to point out the "Filled" sign which was illuminated. My next thought was,"Who needs you, Bub, if you are all filled and the barricade prevents any more cars from entering." It then occurred to me not to argue with good fortune. I'd fulfilled my promise, and it was fate that had prevented us from attending the performance.

I put the car in reverse and slowly began backing out into the street when I heard the attendant say something. Judith reached over and touched my arm, and I stopped the car. I saw headlights coming out of the garage and then a car appeared. The attendant walked out of his little stand and began speaking to me through the window that I'd neglected to roll up. He happily told me there was a space for the Mercedes with the new vacancy. I began wondering why I hadn't rolled up the window. I could understand the joyful mood with Judith, but the parking attendant was another story. I certainly didn't like to think of myself as a xenophobe, but there was a second or two when I wasn't sure.

I grumbled and paid the exorbitant parking fee to my newly acquired benefactor. We spent another ten minutes trying to find the parking space that had been vacated. Our trip in the elevator was somewhat strained as I was still fuming while Judith tried to keep from laughing. "One more chuckle would be the proverbial straw to break this camel's back," I thought.

Timing kept its consistent pace as everyone

was just coming out for intermission when we arrived. Judith and I strolled about the wide foyer, and I was sincerely filled with admiration for the wonderfully sculptured JFK bronze. Judith felt that we had time quickly to visit the gift shop at the end of the intersecting hall. I purchased a cup to add to my collection, and Judith couldn't leave without an expensive commemorative bookmark.

The lights began flashing as the incredibly slow clerk returned the credit card, and we began hurrying along the lengthy hallway. Breathless by that time, we scurried to the main level. We found our seats which were closer to the stage than I'd been in my entire life. Two young ladies in adjoining seats appeared annoyed as they removed their coats from our seats. I was also sorry that I had to be there to deprive them of their makeshift cloakroom. The remaining performance of the Beethoven violin concerto and other works was more pleasing than I had imagined they might be. I only wished the fellow sitting in the next row would have refrained from humming the melody just one instant before the symphony orchestra played it.

I believe that I became a convert to classical music that evening, much to my dismay. I don't mean to imply that I was now a total fanatic. I found that I could enjoy the music more if I took it in small doses. I was still hooked on the Peter, Paul, and Mary sound with a spicing of R & B for good measure. People will find me snapping my fingers to almost every other type of music except hillbilly. I haven't had that lobotomy yet. Others might say the same about my musical tastes. Very good chance they could be right.

I was considerably more relaxed afterward than when we'd arrived. We both looked around before and after we reached the Mercedes, but saw nothing unusual. The bumper-to-bumper traffic didn't seem to disturb me as we were leaving the parking garage and immediate area. I slid right over to the parkway, and we were approaching Bethesda before I knew it. I was about to thank Judith for sharing the concert tickets, but she broke the ice first.

"I believe that I'd have skipped the Kennedy Center tonight if I had any idea it would have been like this," she said with an apologetic tone. "I'm sorry that we had to go through such a wild evening, and I'll do anything to make it up to you."

I took a big gulp and waited a second before I shot off my big flap. This sounded like a great opportunity to put my medium size foot right into my big yap. Sometimes I found it better to leave some things unsaid.

"Maybe, it was better that I was the person who was with you when all that previous nonsense began."

"Yes!" she said immediately. "I certainly can't think of anyone who would've been as calm as you."

"I'll bet you could find better drivers than me, Judith. This bum left hand was almost impossible to deal with. Don't give me all the credit. You were a pretty cool customer when things started popping.

You didn't come apart like many would have. Your composure kept me on task. I certainly couldn't have been nearly as effective if you weren't with me. You performed remarkably well under some very heavy pressure."

"You make me sound like some kind of saint, which I'm not," she admitted somewhat shyly at first. "I'm even thinking about a little mischief at this moment which might change your opinion of me."

"In for a penny, in for a pound," was the only thing my numb senses could conjure up at this late hour.

We turned the corner off the main boulevard and entered Judith's exclusive neighborhood. I was very careful to observe everything that I thought might be relevant to the earlier occurrences. This wasn't a Chevy neighborhood which made spotting one even more likely. I watched for any vehicle with someone inside and also scanned the area for any unusual pedestrians. Everything appeared reasonably normal, as we slowly rolled down their street. We turned into the Rogers driveway, pushed the garage door opener, and slid into the garage without any mishap.

As I was turning off the car and triggering the remote to close the garage door, Judith gently touched my right arm and smiled. She asked if I might want to come in for a night cap in her room.

Smiling, I said, "You must be reading my mind."

She blushed slightly and gave me a little mock slap on my wrist as she returned the grin. Like two teenagers sneaking in late, we quietly walked upstairs to the top landing. A door opened and Evelyn stepped into the hallway to see us as we were about to reach the second floor.

"Just a quick nightcap," Judith whispered to her smiling sister. "We won't be too late."

"I might need a little legal advice sometime also," quietly chuckled the sister with a sparkle in her eyes.

I winced and averted my eyes. The last thing I wanted to do was to become the source of a family dispute. I looked at Judith to see her expression. She squeezed my hand and then gave it a slight tug in her direction. Evelyn gave an additional quiet laugh and closed the door behind her slowly. We continued up the last couple steps where Judith and I eased down the hallway to her room. After she closed the door, we both heard another door creak open and close again. Maybe a full parade with a booming base drum wouldn't have been noticed as much as our sleuthful entry.

Judith's room adjoined her sister's with a shared bathroom separating the two. Her room was larger than mine, but didn't have the accommodations that I'd expected. The furnishings were feminine and very tasteful. The canopied queen size bed was the centerpiece from which other pieces echoed the theme. Cherry with scroll trim wood, matching chest and dresser completed the major items, but the trim and splashes of color brought it all together. I wondered about the art displayed on the walls. Some appeared to be originals by some very talented artisans.

I walked around slowly from one picture to another while Judith went over to the half size refrigerator next to the dresser. She began to fill one glass with ice and then thoughtfully asked me what I might prefer. White wine seemed to fill the bill, so she divided the ice cubes into two glasses and handed me the wine bottle for the honors. As I began filling the glasses that she was holding, she moved closer and began kissing and nuzzling me near my left ear. Needless to say, a few drops of wine missed the intended targets. I wonder why females always enjoy filling a guy's hands with something and then plying their skills while we are helpless. I squirmed and giggled like a teenager on his first date.

Judith stood at the end of the bed with a smile as I set the bottle on top of the half fridge. As I turned, she'd placed the wine glasses on the dresser and then began embracing me. My pulse raced with excitement, and I could hear her breathing increase as she gently began kissing me again. She started to ease me back toward the bed, and we slowly lay across the floral comforter. I heard another door creak and looked around slowly. I had that guilty feeling like school kids get when they are spot-lighted in a car in Lovers' Lane.

About an hour later, I sneaked down the hall with only a small hall light to keep me from breaking my neck. I wasn't completely sure if I had the right shoe on the right foot. I looked at Evelyn's door as I passed and saw no light at the bottom. Carefully I made my way to the main floor foyer and strode gingerly out the door. My faithful old Mustang was there waiting for me as always. I sure wished that someone could say as much for me, but alas, I still had all the morals of the neighborhood tomcat.

The next morning Romney gave me a grin, and Renate asked me how I'd enjoyed the concert. I sheepishly replied that I thought maybe I'd become hooked on a new style and knew Romney was thinking something else with his wide smile. I thought it amusing that he would chuckle at me after his excursions down the hall at night to see Renate. I was in the process of really boring them to death with my new found love of Beethoven when pops arrived for breakfast. He appeared shocked to find his only son sitting at the table and looking wide-eyed to boot.

My ravings about my new music interest ended abruptly as I began to relate my tale of our trip to the Kennedy Center. Father changed from his usual form of polite neglect and switched to give his full intense attention. He sat there and nodded as I indicated how I'd brought Amos Freyer into the action.

"Have you heard anymore from the police?" father asked with concern in his voice.

"Nothing yet this morning."

"And you believe this may be a professional?"

I answered in the affirmative with all the same reasons that Freyer and I'd discussed the previous night. I was about to continue when Renate set a beautiful plate in front of me full of buttermilk pancakes and sausage patties. She'd even taken care to cut everything so I wouldn't need to fumble around with my wounded paw. I promptly thanked her, but Romney explained that they didn't wish to see me with a knife in my hands so soon after the episode with the bagel. After that explanation, I wouldn't have felt too bad if I'd dribbled some of that wonderful maple syrup in some of the most difficult places to clean. I wasn't usually that mean spirited, but I did have my warts.

"I have two concerns, Prich," father began again with that worried expression he always brings out when he wishes to imprint his feelings rather than just convey a thought. "One individual who was a founder of this company-client has been killed under very suspicious circumstances. Now you tell me there was some sort of underworld professional following your car. This..."

"He was following the car I was driving," I interrupted.

"That doesn't make the slightest difference," he continued. "The point I want to make is my only son is becoming directly involved with incredible danger that I initiated by asking you to look into their problem. If something should happen to you, I-"

"Father, you may very well be making more of this than there really is."

"If you were only scratched, it might kill your mother!"

"Let's take this one step at a time. People make more out of a problem when they don't understand the facts. This might even be something we'll both laugh at later."

"I know you want to continue, but I'm right on the edge of terminating our entire involvement with Rogers & Emory."

"I'm probably more dangerous to myself," I interrupted as I held up my bandaged left hand.

The stern patriarch almost broke out in full laughter. This was the first time in the last several days that I'd seen the tension leave his face, even if for only an instant. He was truly concerned for my welfare, which brought a warm thought for him in return.

"The second point I want to make," father started again after regaining his lawyerly composure, "we always work for clients to keep them out of the headlines."

"There isn't anything on the front page."

"Emory's death brought out some curiosity seekers, Prich. The signature of our firm is confidentiality. That certainly appears to be compromised!"

"That's nothing we did."

"Correct, son," he continued. "However, just our association with this taints our good name."

"Sure, but just a little," I countered quickly. "However, that is water under the proverbial bridge. What little problem has occurred is over, and I don't really believe it was that much damage to us. The one thing that I could see hurting our reputation, though, is quitting clients when they really need us the most."

"Your point is well taken," father stated in his best legalese.

"Let's give it a little more time and see what develops," I said with my most earnest inflection. "We might be finished with this in a very short time anyway."

"How so?" came father's curt inquiry.

"Well, what if all Rogers & Emory really needs is a management consultant firm? We could simply refer them to some other firm that specializes with that function, and then we could step away very easily."

"That sounds like the most prudent course, but I want you to be extremely careful, Prich."

"Father," I said with my best convincing voice, "my sense of self preservation is always paramount. I deeply appreciate your concern for my safety, but I'm the biggest coward in the country. They can't hit what they can't find. If the action starts to get rough, I'm out of there!"

Father nodded, and I began to pay more attention to those wonderful aromas drifting to my olfactory senses. I certainly didn't wish to get him started back in the other direction again after opening my mouth. I misjudged my father and thought I could update him and be done with it. He was either becoming very protective of his only son, or our firm was flushed with more business than we could handle.

I liked to believe it was the former rather than the latter.

I'd run out of index cards through inefficient use or clumsiness. I didn't believe the coffee stains all over my current package helped me concentrate on the task at hand. Renate was somewhat unhappy to part with half of her remaining cards destined to contain many of her wonderful recipes. I thought I might also combine several strange and mysterious ingredients of my own with the very same cards. The outcome would be very pleasing, but not nearly as tasty.

I climbed the two long flights of stairs again and wondered if I'd still be able to do this in another ten years. The legs were supposed to be the first to go, and I was huffing already. Mom and pops had another thirty years on me, and they were making the climb to their quarters on the second floor very well. I was wondering why there was an unwritten rule of nature that everything that tastes good puts pounds around the good old midsection. It probably is related to the same nature's law with females: the more attractive the gal, the more trouble she is for you. I hated to think of using that stationary bicycle again, but my wardrobe was beginning to get a little snug. I've heard the metabolism changes about every twenty years. I couldn't wait to find out what changes lay in store for me.

The old cards came off the wall, and I went about writing new entries into my diary. I made several new cards, added the old ones and reshuffled the deck. Maybe I should've kept the coffee stained cards as the new arrangement didn't make any more sense. Why in the world would anyone want to chase me or the Rogers' family vehicle? Why did he stop chasing me? Why did the chase car seem like a professional, and why would a professional be following us? How did the Chevy avoid the cops so easily as the police had the area ringed very quickly after they knew the chase of our vehicle had ended? I was still pondering these questions when my phone rang with Amos Freyer in one of his rare moods.

"Give me some good news for a change, good buddy," I said with one of my more happy tones to try to get Freyer out of his grumpy mood. "I've looked at this thing from every angle I can possibly think of, and I've come up with zilch."

"Yeah, we've got a big goose egg here too," answered the cop with an improving voice.

"Anything on the car?"

"When you said zilch, you summed it up real good."

"Doesn't make sense about the car disappearing so cleanly. Think he had a rabbit hole nearby?"

"You might have something there, Prich. I'm willing to look at almost anything at this point."

"If you find anything, get on the horn to me ASAP, will you?"

"I told you that I would, didn't I?" yipped the cop. "Oh, before I let you go, what's the deal last night with the Rogers' gal? I thought you and Kate had a thing going."

"Good-bye," I said without any inflection in my voice. "I'll continue to keep you updated too. And thanks for the help with that Chevy last night. We could've been in some real trouble if it hadn't been for you."

"God bless cellular phones," Freyer stated as he ended the conversation and hung up without any further inquiry into my companionship of the last evening. I sure wished that he hadn't been involved when I was out with someone other than Kate. He would probably work on me for some time to come up with that jewel.

I wanted to meet with Franky, but thought it was too early for my ex-rummy buddy to be up and about. People like Franky could become my life-long friend after a couple of hours while others were merely acquaintances after many years. I guessed it all came down to caring and trusting. I decided to head back to Rogers & Emory, but wasn't sure how much more I could do out there. I waved my farewells to everyone with my one remaining good upper appendage and tied pops in the driveway with our exits. The grand master with the mist gray Lincoln Towncar always took precedence in this household. I wondered when I might be driving something like him, but the thought quickly vanished when the old foggie syndrome came to mind. I had quite a few years before I wanted to be associated with that class.

The bright sun disappeared along my uneventful drive to Gaithersburg and was replaced with a thundering spring deluge. At first the grand old lady's windshield wipers worked as usual, but that ended quickly enough. A strange groaning noise was replaced by a thud, and then the wipers stopped. I pulled off at the corner service station and was just in the process of getting out to talk to the service attendant when I thought I saw the Chevy of the night before pass by. I closed my door and started to pursue the car when it drove into the service station across the street on the opposite corner. I promptly followed it and parked at the adjoining gas pump. A middle-aged Hispanic lady emerged from the car and began pumping gas. She was somewhat plumpish and small in stature. I started to pump some gas into the Mustang and then casually asked her a question about the mileage on newer cars. She appeared normal as anyone in the community, and I couldn't associate her with the previous night's occurrences.

"I thought I saw this car last night when I was heading downtown," I stated with the same nonchalance.

"My God!" she exclaimed with a bewildered expression. "This car was stolen last night, and the police just found it a couple of hours ago."

She indicated that the plates were changed and also partially covered with mud. She went on to say that the car was stolen from a house where she worked as a housekeeper, three blocks from the Rogers' house. She'd worked at that residence for over six years. Evidently, her employers liked her work, and she enjoyed working for them. She appeared to be a stable, hard working individual who was also a victim in this process. She told me her employers had a house party that evening which accounted for the vehicle being taken near the time I'd encountered it. She also said that as soon as she ended her duties, she noticed the car missing and immediately reported that to the police. The police told her the plates were taken from a car in the next block, and her plates were still missing. She said that she thought it was just some kids looking for a joy ride. I asked if she'd found anything different inside the car, but she didn't believe anything was changed. I knew it hadn't been kids. They wouldn't go through the trouble of changing plates and then partially obscuring the new ones. I also knew it wasn't a kid that had those expert driving skills I'd witnessed. I asked her about the tinted windows, and she explained her son had them tinted dark for effect with the ladies and his peers. He now had his own car, but she was stuck with the darker windows which didn't thrill her. I thought he should appreciate his mother more, but I guess many kids were more involved with themselves. We exchanged names and phone numbers, and I assured her that I would help the police with the information that I had.

I spent the next two and a half hours twiddling my thumbs while the service station mechanic took his grand old time replacing my windshield wiper motor.

I called Freyer again and explained what I'd learned from the lady with the Chevy. I told him that

I felt he was sandbagging me. I should've been hearing about that Chevy from him several hours earlier. His temperament soured, and he wasn't too happy to hear about the Chevy from me either. He grumbled something derogatory about his own department. It also didn't help to get my ribbing along with the information. I further impressed on the nonplused cop that I was providing a great deal more information his way rather than the reverse. I suggested he might start pushing a minuscule amount more of effluvium through his tin horn than he was currently doing. He was still growling when we hung-up.

I also phoned Rogers and Emory to let them know why I was late and not to be concerned. I indicated that I would probably show up after lunch and make it a longer day than I'd originally planned. I didn't believe that made either of us any too pleased, but they saw and accepted the logic of it all. I then called Franky Angelino and found that he'd been up and about earlier than I. Franky was certainly behaving differently now that he was sober.

As soon as I'd dished out half a fortune to the service station for the repairs, the rain stopped. Oh, well, win some, lose some. God bless credit cards as well as cellular phones. I began rationalizing that the repairs were a legitimate cost of my current business as I had gotten some new information from the owner of the Chevy in the process. It made more sense to me, the more I thought about it. I punched-up an old time rock station on the antique push button radio and was off to the Chain Bridge Club for lunch with Franky boy. I recalled some great memories on the way with music from groups like the *Platters*, *Impressions*, *Fats Domino*, and *Buddy Holly*. I believe that I even saw *Elvis* on a street corner as they played *Jailhouse Rock*.

Chapter 8

Bytes and Bits

The blackboard that displayed the menu and specials for the day at the Chain Bridge Club proclaimed crab cake subs with slaw and steak fries for the Monday Grand Delight. They certainly wouldn't get any argument from this poor soul with my pedestrian tastes. I might have been tempted to sell the Mustang or the rights to my first born for the pleasure of crab cakes at the club. I wasn't entirely sure what George was paying Jenny, the cook, but I prayed it was enough so some other restaurant didn't pirate her away.

George seemed to be in good spirits as he and several other patrons were discussing the merits of the Sweet Sixteen in the current NCAA basketball playoffs. It was obvious that George was a big supporter of what he considered his namesake, Georgetown University, but try to reason that with a North Carolina State and a Kentucky alumni. Georgey Boy barely acknowledged me a slight wave in between basketball hand gestures and grunts. One would've thought that some of his sons were on the court.

Suzie Q came out from behind a screen that led to the kitchen. A table full of businessmen sitting by the window appeared extremely appreciative to see her with a large tray full of their midday victuals. After serving them, she swiftly returned with another steaming pot of coffee. I could imagine her tip account increasing by the second, and they were lucky to get her for that small pittance.

Suzie spun around and spied my lonely soul at the usual corner table. She gestured to me with the coffee pot, and I gave her the thumbs-up. Just then, Franky Angelino's head came poking through the door, and I looked back to Suzie and held up two fingers. She quickly slid by the table and said she'd be back in a minute with a fresh pot. That only confirmed she was mentally endowed with the tip account, and I even thought she might have been a gifted attorney too with a little encouragement.

"Yo, Prich," Franky called as he turned to catch a few phrases from George yipping away about the merits of the college basketball draft. Franky smiled and shook his head before turning to finish his walk to the table. Franky and Suzie arrived at about the same time. Both came with a smile, but Suzie was more welcome as she had a fresh pot of coffee in her hand.

"You're sure a sight for these weary eyes," I said as a welcome.

Both beamed a bigger smile and answered with a thank you in return. I thought it much wiser not to tell either one whom I was referring to as I wasn't even sure myself. I was somewhat disappointed, though, when I didn't get a statement from either of them that I was also missed. Instead, Suzie seemed very interested in Franky's well being while I was left to twiddle the proverbial again.

"We'll start with two coffees," I happily interrupted the mutual admiration society duo.

"Must be a pretty good mind reader," joked Suzie Q.

"If I were, you might have a red face and be in Dutch with Kate, my dear," I ragged the smiling waitress.

"Only in your dreams, sweetie," she said in return. "What'll you two big hunks have?"

"Now she's fishing for a bigger tip," laughed Franky. "I'll have the crab cake special, but if it's the last one, give it to Prich and I'll have the Alpo on a shingle."

We all howled, and I told Franky to keep his voice down so he wouldn't be giving away any secret recipes. Suzie poured us our coffee and then tossed us both a raspberry with her tongue stuck out between her pretty lips. She then headed to the kitchen with our orders and a smile on her face. Franky looked bright eyed and fresh as a fellow who could pass as fifteen years younger.

"Looks like clean living agrees with you, good buddy. How's Sandy doing with this new lifestyle?"

"You know, Prich, it's a strange way of life. Sandy, God bless her, has put up with me all these years, but I'm not sure if she was ready for this."

"How so?"

"Well, I believe she might've been happier with me out from under her feet all the time. Now that I'm sober, I'm always asking questions and looking to her for some company. I think I might be driving her nuts. She even told me that our marriage contract didn't include lunch. Maybe she was just happy to tell everyone that she was married with a family rather than one of those divorcees that's always flocking over any bachelor that shows up."

"I think I know what you mean," I said only half telling the truth.

"Even my dog, JD, looks at me strangely. Damn thing almost bit me the other night when I came in a little late after bowling. He was growling as I was unlocking the door and didn't stop after I called his name."

"Maybe you sound or smell different when you're sober."

"Everything's different. I'm just learning to taste food again. Already put on five pounds, though."

"Why is it that food and females are the same for males? If it tastes good, then it's probably bad for you."

"Right, and if she's a real sharp looker, she really knows it. She'll zing you every time you turn around."

"Got that right!" I quickly agreed with a slap on his shoulder. "Which brings to mind those two great-looking gals we saw here the other night."

"Like a moth goes to a lighted fire, you know there's trouble, but you simply can't resist the temptation."

Franky began to explain that the gals were only in town for a couple of days and were guests of another member. He said they were flying out that afternoon so I'd been saved by fate. I felt that fate should mind its own business and let this somewhat single fellow enjoy what time remained with his bachelorhood. Suzie returned with our lunch and refilled our coffee cups. She was even good enough to drop off a couple of extra creams as I put everything I could find into my coffee. I may not have been a coffee purist, but I certainly drank enough of it to keep her busy.

I told Franky about the Chevy incident, making him almost choke on a bite of the crab cake sub. His lighthearted mood changed to an intense interest as he caught every word I said. His eyes narrowed and he stopped eating.

"What's going on with this thing, Prich?"

"Beats me. I thought I was just doing a routine snoop around, but some real strange things have been happening."

"Looks like we're on to a real good one," Franky said with a rising enthusiasm.

"Hold on, amigo!" I interjected quickly. "I'm not sure where this is going, and I don't want my best friend hurt in this thing."

"I might be your only friend right now, and that may not last if you cut me out of this," he said with a little humor returning. "You know that I'm always careful."

"Right?"

"Well, I'm different now. I'm sober."

"Maybe so, love, but if this gets too sticky,

I'm pulling out of it quickly, too."

I told him about more of my concerns, how my father felt about my involvement, indicating that this had initially been a few simple questions and a transition of business to our firm. Now one owner was killed, and some very curious things were occurring.

"If it gets out of control, I'm stepping out of the entire affair, and our firm is too. Pops doesn't want to take any chances, and I'm in full agreement with him there. I don't want to get his only son hurt either!"

Franky and I began to see things somewhat more in the same light after I brought up the Emory killing and added the Chevy incident. He didn't have a death wish either, but only wanted to have something challenging happening to keep his life a little more interesting.

We finished lunch and cultivated the happy mood in which it had begun. We even got a few needles ahead of Suzie Q, surprising us both. She did get in one good one about my eclectic, geometric tie that she described with cat paw prints and puppy dribblings added to my previous lunch spills. She was always after the bigger tip, but had never been known to back down from a hot exchange. Maybe I'd gotten a little sharper in my old age, or maybe Franky was back on his game after drying out. I liked to believe that I was on my own game a little better.

As we parted in the parking lot, I promised to call Franky when I needed him and assured him it would probably be sooner than later. I could see his eyes sparkle when I told him that, and it also helped assure me that I wasn't in this thing alone either. I felt as if the moth syndrome were working with me on this case as well as my female failings. I didn't consider myself a fatalist, but I believed some things were just my nature. I had little choice in the matter. Maybe my halo was on just a little crooked.

My timing was good when I finally arrived at Rogers & Emory. Almost everyone was back from lunch, but not fully into their routine. As I was returning to the marketing department, David Rogers saw me and waved. I eased into his office, and he shut the door.

He appeared worried and began pacing before he even offered me a seat. I could see that he was struggling for the right words before he spoke. He gestured to a chair finally, and I slowly sat down. I was more interested in his behavior and expressions than anything he might have to say. He could say something, but his behavior usually told me the truth, though extremely cryptic. Rogers was very concerned with the Chevy incident, making me cautious and very suspicious.

"Judith told me about you two being followed the other night on the way to the Kennedy Center," he started in a somewhat shaky beginning. "That certainly has us all very worried."

"I'll bet it does!" I thought, but did not say. I wondered who all the "us" was and what each one of the "us" was worried about. I would've bet my last shekel that they didn't have the same motives. Some people take everyone for some kind of bungling schlemiel; however, some of us weren't so deaf that we couldn't hear a train that's about to run us over. I was amused and yet extremely interested in seeing how he was going to schmuck me around.

"It was very trying for a few minutes," I said to fill the void while waiting to see what he had up his sleeve.

"Notice anything unusual or see the driver's face?"

"No," came my curt answer.

"Nothing at all?"

"I was pretty busy just trying to handle a car that I wasn't familiar with," I stated with some annoyance. "Have you noticed this left hand of mine in the sling? It's lucky we didn't pile it up in the process!"

"Oh, yes, please excuse me," he said acting as if it just slipped his mind. "We're very thankful you were able to control the situation."

"Thanks, so was I," I replied grudgingly.

"Certainly," he again acknowledged, but then continued. "Did the police find anything, or were you able to tell them anything?"

"Ah, ha!" I thought again, but didn't say. "Now we are getting to the crux of the matter!"

"Not much," I said.

"What do you suspect?" came another searching inquiry.

"I'm baffled, to tell you the truth. I wish the

cops would've been able to catch whoever it was, and then maybe we would know something."

"Yes, so do I," said Rogers, but I wasn't too sure about his credibility with any of this.

We continued our discussion with the direction changing to my continued purpose at his company. He seemed pleased that I indicated my visits might be diminishing in the near future. I did indicate that I thought they would probably need a management analysis team after I concluded my work, but that they would have the option of choosing any firm with that specialty. He inquired about our firm. I gave him the standard answer that we did that type of work, but it was on an exception basis rather than the rule.

I asked him more about the prime aspects of the business and their legal implications. He was partially helpful when he indicated that they were developing an enhancement piece of software that would assist all games developers. That was news to me and I pursued that line of information. He added that the current computer operating system had only a limited amount of memory and that usually wasn't enough for computer games that were being developed. He mentioned some technical things like computer RAM which blitzed my mind. I believed he saw my eyes glaze over when he said the techni-world acronym, and that made him extremely happy. I thought, "Just wait until he gets my bill and we'll see who's laughing then!"

"I appreciate your assistance," I stated.

"Could you be of further help in indicating additional areas which should be examined while I'm here?"

"Other than this department," he began, "I understand that you've been to marketing and our resource management departments."

"Right," I said, "I'll be with both of those departments for a short time, and maybe have a question or two more for you."

"I also think our shipping department is one of our most important areas other than our software development division. If we can't get it to our customers promptly and undamaged, then the entire process of developing and marketing is worthless."

"You sold me," I responded politely. "I might give your development division a few minutes, but they'll probably snow me in the first ten seconds."

He laughed a genuine laugh, the first time that day I felt he was being honest with me. Anticipating my next question, he suggested that I contact Ken Hobbs in Shipping and Lew Winston in the Development Division. However, he did indicate that he probably knew as much as Winston because that was how he started with the company.

He told me that his father initially began the business because he wanted to help his son develop the computer software that he was already doing for some other company. The elder Rogers felt that his son was being exploited and wished to assist him to start his own enterprise. As the business progressed, the father wanted to step away more to enjoy his semi-retirement while transitioning the management of the business into the son's hands when he brought on new talent. Evidently, the new professionals were very difficult to obtain. Most individuals who had innovative ideas for new products tried to do the same as the younger Rogers and start their own company.

Many weren't as large or developed as Rogers & Emory because they didn't have the backing or a wealthy father as he did. Some were even started in a garage or family basement. It seemed everyone wanted to become an entrepreneur, and many small software enterprises popped up throughout the industry. The competition was fierce, and everyone strived to be first in the market.

I indicated that I would probably visit Shipping first, but Rogers remembered that Hobbs often helped Patsy, his wife, on Monday afternoons at the horse farm in Middleburg, Virginia. He said she was shorthanded on Mondays, and Ken Hobbs once worked summers at a riding stable in southern Maryland when he attended college. Evidently shipping wasn't as important to Rogers as he had wanted me to believe if he gave the chief of the department a half day off at the beginning of the week.

I left David Rogers in a reasonably good mood as he was still chuckling about my lack of expertise in automation. I wondered if he understood how many in my age group and older generations were considerably inept around anything that contained bytes and bits. I never could understand even simple terminology about automation, like why do they spell disc and disk differently? I wondered if a disc was a disk or what the heck was it. And what's a diskette then? And don't get me started about RAM and ROM and some other sort of memory. It was kind of like and Abbott and Costello, "Who's on First?"

I trudged off to the Marketing Department and saw Judith in her office with another lady. She appeared to be busy at the moment and didn't look up as I walked past. Evelyn skittered past while I was looking in the opposite direction and caught me by surprise when I turned back. She was delicious as ever and even wore a smile. She was also carrying a suitcase that she just set down.

"Understand you had an exciting evening," she said with the same smile.

"Oh?" I responded with some embarrassment.

"I mean the police and all the rest. Uh, the chase sequence," she chuckled with a little too much glee.

"Well, yes," I said as I felt my face getting red. "It was more than I ever hoped for that evening."

"You mean the car chase?" she said with all the mischief clearly beaming through.

"Yes, the car chase," I dragged out slowly, feeling my face and neck getting redder, if that were possible.

"Wouldn't mind trying that sometime myself," she said with a quiet laugh."

"You mean the car chase?" I now asked with a touch of revenge in my heart.

"And that too," she gleefully snickered.

"Okay," I conceded, "I guess you've gotten the best of me. I'm probably blushing like a teenager with acne and bad breath, and you're having a grand old time."

"How did you ever come to that inspired conclusion? You're the lawyer. Can't you object on some grounds or take me to task with your debating skills?"

"Well, you smart patutie, let the contest begin!"

"Hey, bub, you called me a name, and I could nail you real well on a libel motion," she laughed.

"Not likely," I howled in triumph. "It's only libel if I scribbled it down and nailed it to the church door with my ninety something theses. I only called you a name and that's slander my dear. Pretty darn hard to prove without a witness, unless I was foolish enough to fess-up."

"I'll bet if I bat my eyes at you several times, you'll confess."

"You forget that I'm a lawyer, and we're immune to all those temptations."

She fluttered those beautiful eyes at me a couple of times, and I said, "Mea culpa, mea culpa, you win." She indicated that we both lost because she'd just called a cab and would be out of town until Wednesday afternoon. I thought that I was probably saved by fate again, but sometimes it would be much nicer to make the mistake. With that bullet just dodged, I made off for the Resource Management office, but was caught by Cassy who told me Judith wanted to see me in a couple of minutes. Just to kill some time until I could see her, I kicked around Cassy's desk and made small talk about the people at the company. I asked about several people and got the low-down on a few. John Evans was bright, but a mama's boy and a little nerdy. The Rogers sisters were the good and bad witches in the *"Wizard of OZ."* Lew Winston in Development was a wimp and some thought more fond of the fellows than the gals. "Live and let live," I thought. However, it was obvious that she had another opinion. I asked about Ken Hobbs as Cassy had run through the entire staff, and I hadn't heard his name yet. I was curious as I intended to see him the next day and hoped to understand him better with the down and dirty facts from her.

All I got was, "Oh, I date him," and not another word. I expected she might say that he was handsome or bright or maybe even a nice guy, but not a thing. She even tried to change the subject when I perused the point, and she seemed relieved when Judith waved me in. I thought he might be a hunk. Cassy ran a close second to Evelyn Rogers, and she would want to be seen with someone who was her peer.

Judith seemed to be in fine spirits. She'd just concluded a deal to have two of their products marketed in a new automation retail chain that was opening next quarter. If sales started to increase, this might add new momentum to initial development and expand the upgrading of current products.

I thought she would be curious about any

new developments with the previous evening's car chase. However, she wanted to speak about the potential she envisioned for the company. She also wanted to know what I thought about the performance at the Kennedy Center, and I believe my answer pleasantly startled her. I think she expected me to tell her something like "very long" or "boring," but my answer was somewhat of a revelation. I believe my attitude may have even surprised me to some degree. I honestly, as a lawyer can be, immensely enjoyed the performance and wished I could understand why. However, I wasn't too proud of that fact. It was probably because I'd spent so much time in my life making fun of anyone who listened to classical music. It was sort of a reverse snobbery. Things seemed to have a way of coming full circle.

I was about to beg my pardon away from her charming companionship when she reached for my arm and headed towards the coat-rack.

"I'm going to prevail upon your kind manner and ask you to escort me again," she said with a bright laugh and a cheery attitude.

"Where now?"

"I just made a potential big killing with a likely new customer, and I wanted to get out and shout for a bit."

"Well, I'm always game when a pretty gal grabs my arm and wants to kick-up her heels," I said with several purposes in mind. First, I was being truthful about enjoying good looking females who also found me handsome enough to initiate what she had the night before. Second, I was still on the billable clock, and it was their nickel she was spending to have me sit by her side. I had all day and night if she wished, but I would stop the clock at one point if she wished to repeat last night's ending. I know what many say or joke about lawyers, but there are some things I would never bill.

Chapter 9

Peep Show

Judith and I went swinging out the front door like two high school kids skipping out on the afternoon classes. As adults, there are some things we never grow out of which enriched our lives as teenagers. I also thought that she saw me outside her glass-walled office with Cassy and then dear sister Evelyn. That may have been a way to put her mark on me. Sure, the other women could make their plays, but everyone could plainly see whom I preferred. I looked around at both of my sides to see if I had a brand on me.

The blacktop parking lot had tiny, wiggly heat rays rising like a desert mirage. A fine day for still being very early in spring with the hint of frost just the previous morning. It was a sailor's high sky and we both searched quickly for sun glasses to avoid the glare. She looked at her Lexus and then over at the Mustang. I could see a glint in her eye, and I didn't believe it was only the sun.

"This is such a beautiful day," she began. "Why don't we take your convertible and put the top down?"

She must have seen me give a slight glance at my left arm which I still had in the sling. She started to continue speaking, but seemed to stop in mid-thought and reached over to my left arm.

"I didn't think about your problem with your

hand," Judith said with an apologetic tone. "I felt so badly last night after you had to drive like you did with only one hand."

"It really doesn't hurt, you know."

"I know but if you had hit something with it during that fracas, then you might have been in screaming pain. I felt so inconsiderate."

"Is that why you took pity on me later?"

Judith broke out in an almost silent laugh and blushed at the same time. She then stopped and shook her head.

"That wasn't pity or even gratitude," she stated earnestly. "I was very attracted to you, and it just felt right. Now that you've got a big head too, why don't you hand me the keys and I'll drive."

"Okay," I said feeling like a despicable heel of a traitor with not one ounce of loyalty. "But please be very careful as I'm not too sure how my insurance looks today."

There was some truth in that statement as I didn't have an actual appraisal of the car by an authorized individual who was a knowledgeable collector. If the car were in a slight accident, the insurance company might want to total the entire vehicle for a mere fender bender. There was no justice in this world, and I wasn't exactly sure how firm the ground was that I currently stood on. That might not be the best endorsement for a lawyer to admit. Maybe that was why I was out there in the sunshine rather than fleecing a client in a plush office.

I handed her the keys, and she even walked

around to the passenger side and unlocked the door for me. That really felt good, but I wouldn't recommend a sex change for that privilege. It would be my luck that the attitudes would change, and I would have nothing at all to show for my trouble.

Judith was a quick study, but I know it was quite a let-down to return to sixties technology after wheeling around in a new Lexus. It was novel to watch her find things that were obvious to me. The windshield wipers, for instance, were on a knob on the dashboard rather than a complicated shaft on the turn signals. The turn signals, by the way, were just that, turn signals. Her Lexus had darn near everything with the turn signal lever: cruise control, light dimmers and wipers. It was a wonder they still manufactured a turn signal lever at all as there was so much on it. It might signal left automatically because of all the weight pulling it down. The Mustang actually had a real horn ring that you could find when needed.

She took it slowly at first as she began to get the feel of the suspension. The steering was so loose compared to new cars that turning a corner was a real experience until she became accustomed to the slack. She accidentally tooted the horn once and gave me a slight chuckle. We'd gone about five blocks when she asked if she could put the top down. I thought that I could shiver in silence on such a bright sunny day. We pulled the Mustang over to the side and stopped. I showed her how easy it was to bring down the top. Surprisingly, the sun rays warmed us just fine. The needle on the gas gauge was looking a little anemic, so we stopped at a gas station. We replenished my mechanical wonder which had never been on a diet or even a budget. Regular gas made it ping and premium cost like the dickens. It was sure a good thing I could write most of this off on the expense voucher. I even had a client in the car this time so all was kosher.

After catching the outer loop beltway, we turned south across the Potomac River into Virginia. It was extremely gusty in the car with the top down, and I was happy that we didn't stay on the expressway very long. We exited into the congestion of the suburb's secondary roads where I was happy for once that I wasn't at the wheel. Judith kept her good humor while continuing her casual chatter and laughed at my returning prattle. I watched the other drivers grumble or show a variety of frustrating behaviors and wondered how I might appear if I were behind the wheel. The few glimpses of Judith remained consistent as she appeared unstressed and happy to be exactly where she was.

Struggling along for several additional miles, we exited to a small feeder road which quickly became very rural. I wasn't completely enamored with the pinging gravel in the wheel wells, but this ended after a time. We were rolling along slowly in a deeply rutted earth bed while I was enjoying the wonderful pastoral views. As we came to a Y in the road, Judith pointed to the right and said we were almost there. I was happy we started moving again when the gnats zeroed in the moment we slowed to turn. Sharks could learn a thing or two from those tiny carnivorous creatures. They appeared more like miniature piranha with wings and snapping teeth. We both were slapping our arms and neck, and I was about ready to reconsider the wisdom of a convertible in that locale.

The next opportunity to make a left turn resulted in our entry through the gate after Judith produced a small transmitter from her purse. White fences framed an elegant rising landscape. The road led around a small mound where the stables came into view. I saw about half a dozen cars parked at the side and also one very fine lady who appeared to be approaching middle age. As we pulled to a stop, she waved and greeted Judith. Judith responded by waving back and addressing her as Patsy.

"I didn't recognize you at first," Patsy Rogers said as she walked over to greet us. "This must be the handsome fellow you told me about."

"Patsy," Judith responded with a blushing face. "You could be somewhat more discrete."

"Oh, I thought you wouldn't mind if everything were out in the open," the sister-in-law stated with a smile.

"Nothing delights me more than young ladies squabbling over me," I chimed in with a hope that the initial conversation would not diminish beyond where it already had been.

"Oh, great!" answered Patsy. "This young fellow seems like a real live one."

Things were looking brighter by the minute as Patsy seemed to have that flirting glimmer in her eyes. My ego was working overtime, and I certainly could use it after the bagel incident. Maybe the wounded paw brought out special things in women that I'd never known before. I wondered how it would appear if I had this bandage with me permanently.

"I thought I would bring Mr. Hale and show him the place today," said Judith.

"Great," came Patsy's response.

"Where's Ken?"

"Out with a student," Patsy said brushing hay from her hair. "He should be returning in a few minutes."

"What are you doing now?"

"Just waiting for them to return from their ride. They'll be back shortly. Two more are coming in about forty-five minutes."

"Sounds like you're really busy," I stated.

"We surely are becoming that way since spring has arrived."

"Is the Ken you mentioned the same Ken Hobbs who works in the Shipping Department?" I asked.

"The very same," answered Judith.

"He helps me on Mondays, and he managed to make it here today also."

"Things a little slack at work?" I said to Judith.

"Maybe they'll pick-up some after the deal I closed today," she answered.

"Hey, here comes Ken," stated Patsy.

Two riders on shining horses came galloping

up to the fence rail and hopped down. Hobbs took the reins of the other horse from the young lady and began walking both horses toward the stable. He was a big, handsome brute of a fellow with an athletic build who weighed about two-thirty with a thin waist and massive chest. He had a broad forehead and wide-set eyes with one eyebrow heavily scarred. I could see that he'd misjudged some fellow earlier in his life as his nose tilted slightly starboard. I estimated him to be about six-two or three. He had a gruffy tuft of blond hair that appeared as coarse as a German shepherd.

The young woman stepped through the fence and walked over our way to speak to our group. I excused myself and strode towards the stable. I was hoping for a few words with Hobbs before he became busy again. As I walked through the partially opened doors at the opposite end of the stable, Hobbs was just putting the second horse into its stall.

"Glad I found you here today," I said as I started to introduce myself.

"I heard that you might come by," he stated.

"Just trying to get a handle on the business operations as your company transitions over to our firm."

"I didn't know that we needed any legal help," he said with a slight twinge of annoyance.

"Most people don't until it's too late."

"Okay, well, let's get it over with. I've got some more people coming over in a short time."

"If this isn't convenient for you, I'll be happy

to see you later."

"What do you want to know?"

"Let's start with who's minding the store when you're out here."

"I've got a good assistant plus two others who are there all the time. They can handle almost anything that comes up, and they know where to find me if I'm needed."

"Do you get called here very often?"

"Haven't yet."

"Then maybe they can cut costs."

"Don't worry, fellow. They more than get their money's worth!"

"I didn't imply that they didn't. I only meant that maybe..."

"I know what you meant!" he snarled as he cut me off in mid-sentence.

"Maybe we're getting off on the wrong foot," I replied as I tried to cool the man down.

"Let's just say that I'm not too fond of lawyers."

"That's okay."

"So get lost!"

"Listen, sport," I began. I was becoming a little steamed under the collar. "I'll leave you alone today and let you play whatever game you want. Tomorrow you're on my time, and if you don't wish to cooperate, I'll pass that along to Mr. Rogers with my invoice, and you can do the explaining. They can find another law firm that would condone your type of behavior."

"You threatening me?" he growled.

"Now you're getting the drift."

The angry man slammed the stall door and glared at me. I began to wonder what I was doing in an argument with a guy who was fifty pounds heavier than I, while I only had one hand to operate. Sometimes I marveled how smart I really was. I hoped I could wriggle out of this one.

"The last lawyer I was involved with took me to the cleaners," he continued to growl.

"Sorry to hear it," I responded in an apologetic tone.

"Sure, I'll just bet you are!"

I became frustrated with that man and decided to back out of the confrontation. There was much more to life than spoiling around a smelly stable with a low life. I did a quick about face and walked back through the same doors that I'd come through. I guess that sobered his mushy mind as he did a fast step to follow me outside.

"Hey, where you going?" he yelled after me.

The women looked over in my direction and saw me heading their way. The three females waved, including the one young horse rider who said that she really loved my Mustang. Judith walked toward me and reached for my free hand.

"You sure finished quickly!" she said with a questioning look. "Hope everything worked out okay."

"I had a little difference of opinion with Mr.

Hobbs, but it doesn't make any difference now."

"I'm not sure I understand."

I wasn't aware that Hobbs had been trailing us. As we moved close to the car, he appeared next to the fence. I was about to discuss our future activities for the day when Ken Hobbs interjected.

"Sorry, Mr. Hale," Hobbs began. "It seems that we got off on the wrong foot. If it won't take long, I'll be able to give you a few minutes."

I wasn't in the mood to see any more of that jerk on that fine day, so I begged off until tomorrow morning. He seemed pleased as well, so everyone was happy and we could get on with life. My initial opinion of him was that he may have missed several days when they handed out higher reasoning. His emotional shortcomings likely began after being left behind by the mother ship.

Patsy volunteered to give me the special half-hour tour, but I indicated that we were about to leave. She walked Judith and me back to the car and was gracious with her offer to show me around any time. I thanked her and indicated that I would probably take her up on her offer soon, but made it clear that large animals and I didn't necessarily see eye-to-eye. She consoled me by indicating that I wouldn't be required to become an equestrian. She also said that she hoped to see more of us and thought that we might find some occasion to socialize or to have dinner together.

I decided that I would drive on the return as I probably had exposed the Mustang to enough hazards for one day by delegating my responsibility. We said our good-byes and started down the road with the young lady driving her car behind. I was sorry to look back to see her eating all the dust I was stirring with the Mustang. The unpaved road didn't last too much longer, though. Judith looked down and then looked over to me in a strange way.

"What's wrong?" I said, knowing she was bothered by something that I couldn't explain.

"I've forgotten my purse back there. Sorry, Prich, but could we please turn around? I'll need it before I see Patsy tonight."

"No problem," I replied as I pulled the car to the side of the road so the young gal could pass.

As I stopped the car, she pulled over to see if we were having mechanical trouble. Judith explained that we were okay, but we were going back to retrieve her purse. The young lady just smiled and indicated that we might want to wait a little longer before we returned. I asked why, but she just smiled again and pulled off. I looked at Judith with a puzzled expression, but she simply shrugged her shoulders and returned the questioning look.

"Maybe she meant that he was still hot under the collar," I said with the same unclear expression.

"Don't worry about it. Let's just go back. I have a couple of things I still need to do today."

I turned the car around, but waited a minute for the dust to settle somewhat better. Judith took the opportunity to thank me properly for all my trouble and time that I'd spent with her by reaching across and kissing me fully on the lips. I thought while we were out in that lonely place, we might get into this a little further. The dust was clear by that time, and she did say that she was in some hurry, so I didn't push it. I reluctantly put the Mustang into gear, and we started back. The return trip seemed even more relaxing, and I guessed it was because I had regained control of the steering wheel.

I didn't see any sign of life as we came over the rise and neared the stable. I slowed to a stop, surveying the scene. Both cars were still there by the fence. I didn't see either of the people or Judith's purse. I began looking beyond the fence, out into the pasture when some movement in my peripheral vision barely caught my attention. I pointed to the nearer vehicle and saw a woman's leg move in the air from the back seat. Judith put her hand over her mouth as I turned off the engine at a distance of approximately two hundred yards.

Judith began to open the door, but I stopped her before the passenger door could squeak. I put my finger to my mouth to shush her and then I leaned over and whispered in her ear. I told her that we should do this as quietly as possible, but she whispered that maybe we should leave them alone and slip away. I considered her idea for a moment. I did have a feeling of someone who threw water on two dogs in the heat of love making.

"Damn it anyway!" Judith cursed under her breath, the first time I'd ever heard her use any profanity.

"What are you thinking?"

"Prich, if she is cheating on my brother, I guess I should find out about it."

"Maybe she might just be lying in the back seat by herself while he's out somewhere with the horses," I offered in an attempt to put a better spin on what I suspected was really occurring.

"Come on, Prich," she protested under her breath.

"Well, look at us."

"That's different, for Christ's sake," she swore again. "We're both single. Makes a world of difference! We aren't cheating on anyone we gave our vows to."

I held her hand and then saw she had some tears about to drop onto her cheeks. I knew that I couldn't let her see what was happening in the back seat of that car. I told her to remain in the Mustang so I could verify the true story. She nodded in agreement as I breathed a big sigh of relief.

I gently climbed over the side of the car like a teenager would without using the doors and slid onto the dusty road. Carefully walking along the road, I was sure to place every step where I wouldn't kick any rocks or cause a clumsy noise. As I drew closer, I began hearing moans and a grunting sound of a male. I could also see the car move with a gently swaying motion. The thought occurred to me that Patsy may be having sex, but it might not be voluntary on her part. Then I heard her giggle, and that well-meaning charitable notion quickly faded. I stopped about fifteen yards behind the car and wondered what I should or even could do next. I had a strange thought like, "What am I here, the sex police?"

Looking back to the Mustang, I saw Judith slowly waving her arms back and forth as if to say that she didn't want to stay. I was in compete agreement, if I were interpreting her correctly. I carefully made my way back to my car and heard Judith say that she just wanted to get away from the area as quickly as possible. Our feelings were truly the same at that point, but I didn't have any emotional family investment with the episode.

One good thing with an older car was it didn't require that the engine be running to shift it to neutral and let it roll. I did just that as we let gravity do all the work and slowly backed down the hill. After we were confident that we were sufficiently removed from the stable area, I started the car and made a quick departure. Judith was dead silent. I thought maybe I should say something, but wasn't sure if anything would sound appropriate. She looked over my way, and I thought I would hear her curse the male population, but I sure was wrong.

"That stupid, unfaithful cow!" she groaned.

"It always takes two," I reminded her as we now drove down the suburban street.

"Sure it does," she began to agree, "but most often the woman lets it happen. I'll bet we could stop the car, and I could get many of the men you see into bed in a very short time."

"No doubt about that."

"Let any or all of those men come after me any time, and they'd leave very disappointed."

"What about us?"

"That was my choice, not yours."

"Yes, but I had to agree also."

"Sure you did, and I was happy you decided the way you did. You see, though, it was still my choice, and it's that way most of the time for other women. We women normally can stop the sexual activity even though a man has initiated the process. We can usually start the process even though the thought hasn't occurred to the male."

"I'll have to remember that the next time I see that glimmer in your eyes."

That was the first time in the previous half hour or more that I'd seen her smile. She had a pretty smile, and I was happy to see it return. Judith must have had a thought that was somewhat funny with just a twinge of Machiavellian playfulness. I saw a spark in her eyes, again.

"Why don't we stop at the corner gas station?" she asked with a grin.

"Need to use the restroom?"

"The phone."

"The phone?"

"Right."

"Okay, if you don't want to tell me it's all right. I've got to use the restroom anyway."

"It's not that I don't want to tell you. It's that I'm afraid your opinion of me will diminish."

"Just tell me, please."

"If you won't think too harshly of me. I remembered that Patsy has a cellular phone, and I thought about calling them."

"So what's wrong with that?" I said.

"What if they're still at it?

"You don't think they would be, do you?"

She shrugged her shoulders as I pulled the Mustang into the gas station. I wanted to hear that conversation and thought I might pile it into a telephone pole if we used my cell phone. I didn't need to use the restroom that badly, and I wouldn't miss that call for all the world. We walked over to the phone on the outside wall, and she asked if I had some change for the call. I pulled out all my change and held it in my palm as she dropped several coins into the phone. She dialed the number and it rang over five times. I thought we would receive the message that the user was either out of the calling area or the phone was shut off. Just as we were about to give-up, Patsy's voice came on the line.

"Yes!" she said with a huffing and puffing voice similar to what I'd heard about five minutes previously. Those two folks must certainly be in tremendous shape, and I envied that Hobbs fellow! I also felt like Mr. "Climaxtus Interruptus."

"Patsy, is that you?" asked Judith as her grin became wider and wider.

"Judith?"

"Yes, you sound out of breath. Anything wrong?"

"Nothing's wrong. I was some distance from

the phone, and I had to run over to pick it up before the call was disconnected. Oh, I also found your purse and was going to call to let you know after you returned to work."

"That's why I was calling. I was positive you would find it, but I wouldn't feel comfortable until I knew for sure. Thanks for all your trouble."

"No problem, dear, I'll just drop it by the office on the way home."

"Thanks, Patsy, that will be a great help. I'm becoming so forgetful lately."

"That's probably because of that handsome guy you were with today."

"Maybe so and thanks again. Oh, please don't run so hard and get so out of breath next time," Judith said with a half chuckle that she was trying to mask.

Judith replaced the phone in the receiver as we both broke out into wild laughter. I started hopping around then, and she gave me a cross-eyed look, as we both took off to our respective restrooms. They sometimes refer to those places as "filling stations," and I certainly did my part to add to that reputation. It was great to be able to smile once again without the feeling of incontinence.

Chapter 10

Menage a Trois

I thought the gas station attendant appeared annoyed with our flagrant use of their facilities without filling the tank. My classic beauty was a genuine gas guzzler, but I'd just filled up the darling. I couldn't really understand the attendant's problem as I'd purchased two highly over-priced candy bars from their vending machine. Our journey back to the beltway was about as uneventful as I'd hoped under ideal conditions. I saw only one taxi in an accident with a touristy looking mini-van which had several pieces of luggage tied to the roof, one of which was spilled all over the highway. I imagined the lady in the van wasn't too pleased to see her personal garments on display for all the world to view in two and a half lanes of road pavement.

Judith quietly munched on her candy bar and even found a napkin in the glove compartment to help me wipe some of my dribbles that I developed in my endeavor to drive and eat with one hand. She was in a much better mood now as the small amount of time had managed to numb the effect of her recent discovery. I was happy that she could recover so quickly, as some other individuals might drag that thing out, making themselves so miserable with little or no ability to change one blasted thing. Maybe she was reconciled to something she'd suspected previously, but only confirmed that day. Maybe she was also simply giving thanks that she wasn't involved in a situation like her brother. I was curious about what she was thinking now since she wasn't the easiest individual to read.

"Thanks for the wipe," I said with a smile.

"No problem," she said in a partially reflective mood. "I was just wondering what I should do about Patsy. Think I should tell David or lobby to have Ken Hobbs fired?"

"It's difficult to call," I began questioning the sanity of the driver who'd cut me off to cross three lanes to exit while moving along at nearly seventy miles per hour. "You might end up alienating everyone and come out the big loser."

"Why do you think that?" she said with a slight defiant tone.

"You've heard of the messenger theory before, haven't you?"

"What's that?"

"The guy who delivers the bad news get his head loped off for all his trouble. If I get any of my body parts truncated, I would at least want it to be for some reason where I would be the beneficiary of the reward, especially, if I accepted all the risk."

"I see what you mean."

"Maybe you should have David discover the situation by himself. That way you won't get yourself burned."

"What if I left a few hints?"

"Not bad if he thinks he discovered the affair

by himself," I added. "However, if he thinks someone else fed him the information, he'll know someone else knows, and he'll suspect his siblings and close family first."

"You're suggesting that I need to be extremely subtle about the entire thing?"

"More than subtle, squeaky clean," I added with emphasis. "I should probably add, if you do it at all. Is it worth it to see your brother injured? I don't blame you for being infuriated with your sister-in-law, but is getting even with her worth all the family strife?"

"I know in my heart," she began with a sob in her voice, "you're exactly correct with your analysis, but my emotions are pulling at me."

"I believe it's the wisest approach. You should avoid making an important decision while under stress. It's kind of similar to never going to the grocery store when you are hungry."

Her damp eyes splashed with a sparkle as the corners of her mouth turned up. She leaned across the console, nuzzled me with her cheek, and squeezed my arm. I believe she was getting more fond of me than I was ready for at that point in time. I wasn't a "love em and leave em fellow," but her speed made me more uncomfortable than breaking the speed limit on the beltway.

I hoped that she would cool off in several ways now and perform more in a left brain mode. She'd become too emotional with her sister-in-law problem and made me uncomfortable with her added warmth. She would hopefully cool down with both, and maybe her perceived problem with the family *menage a trois* would become resolved. I didn't wish to spread rumors and add any problems, so I didn't say anything about Cassy Lewis in marketing, indicating Ken Hobbs was also her boyfriend. I considered everything that came my way as confidential and would only divulge something under exceptional circumstances.

We headed toward her office as she hadn't given me any additional advice about another destination. I guessed since the first place was such a bust, why press her luck. That was just fine with me. I needed to clear up some things with John Evans which were a concern to Joe Lindsey in our accounting department.

It was getting late in the afternoon when Judith and I hit the entrance and parted our ways. I still wasn't completely sure what she would do with the new information about her sister-in-law, but there was little more I could do. After all, I was hired to perform a business function, not to be a family baby sitter and some sort of morals police. We were all adults, which gave us the right to behave as we wished with our bodies.

While I was on my way to the resource division, I ran into Cassy Lewis as she was depositing some accounting forms on another desk. She asked if I'd seen Ken Hobbs today, and I was tempted to tell her how I'd really seen him. Being the nice guy that I am, I fell into my normal role of enhancing the truth just a smidgen. She had the appearance of someone who was haggard or under some unmanageable stress. Her face was drawn and her eyes had a tinge of red, but appeared sunken in deep, discolored sockets. She nervously ran her hand through her straggled hair and then tried to straighten her ill kept clothes. I wasn't sure if she'd had a good cry or a wonderful night on the Georgetown night owl strip. I thought of asking if she'd had a bad night, but remembered some of my previous jaunts with Franky, how I didn't care for the inquiries the following day. Cassy and I were slowly walking to her desk when I saw John Evans returning, and I excused myself to meet him.

Evans also had an arm-load of accounting forms, and I was beginning to wonder if those accountants were going to kill all the trees. I clearly understood the importance of numbers, but I hadn't ever seen any figures hold up that bird nest in the back yard, even though the bean counters might have given me a good argument. Evans had a smile on his face after he turned my way. We both surveyed the area to see if we were being observed or could be overheard.

"You haven't made any connection yet, have you?" he asked with an air of satisfaction.

"Nothing substantial, but still looking."

"Did Mr. Lindsey get the documents that I sent over to him? I'm not sure if it's the information that he needs."

"I guess he did, but I can't say for sure as

you and he are working together, and I'm not keeping current with every detail."

"I thought that was what you were doing," stated Evans with a startled look. "You were looking into this matter for me and he was helping you."

"He is helping me, Mr. Evans," I answered with a softer tone than he'd just used. "He's our accounting expert, and I would be just getting in his way if I were peering over his shoulder. He's a very good man, and he'll let me know if he spots a problem."

"Then he hasn't found anything yet?"

"I believe he's still in the information-gathering mode. That's the reason he asked for more data."

"This is taking longer than I had hoped," stated Evans with a frown developing on his face.

"It's only been a couple of days."

"I came to your house last Thursday," he said more argumentatively.

"So it's Wednesday now, and that's less than a week," I responded with a more forceful attitude. "You've been at this a great deal longer, and what have you discovered? We're just getting started, so give us a little time."

"How much time will you need?"

"I'm not exactly sure what will be required and can't give you a guess until we see a problem. Why are you so impatient?"

"I've got to know something soon if I want to break away from this place and not be tainted by some sort of scandal."

"If you're that concerned, just make the split and start with another company."

"I hate to give up all the progress I've made here. If I leave in haste, I'll be throwing away several years of advancement that I'll have to repeat elsewhere. It'll be difficult to take that pay cut and begin all over again."

"I certainly understand your position. We're using our resources without any compensation. Joe Lindsey is a good man but he has other duties, and he's also dependent on the information that you provide. We can't come in here like storm troopers with search warrants and have a large team of individuals work on this with unlimited resources."

"But you should have something by now."

"All right, how much have you paid the firm to date?"

"Why, ... nothing," he stammered.

"That's correct, Mr. Evans," I added with emphasis, "and you aren't likely to receive any billing. We're simply doing you a great favor. I'm here because the company is paying my fees, not you. I only help you on the side, but my first responsibility is to the client who pays the freight."

"I understand," came the diminished response. "I was just hoping ..."

"Hang in there, friend," I added in closing to reassure him. "We're working on this, and Joe Lindsey will find something if there's anything to find."

We ended our discussion with a better understanding of our current positions. I felt as if I were standing on firmer ground. I didn't believe that he clearly had any idea of our relationship because it was so unclear from the beginning and never completely out. That was our fault, in large part, but we seldom ever had someone ask us to do something like he had. I couldn't remember a potential client asking us to investigate one of our clients. That isn't to say that we didn't look into a client, but that was for our needs and not for someone else's. We usually wanted to verify that clients were exactly what they purported themselves to be. Surprises from the other side were troublesome enough without added trouble from one's own client for which one was the advocate.

I looked at my watch and then caught Evelyn Rogers' office out of the corner of my eye and mentally salivated. I thought that I'd better keep my intellect in control since I was regressing more every time I came close to her. I was becoming a teenager again who made too many decisions below the waist. My intellect should have developed better, but I was still struggling. So many of my peers were regretfully doing the same.

My hand was beginning to be more of a pain in the posterior rather than a physical discomfort while I thought about the humorous young doctor. I left my current location a little early and thought I would spin by the hospital to have my bandage changed before I continued anything more physical. The drive was slow and pleasant which was fortuitous as I received several hard stares half the way there from two cops pointing a radar gun in a speed trap.

Unsure about who or where in the hospital that I needed to go, I marched directly into the same place which I previously had gone when it truly was an emergency. I was about to find the men's room and then leave that place of human care when the wise-cracking physician who first treated me appeared and I was recognized at first sight. Lucky for me, I was in and out in a blink with a quick snip here and a re-bandage there.

I thanked the good-natured young doctor and then left, feeling some stress come off my back. Nothing turned up my blood pressure more than the smell of a hospital. I knew that I wasn't hurt very badly in there, but it seemed as if all the weight of the world was lifted off my back as soon as I walked out of their front door.

As I strolled out to the parking lot, I saw several suspicious characters giving the classic Mustang the once over. I made some noise by clearing my throat, and they promptly moved away. As I was pulling out of the lot, I watched the two shady individuals in the rear view mirror do a quick force job on a Jaguar's door. It boosted my ego to think they considered my Mustang. It also did my heart good as I dialed the police station on my cellular phone and relayed what I'd just witnessed.

I headed back to my office hoping to arrive before Joe Lindsey ended his day. I was in luck with the traffic, but out of luck with Joe as he wasn't in the office when I arrived. I was told that he would return shortly, so I made myself busy at my desk with some paper work as I tried to ignore the country music through the partition. I was just thinking about disconnecting the surge protector that would pull the plug on the music when the phone rang.

"Why don't you return your calls?" came Amos Freyer's voice over the receiver.

"I just hit my desk, Amos."

"Guess whose name I just heard?"

"I give up."

"Yours."

"Mine?"

"Right, I heard the desk sergeant relay some call about a car theft, and then your name was mentioned. That perked up these old ears. Can't you do anything without becoming involved in some sort of screw up?"

"I'm only a concerned citizen who takes an active role in community affairs."

"Bull! You sound more like a lawyer every day. When are you going to behave like one and chase those car thieves around so you can represent them for a big fee, instead of calling us to turn them over for prosecution?"

"Need to pass that along to Pops. Maybe he'll get me started on litigation rather than this Mickey Mouse that I'm doing out there now. Can I use you for a reference, old buddy?"

"Sure, any time you wish. I'm getting to be like you. I can be bought, too."

"Yeah, but you're cheap, only a Grand Slam and ten cups of stiff coffee at Denny's."

"Okay, so I'm predictable. What about you? Got any news about the Emory killing or the Rogers' operation?"

"Nada, amigo."

"Sand-bagging me again, sport?"

"Wished I had something to do that with, but you know where I've been for the last hour or two. That's been the highlight of my day."

"Okay, Prich, but I expect to hear from you when you have something."

"Right-O, and likewise from you, good buddy," I said as we ended our conversation. Give-a-little to get-a-little, and I didn't see much coming my way either. What the heck, at least I reported a car theft, and all I received was a little grief from Freyer for my trouble. I returned several calls which had piled into a neat stack since my latest involvement. Nothing seemed attractive enough to pull me away from the current involvement, though.

I was about to call the accounting department when my phone rang. I thought the word had gotten out that I needed to speak with Joe Lindsey.

"Joe?"

"Not unless I've had an operation for which I'm completely in the dark," laughed Kate. "Where the devil have you been, sport? Seems as if you dropped off the end of the world."

"I've been very busy, love," I answered, and then felt my halo slip a smidgen.

"I was wondering about how busy was busy, so I asked Suzie if you'd been with any more gals."

"Oh, ye of little faith."

"Oh, ye of little faithfulness!"

"Well, you lucked out this time as Suzie swore a blood oath that you weren't on the lamb with some other poor unsuspecting woman. Have you been tipping her an extra large amount?"

"Who me?" I said with a loud howl.

"No, I should know better than that, you cheapy."

"Hey, you say that we should go Dutch most of the time, and now look who's calling whom cheap."

"Well, you owe me a Chesapeake Bay weekend, and I'm trying to find out what you intend to do about it. The last weekend I spent with you ended up with your getting injured and meeting a goofy doctor."

"I thought he was a fine doctor."

"You would!"

"Well, I saw him today and my hand is doing very well."

"Do you mean that you went back to the emergency room?"

"Let's not get into that. This weekend on the Bay sounds wonderful. I'm looking forward to it, and I'll give you a call tomorrow."

"Sounds like you're getting rid of me with a rush, so I'll say good-bye until I hear from you tomorrow. I will hear from you tomorrow, won't I?"

I promised on the head of my ancestors, and

we parted. Kate was becoming too suspicious for my own good. She seemed all together too righteous. I wasn't checking on her and making her accountable for all the time we weren't together. I wasn't certain if she wouldn't have been better suited as an auditor with her cold reasoning of every small detail. With her spy network, she could even have been a Mata Hari. She hadn't found me out yet. She had only her constantly reoccurring suspicions which didn't hold much weight against a good lawyer in modern courts.

I finished what little house-keeping remained at my desk and skipped out without much notice. Joe Lindsey was easy to find because he was beaming the widest smile as his buxom friend left his work area. The moment I saw her, a wide grin appeared on my face too. I thought Joe was a lucky young fellow to find such a gal with all those wonderful mental and physical endowments who also was interested in him. Joe waved me over and began looking for an extra chair. He appeared pleased to see me while he was reaching for a small group of forms beneath a larger stack of printouts.

"I was just about to give you another call," Lindsey said with some eagerness. "I tried earlier, but they told me you were out."

"Sounds like you may have found something, my good man."

"Maybe and maybe not."

"First, give me the maybe."

"Okay, Prich, but I'm not certain you'll understand this thing. I'm not sure that I do either."

Lindsey turned and began shuffling through the stack of forms until he found the sheet he required. He gave a groan of happiness and proceeded to rummage through more forms while he scratched his head with a sigh of wonderment.

"I thought I had this all figured out, and then another task came along, and somehow I mixed the whole schbang together," groaned the young accountant. "Please have a little patience with me. I know it's around here some place. Just got too much junk on this desk. I believe I need a course in filing. You'd think they would teach something like that in one of those accounting courses."

"You sure do have a mess, but I'll bet my desk is the only one around here that's worse. I skipped that neatness 101 course in law school."

I spied another short pile of forms lying on a cardboard box by the window. Joe was working the depths of the wasteland of paperwork on his desk and had his back to the window.

"Strike oil yet?" I said.

"Dry hole so far."

"What are those on the box behind you? All accounting forms look the same to me, but they look sort of like the other stack that you first showed me."

As soon as Lindsey spun around and I saw his eyes, I knew he was home free. Joe pushed some of his mess aside as I pulled up a chair. I bent over and gave the appearance I was truly interested in those columns-after-columns of figures. The first thing before me was one spreadsheet which was a feeder into the bottom line of another spreadsheet. I wondered if this was the input for the next one.

Joe poured over the documents with the precision of a diamond cutter and then came to several subtotals which he pointed to and marked with his red pen. He then went into the newly found stack and did almost the same thing; however, the figures in the new stack were in quantities or number of items rather than dollars.

"What's up, buddy?" I said again while still feigning interest.

"Doesn't appear that it's a big problem, but there's something that may be interesting."

"Oh?" I mumbled with less than wild excitement.

"Right," he began. "I was looking for a direct correlation between product sold and revenue."

"That sounds about right."

"Well, their bank balance looks nice and healthy with the steady stream of revenue, but the product shipped doesn't match those totals."

"That just puts us back to where we were with that John Evans fellow. His complaint or question was something like that, and he had some ill feelings."

"I can understand why he became concerned, Prich. It's a little cryptic, but I like a good puzzle. I kept digging, and I believe that I might have a partial solution."

"Wonderful, Joe," I yipped with real delight, "this couldn't have come at a better time."

"Now don't hold my feet to the fire on this analysis, as I'm working third-hand knowledge here at best," Lindsey cautioned. "I'm not sure if I have all the accounting information they have available at their facility. There very well might be some other pieces of information available that would have cleared this whole jumble in a jiffy. If this is all Mr. Evans has available to him, it's no wonder that he's concerned. I would have raised a red flag a long time ago."

"Evidently, he was concerned, but very insecure. It's a long story and I'll spare you. At least he's come forward now. I don't believe he knew anyone he could turn to before."

"I wasn't trying to be critical," the young accountant apologized. "I was just trying to state the poor form used here from the technical sense, and I was amazed he went along with it if he has the background that you indicate."

"I suspect that this was only a very recent development from what Evans indicated. I don't believe the anomaly has existed very long. Now, what can you show me that won't start me talking to myself in a couple of minutes? Let's try to follow the KISS rule with me. That's 'Keep It Simple, Stupid,' but I guess you have heard that enough with me around."

"I say the same thing about legal matters. That's why you folks hired me. I am supposed to know something that you don't."

"I never looked at it that way before, but it makes perfect sense," I told the accountant as he yawned, and I scratched my head.

"Well, we've been looking at Rogers & Emory as a software company which makes games and delivers their product through a wholesale distribution system. Then that product enters a much wider retail distribution chain which ends with my seeing computer software selling at the shopping malls and all over the place. Even K-Mart is selling the games and other computer software items like word processing and spreadsheet programs. I expect 7-11 will be marketing software, if they aren't already."

"I'm with you so far," I said with pride and my chest puffed out.

"Well, there's another form of product called a service type product."

"Like what we do here at this law firm."

"Right, Prich," Lindsey said with a smile. "Sometimes we provide a physical product, such as a will or a contract, while other times we provide a service type product, such as advice or representation in court or anywhere else. Have I bored you yet, Prich?"

"I'm still with you," I responded and then gave him a mock yawn.

The young accountant laughed and then offered me a cup of coffee. Not wishing to damage my reputation as a "Mini the Mooch," I quickly accepted to catch my breath.

"Ah, ha," Lindsey said with obvious happiness as he pulled out the one sheet that he'd been alluding to, but now he had the documentation to support his theory. "Here's the reference that I'd been talking about. It's somewhat vague, but gives clear reference to the problem."

"How so?"

"The most important thing about the line is that the numbers add to the correct final total."

"So what?"

"That's your job, Prich. You're the 'So What' guy. I'm only the 'Here It Is' fellow."

"Okay, Uncle!" I cried softly with a laugh.

"I don't know what else to tell you, Prich," Joe Lindsey said with a slight groan as he pointed at the line on the form. "This line entry entitled 'Assistance' adds to the correct total. Now don't ask me what 'Assistance' means since I can't find any other reference to it anywhere. It sounds like a service type entry, but your guess is as good as mine. If I hadn't gotten those additional sets of forms which I asked for later, we would still be whistling in the dark."

"You're right." There was some more glee in my voice as I was so surprised that I did grasp what that personable young man was conveying to me. "I understand your dilemma too, and that scares me. I just wonder why Evans never caught this anomaly? You would think that if he was as competent as he states, he would've been on top of this already. He had access to this information before any of us."

"I'm not sure if he did, Prich," he said with a thoughtful expression. "These latest forms are something which I'd asked for later in the process. Evidently, this information was still in the processing stage in the marketing and development departments. It'll probably show up soon in the regular accounting journal and ledger accounts, but the funds beat everything else to the punch. It's the old axiom which I hear you saying, 'If you can't understand the system, just follow the bucks.' That got everyone started this time, and it'll probably follow through to the end."

"How did Evans get his hands on these documents?"

"He didn't really say, and I didn't ask."

"I hope he didn't put himself into any sort of jeopardy if he went outside his department or beyond his authority."

"I don't know," responded the thoughtful young accountant with a wrinkled forehead and possibly a small twinge of guilt. "He seemed like a sharp fellow, and I'm sure he wasn't reckless. I certainly do hope that I didn't push him too far with my eagerness."

"It's his job to keep the books straight, and he was only doing what they pay him to do. It was also his idea to start the whole inquiry. He seemed impatient to find out something the last time I saw him. Don't get upset about Evans. He's the one who is making an issue here, not you."

"Thanks, Prich."

"Nothing to thank me for. It's the truth."

"Right, but thanks all the same."

We finished with my still trying to tell Joe Lindsey that he'd done a great job, and now we had something to work with. I collected the pertinent forms with the important accounting line entries and asked Lindsey to highlight each entry to make it easier for me. It looked easy when Lindsey explained it to me, but I wasn't sure if I could describe the process to another party without a little assistance.

I had everything tucked under my arm and was whistling my way out the door ten minutes later. It felt good when I could truthfully say that I was earning my paycheck. I'm not all together sure about that, since I also felt good when I wasn't actually earning my keep either.

Chapter 11

The Great Butt-in-ski

I bounced back up the stairwell to my floor and whizzed over to my desk in a spry mood. I'm not sure why I was so proud of myself, as Joe Lindsey and John Evans had done all the work. The best I could rationalize was that I'd become a facilitator and brought several principals together. That was my sole attempt at humility. I was about ready to high-tail it out of there when the intercom buzzed, telling me Franky was on the line; this was the umpteenth time he'd tried to reach me today, but would never leave a message.

"Hey, Franky," I said lightly, "what's happening on easy street?"

"Was gonna ask you the same. Anything new popping lately, and more to the point, do you need any additional help?"

I felt somewhat guilty and obligated at the same time, and I wished that I had something to keep my good friend occupied. Maybe I was like the fellow in another culture, who after saving a life, became responsible for that person the rest of his existence. What had I gotten myself into?

"I believe this thing is just a little spooky, Franky," I stated out of the blue.

"How so?"

"It's not anything that I can put my finger

167

on at the moment, but I have this strange feeling about the whole thing. Call it a sixth sense or anything you want, but there's an under-tow in these seemingly calm waters and that means trouble somewhere."

"Sure you got nothing to pin it down with?"

"Just some hints."

"Like what?"

"Well, one big 'Like What' is the murder of Joseph Emory. It surely wasn't a mugging or the work of a professional either. Now what does that leave?"

"Well, who stands to gain from his death?" came Franky's well pointed question.

"Everyone and no one in particular. The company goes over to the Rogers. However, that wasn't the bulk of his estate; some went to charity, and the greater percentage to a Johnson lady, whoever and where ever she might be."

"Is that it?"

"Nope," I exhaled. "Just can't bring it all into my consciousness."

"Try harder," Franky prodded.

"Tell you what bunkie," I said in a more weary tone. "I'll see you tomorrow for lunch at the Chain Bridge Club, and we'll chew on it over the special."

"What's the special?"

"Whatever Georgey hasn't peddled the previous week. If the corn beef and cabbage didn't slide down the old gullet too smoothly last week, then it's corn beef hash this week."

"What happened to all that cabbage then?"

asked my puzzled good buddy.

"Remember all the wonderful slaw that you always brag about? Ever notice how it appears as a staple with all the other menu selections?"

"Never gave it any thought."

"What about now?"

"Geez, Prich, now I'll be analyzing and scrutinizing every last thing at the club. I won't be able to enjoy a darn thing anymore. Thanks a million."

"You're welcome," I said meekly as we parted. Well, what the heck, what are buddies for if you can't have a little fun with them?

I gathered myself together and slipped out the door in an effort to get home early and indulge myself with some extra rest. I'm not an old timer, but I'm also not a teenage stud anymore either. Come to think of it, I probably never was a teenage stud with my lanky, awkward appearance and my Clearasil complexion. Most of the zits had vanished. However, my appearance and posture could still have used some improvement.

Some days my body felt better about pulling into my own driveway than others. I felt weary that day and wrote it off to another visit to a medical center and the stress associated with the white coat syndrome. The safety and security of one's own abode has a calming and renewing effect which fit my needs to a tee that fine day. As usual, I'd beaten father home, but that was his nature. I was more than happy to concede that aspect of a good character trait had failed to be passed along to yours truly. I was always thrilled to be the very first warm body out the office door rather than the last. To heck with that nonsense about the captain staying on the bridge with the ship. I preferred the roles of the women and children - I was out of there on the first life raft.

As I was entering the house, I saw Romney and Renate through the corridor. Smelling the wonderfully satisfying coffee aromas wafting across my pleasure zones, I headed directly to the kitchen.

Renate smiled her pleasant welcome and then began making her departure to the supermarket for the evening meal. Being from the old world where everything must be completely fresh, she made her daily jaunts to the market to assure everything was at its peak of freshness. You could never catch any item in her grocery cart that was an over-ripe special.

"What's for dinner this evening?" I asked while she was leaving the house.

"Roast loin of pork with dill sauce and new potatoes," came her response.

I took a sip of that luscious tasting java with the steam wafting into my nostrils and ummed with a vocalizing delight. It had occurred to me again that I was neglecting a great source of back-door information about the Rogers family. Romney had provided valued data more than once before through the domestic-help gossiping grapevine. This information had always proven invaluable in the past and had even contributed to the break-through clue on one previous case.

Romney had contacts upon contacts who

lived with and knew every intimate detail of their employers and benefactors. They could tell me who was running around with whom, who had what medical condition, or what brand of toothpaste they used. I just wondered how much of my private life was more public than I would have wished? If I could purchase data on any Bethesda blue blood, were they doing the same in return? I was consoled by the next thought: who would want to know anything about me as there wasn't anything worth paying to find out about me?

"Romney, are you still in the information-gathering service?" I asked with my natural finesse.

"I was wondering how long you might string your current situation along before you came knocking. I was beginning to feel neglected."

"I've been just so wrapped up in this process that I haven't been able to use all my sources. This thing has also been ballooning beyond what I had originally thought, and I've been trying to play catch up ever since."

"I can understand that. I've gotten swamped with a load of things lately, too."

"Well, I was going to ask if you still had your active network in place."

"Alive and well," came Romney's response with an indication of some pride.

"Believe you can do any good with the Rogers family who live over by the park? They have a staff there too."

"I already know who they are," he said with

his reputation in tact and his pride swelling.

"Have you any knowledge about them?"

"Nothing specific yet, but I do know they have a skeleton or two."

"Oh, really?"

"Hear the old man is becoming a touch less than he was before."

"In what department?"

"I don't think he's simple, but he's also not wrapped as tightly as before."

"Okay, is that all?"

"Heard the son is a real jerk."

"Amen! I like your source!"

"That's just for starters. I'll have more later on after I put a couple feelers out."

"Need to grease any skids?" I said.

"Never hurts."

"What do you think it might take? Would a couple of hundred help to begin with?"

"Couldn't hurt."

I pulled my check book out of my briefcase and wrote a check to cash for three hundred dollars. Romney smiled when I handed him the greaser, and I indicated the extra hundred was for him. He'd always seemed to supplement his income with a touch of confidential dirt from the rich class. Maybe we Bethesda folks needed to pay our home staff a little better for some compensation of tighter lips. I clearly anticipated that he would hit me up a time or two more with this inquiry, but he'd never overcharged me yet. I always seemed to get my money's worth and never begrudged him of one thin dime. I wasn't even sure if I could call it my money as it surely always hit the expense voucher. That thin dime didn't slip out of my pocket.

With about all the work done which I could grasp at the time, I blended away to my loft for a couple of winks with my feet up. I quit spinning all the details around in my head and just slipped away after setting the alarm for an hour and a half. I also wised-up for a change and turned off the ringer on the phone.

I thought that I only rolled over when I heard the alarm clock rattle and buzz that charming noise my way. I must have really been tired, but I felt a great deal better after I took a quick shower and dressed for dinner. A little nap and shower did wonders for my disposition too, since I was happy to greet the family, and everyone seemed pleased to see me again.

Renate's meal was back on par again, a gourmet's delight. I guess the same can be said for cooks as well as writers: do whatever you know how to do and do it well. Renate came back to what she knew, which was wonderful. Normally she would frown with my pigging out on seconds, but she took it as a compliment that evening. While we finished our cherry cobbler ala mode dessert, father quietly suggested we have a brief get together for an aperitif in the study for a few minutes. We both understood what that coded phrasing meant.

After patting my stuffed tummy and finally

pushing my chair away from the table, I rinsed my hands and headed for the study to provide a short briefing to pops. That also meant we would decide where we were heading and if we wished to stay the course. From everything I could read from his demeanor to the inflection of his tone, I didn't find any annoyance or alarm.

He still appeared to be in the information-gathering process, undecided which way to go. He didn't wish to abandon a client in a time of need, but he didn't wish to commit our firm to a process which could bring discredit our way. He was walking a tight rope, and he knew I would pull the plug the minute we might become involved. We certainly didn't want to be identified with any misdeed. Our sole purpose was rather as counsel to a client, merely representing that client to mitigate his risk or penalty. Father raised his hand to greet me when I entered and walked over to the chair opposite his.

"You've looked somewhat tired and drawn the last several days," he began with a concerned tone. "I hope that short nap helped you, son."

"Seems it was just what the doctor ordered. I feel much better now, and the wonderful dinner sure didn't hurt."

"Good. Glad to know you can identify when you need to stop for a pause to let your body renew itself. I sometimes think you push yourself too much."

"I've got that perfect one thousand batting average, and I wouldn't want to spoil it without giving it every chance."

"I understand that you have your pride, son, but sometimes events get out of hand. I have my own practice to show as an example. I haven't been able to foresee every event that has happened. I've made many adjustments throughout my career. I certainly wouldn't think anything less of you if you came to me anytime with a recommendation to end an inquiry before the final outcome."

"Sounds as if you are a little less than directly telling me that you wish to end the Rogers' inquiry. It also sounds as if you're trying to let me down gently, and I sincerely appreciate your concern for my feelings."

"Can you blame me, son? I have several serious concerns with this inquiry. I don't wish to see you injured or our firm's reputation damaged. I'd take this position even if we were talking about an old and faithful client. Rogers and Emory are neither, and I'm amazed that we've been with them as long as we already have been."

"Do you have anything beyond a bad feeling with this inquiry?" I said defensively.

"Only what you've told me, Prich. But let's add them up. First we have an inside chief financial officer come to us with a suspicion of financial malfeasance. Second, and extremely important, Joseph Emory was killed under extremely unusual circumstances. Someone is playing for big stakes. Next, you're chased by someone that you describe as 'probably a professional.'"

"What makes you think that I might be in

some danger?" I said, but knew what the answer would probably be.

"It's the old cliché, son: in for a dime, then in for a dollar. If someone has murdered once, then why not again? It's only the initial murder that's the difficult one, and the others which follow come much easier."

"Father," I began slowly, "please stay with me a day or two longer. I certainly don't believe anything of consequence will occur in that short span of time. I'll stay at arm's length for most of that period, and Joe Lindsey can initiate our billing cycle. It would be a shame to walk away after what we've invested to date."

Thinking that I could appeal to his financial propensity for good business judgment, I could gain several days by telling him we would be paid, and I would keep clear. I knew he had my safety at heart first, but he always held the almighty buck in very high esteem.

"The first new project you see coming my way," I continued, "I can pull the plug at Rogers, and we will be fully compensated for our investment and efforts."

Father seemed somewhat satisfied that I'd appeared to accommodate his position without any significant objection. It seemed strange to me that he didn't ask for any update, for I wasn't willing to provide him with any additional doubts after he expressed his intentions. I thought I might be able to wriggle out of this hot spot as time mollified many strong directions. It also didn't hurt in the least to appeal to his financially frugal side of his character. It simply bothered me to let David Rogers off the hook so easily after some of the comments which I endured. Everything has a price, and I wanted to be there when David Rogers saw our invoice.

I almost forgot the aperitif as I was so thrilled to placate my father that my senses were numbed to the finer things of life. Priorities, priorities, wherefore art thou, the bard might have said, and I surely needed to get mine realigned much better.

I quickly changed the subject of discussion with my concerned parent and brought up my parents' plans for their vacation. It was coming close to their annual jaunt. Father could talk for hours on their ancestral homeland in Europe. We even got around to my wounded paw, and father seemed extremely pleased that it was coming along so well. I only had a small bandage now. After a while, father opened his combined works of Poe volume, and that was my cue to excel in another location.

I made my excuses and slipped out of the study to retrieve an iced tea and cart it off to my lair. I was in luck as I spied several dozen homemade chocolate chip cookies which Renate had left on the cooling rack. I hoped that she wouldn't notice several of the "jewels gone missing," as the Brits might say. I simply had to pay more attention to that waistline of mine.

Back in my loft, I went about my duties with my diary again as it was becoming dated. I felt rather fresh after my nap so the task of recalling the events of the recent past were more forthcoming than I'd anticipated. I again wrote several more index cards and sorted them with the previous cards. I tried looking at the events from a different perspective.

I thought about a new approach by making new "what if" cards by color coding them with a red dot in the corner. I then moved the old index cards around, trying to fit them under the new "what if" categories and occurrences. One "what if" scenario addressed the position of what if the Rogers and Emory company weren't as financially fit as they appeared. Different possibilities occurred to me as my mind raced in every direction.

I began to consider the "why" along with the "what if" and quickly came to the conclusion that I surely could use some help. I had a great answer to that problem and would address it tomorrow. I didn't have the answer to my most immediate problem of pops wanting to end the entire inquiry. The only thing I could show was something akin to a stay of execution. I was hoping that time and other events would soften his attitude toward our ongoing relationship with the Rogers and Emory Development Company.

Up and at 'em early the next morning, I was the first one downstairs again. Renate was busy inventing another culinary masterpiece while Romney was setting the table. Renate asked if she could tempt me away from my corn flakes with a Western omelet; she didn't need to twist my arm too long. The aromas emanating from her work area already had me convinced. Everyone still couldn't comprehend why I wanted my orange juice and banana, but they didn't press the issue.

Pops was just coming down as I was finishing the last bite and pushing the plate back with a satisfied groan. Maybe he stayed up too late or had nightmares after reading Poe. Whatever the reason, his late appearance was uncharacteristic, but he didn't offer any explanation. I didn't make any inquiry as it was my intention to get out and about without any confrontation with the family patriarch. We said our greetings and pleasantries, and I vanished with a whisk.

I was in the Mustang, heading for Rogers & Emory faster than an Indy pit-stop. I wasn't sure if it was a good idea to arrive so early, so I kicked it back a few notches and pulled into a full-service gas station. Luck must have been going with me because I saw the best radar trap hidden around the next turn as I was just starting to build up to speed after leaving the service station. They would've picked me off for sure. I waved and smiled to them as I passed.

The parking lot at Rogers & Emory was over half-filled when I arrived, and I parked much closer to the building. The spaces were numbered, and I hoped that I wasn't taking anyone's reserved space. Reserved parking in this metro area was highly coveted, and I didn't wish to annoy anyone or have him seek me out a short time later. I bounced into the main door and spotted John Evans who waved me over.

"You folks get anywhere further with that additional data that I provided the other day?" asked Evans with some anticipation.

"As a matter of fact, I believe we did," I happily answered the surprised accountant.

"Really!" he exclaimed as he stood there with his mouth open, lost for words.

"Right," I continued so he would close his mouth and not make a spectacle of himself, "Joe Lindsey found a line item that added to the correct final total."

"What type of line item?" Evans snapped loudly before I could finish my thought.

He then caught himself and understood that he shouldn't be drawing attention to himself or even have others notice that I was consulting with him. Everyone accepted me as a normal fixture now, but I didn't wish to have people connect me as a frequent visitor to the accounting department or to John Evans in particular.

I was having a difficult time enough with my own father and didn't wish any more complications here. I indicated to Evans with a smooth downward motion to lower his voice and calm his demeanor. He nodded in agreement and then told me that it would appear better if we sat at his desk.

"What type of line item?" he repeated softly after we were sitting and behaving normally.

"The only thing I know is that it's called Assistance, whatever that means."

"Assistance?"

"Right."

"Where'd you get that name?"

"From the forms that Joe Lindsey asked for later. I don't understand why he asked for them, but all of a sudden this Assistance line appeared, and it balanced the entire process."

"I never heard of Assistance, and I don't have the vaguest idea what it means," Evans stated as he turned up the palms on both his hands and sat there with a bewildered expression all over his face.

"We were hoping that you could shine some light on this mystery entry," I said voicing my concern.

"Doesn't make any sense," Evans mumbled softly.

"Have a copy of those forms that you provided to Joe Lindsey?"

"Sure, right over here," he answered as he rose and headed for a bank of filing cabinets.

Evans opened the file and sorted through the various stacks of accounting forms until he came to the one which he was looking for. He quickly pulled it out and opened it to expose the rows of numbers. He began moving his finger down the first column entitled "account name" until he reached the Assistance account on the next to last page.

"Bingo," he snapped quietly.

"Ah, ha!" I said more as a matter of relief.

"You were correct," he admitted.

"Sure," I replied, feigning an injured

expression. "Now, can you tell me what the heck Assistance means? Neither Joe Lindsey nor myself had any idea what that entry meant, except it was the magic bullet that brought the entire account into agreement. It literally made the books balance."

"I can see that much, but I haven't the slightest idea where it came from or what it means."

"Joe Lindsey indicated that he thought it sounded like a service type entry rather than a product entry," I advised. "None of the product numbers seemed to have any reference to those additional funds."

"Well, that makes sense," he began with a puzzled expression. "I just don't understand what service we have that would add to those kind of figures."

"How long have they been on your books?"

"Obviously, not that long or I would've been concerned about them before this."

"Well, let's see if there's some audit trail somewhere," I said, since I was beginning to sound like a bean counter too. "These funds couldn't just appear out of nowhere. Let's see when they first appeared and who made the first entry. Do you have anything which could shine a little light on this?"

"Sure have, now that I've got a reference to work with," Evans indicated as he pointed to a column on the printout that indicated a reference number.

Evans picked up a slip of paper from a nearby desk and wrote the reference number and several other pertinent facts. He then told me to have a seat and he would return shortly. I went back to his desk and waited patiently. I saw Ken Hobbs walk past twice and made a mental note that I needed to see him after I finished with Evans. The accountant returned after no more than five minutes with a broad smile on his face.

"Any luck?" I asked

"Some," he said with a grin. "Looks like Cassy made the entry about three weeks ago and didn't say anything to me."

"Is that standard operating procedure?"

"Heck, no, it isn't SOP!" he responded firmly. "Anything this significant should always be discussed with me. That surely isn't like Cassy. She's usually right on top of everything."

"Let's talk to her," I stated as I saw her just come in the door to begin the workday.

"We'll give her a couple of minutes to become settled, and then we'll have a talk with her," Evans said with a degree of caring for the feelings of a good subordinate and coworker.

Evans busied himself by collecting all the appropriate accounting forms and supporting documents. I went over to the water cooler for a drink and saw Judith wave as I was returning. I waved and smiled back, then continued over to Evans' desk. Cassy was sitting there as I returned. She smiled a warm welcome while I approached. Evans had waited several moments before talking with Cassy, since he didn't wish to have her repeat anything. He hoped that I could detect her true thought, if I could watch her as she responded.

"Cassy, we've been struggling with an accounting dilemma for awhile, and we may have found the solution. The problem we still have is we don't understand the new line or how it was initially added to the accounts," Evans began.

"You'll need to be more explicit," she responded with a true sense of bewilderment.

"We had a great deal of difficulty bringing the accounts into balance," he continued.

"You folks had more revenue to show for your efforts than the product lines would normally indicate," I added.

Cassy still looked at both of us searching for some reasonable meaning. I had to give her one thing - she was more than patient with us, and she didn't fly into any defensive tirade or make a scene to distract us from our inquiry. I could picture many other individuals breaking into a prolonged outburst of vehement speech to construct a dramatic denunciation of the interviewer. She was only trying to understand our problem and appeared eager to offer us her help.

"We finally found this line entitled 'Assistance' which has us confused," Evans stated.

"The Assistance line?" she asked.

"Right, that's the one," I answered as she swung her attention around to face me.

"Oh, I thought you knew about that," she said.

"What do you mean?" asked Evans.

"David Rogers asked me to add it a couple of weeks back, and I thought he told you too," she replied as she looked at Evans with a questioning expression.

"David never said a word to me," he said in response.

"I believe that he even said you knew about it," she added as everyone became quiet.

"Not a word," he indicated.

"Well, all right. Now that we've gotten past that," I interjected. "The next question is ... what does Assistance mean and how is it used to produce any revenue?"

"I've got no idea," she stated, looking more confused than ever.

"Do you mean that he didn't say what that line was for, and he only told you to install it in the accounts?" Evans asked with a degree of incredulity.

"That's right!" she stated with some degree of firmness. "I thought that you already knew about that new account, and everything had been cleared. I would've come running if I thought otherwise."

"I appreciate that," he responded with a tone of apology in his voice.

"He's also the boss, and I wasn't going to give him the third degree!" she emphasized.

We both shook our heads in agreement. I understood how she could have easily become confused.

We both thanked her and she appeared happy to have been of some assistance to us. She returned

185

to her work station, and we both looked at each other for a sense of confirmation.

"What do you think?" he asked.

"I believe she told us the truth," I responded matter-of- factly.

"So do I and I plan to find out more about it!" Evans concluded as he walked away shaking his head.

I gathered my thoughts together and stepped over to Cassy's desk. She looked up and smiled as I sat on the corner of her desk and crossed my leg.

"I wouldn't worry about that little misunderstanding," I volunteered.

"I'm not worried, but I feel somewhat disappointed, as if maybe I let John down," she replied.

"You were only doing your job. When the boss asks you to do something, you simply get it done," I replied.

"Well, I understand, but I wish that I would've let John know," she continued. "I can see how he would become concerned. I was just under the impression that Rogers had already cleared this with him. Now that I think about it, why would David ask me to do that function rather than following the chain of authority? He should've discussed this with John, and then John would've asked. 'Why skip John?' is my question"

"He's the boss and can do any darn thing he wishes," I answered to her somewhat rhetorical question.

"I know that he can do what he wishes, but I'm trying to figure this thing out. It just doesn't make any sense, and he should've known that it might get me into trouble by going behind John's back."

"I believe John understands what happened now, and I don't think that he is the type of fellow who blames others to make up for his or someone else's shortcomings. He'll get to the bottom of this mess-up, and it won't result in being your fault. John might be a little nerdy, but he seems like a fair guy."

"John isn't a nerd," she quickly defended her immediate boss and friend. "He's only a little quiet, but he's very bright and such a kind man."

"Some kind of catch for the right gal, right?"

"Sure."

"How about you?" I said with my matchmaker mode just beginning.

"I've already got a boyfriend," she answered with a look of pride in her face.

"Sure you have," I chided with some care.

"What do you mean by that?"

"Ever notice how some very bright gals who're very pretty get dumped-on all the time? They could have the pick of any litter, and yet they always end up with the Macho type. Those lovelies just like to get beat around and would feel strange not to see one of their eyes swollen shut when they looked into the mirror in the morning."

"I'm not like that!" she said.

"You're not saying that you aren't bright and very attractive, are you?

187

"Why, certainly not!" she countered.

"Well, there you are then," I said.

"What does that mean?"

"You figure it out, Cassy. You're just too good of a person and don't deserve what you have now. I hope that's plain enough for you."

"You know what? What you're saying might work both ways, don't you think?"

"How so?"

"I've seen you leering around Evelyn Rogers, and I've seen her flirting with you."

"I'm kind of like Jimmy Carter. I lust in my heart, but leave the real thing alone."

"Why, sure you do!"

"The honest to God truth," I protested.

"Keep singing that song, and you might find some poor gullible gal who'll swallow the line."

"Well, heck, I'm a single guy."

"And I'm single too."

"But, I can take care of myself."

"Ditto."

"Just look at who you're involved with."

"Evidently, you don't know much about Evelyn Rogers either, do you?"

"Not really, except that she's a real knockout!"

"I shouldn't be the one to tell you, but she's hot after any guy with pants and something she can swindle them out of. What do you have that she wants?"

"Beats me, but I'd probably enjoy finding

out."

"I'm sure you would for a short time, but just wait until you wise up and find your wallet gone. Are you making a pass at me?"

"Well, no, that never occurred to me," I stated in my defense, but knew that I'd said the wrong thing as soon as I heard the phrasing come from my mouth.

"Well, thanks. You really know how to boost a girl's spirits and self confidence."

"No, I didn't mean to say it the way it sounded. I'm on your side and pulling for you. I just don't like to see anyone of quality, whom I like, end with something less than they deserve."

"Let me be the judge of that."

"Good luck," I said softly as I walked away to meet with her poor choice of a boyfriend. I thought that I had the last word. I should have known better.

"You're the poor sucker who'll need all the help he can get!"

I smiled, but continued walking.

Chapter 12

Mutual Admiration Society

I walked over to shipping and passed through a large pair of swinging doors that led into a warehouse area. There didn't seem to be much activity occurring on the main floor, but I did see the outlines of several people making gestures from a considerable distance. As I drew nearer, they remained unaware of my approach and continued their animated verbal foray. It was apparent there was an argument that had gone well beyond the quiet phase. I didn't need to gain a closer vantage point as my being fifty feet away had clearer reception than my cable TV back at the house. I was beginning to believe that my internal timing device might need some warranty work, and I considered asking my parents for a rebate. Ken Hobbs came storming out of the office and immediately glared at me.

"What the hell do you want?" he shouted my way as two other men came out of the same office shaking their heads. "You sure do have a rotten sense of timing!"

"I was just thinking the very same thought," I replied with a big grin on my face, remembering that last time I'd seen the suspension on the car bouncing. Those were some dandy groans emanating from that back seat at the horse farm.

"Well, I'm up to my ass in alligators, and

the last thing I need is your getting in my way," Hobbs scowled with a screwed up expression of a gargoyle. "Can't you come back here some other time? I sure as hell don't have the patience to be a baby-sitter today."

I wasn't exactly sure which way to go. I knew that I needed to get things wrapped up quickly with pops breathing hard down my neck. On the other hand, I wasn't relishing any type of interlude with the knuckle dragger standing before me. Thinking that I might let the solution appear in the Neanderthal's cranium so it was his idea rather than mine, I gave it the old college try.

"Sorry to come here at a bad time and hope everything works out," I began my spiel. "I know you're always very busy, and I was hoping you might find some other way for me to get a few questions answered. I didn't want to get in your way, and I know your time is very limited."

His expression became less pained, and he was silent for a moment. I watched his eyes move from side to side and wondered if any significant contact was made as they touched the port and starboard extremes. There wasn't any steam or over heating of those little gray cells so we weren't splattered with water from the fire sprinklers. I did, however, see a slight amount of drool in the corner of his mouth from his previous tantrum with his coworkers. Maybe a good dousing would be the perfect thing to clean up that guy's act. Then in a gratuitous gesture, he waved his hands as if a regal figure was ready for a wondrous pronouncement.

"Well, I can shake Stan loose for a time this morning. He knows this place backwards and forwards," came the magnanimous offer from the self-proclaimed mental heavyweight. "I'll need him a little later and don't want you to tie him up long, if you get my drift."

"Gotcha," I stated with more meaning than he understood. "I won't hold him too long. If there's anything he can't explain, I'll get back with you at a more convenient time."

"Right," he growled with some satisfaction in his tone.

"Thanks again for your help," I stated with some enthusiasm that could be nominated by the Academy next year for best performance by an amateur.

I felt that I owed a debt of gratitude to our old friend, Sigmund Freud, who may have instilled the theory of the "not invented here syndrome." It always worked well with intellectual giants like Hobbs if I could convince them it was their idea in the first place. If I proposed the idea, then they'd think that it wasn't their idea, and the "not invented here syndrome" theory comes immediately into effect with an undesired outcome. If they didn't invent the idea, then it wasn't worth the mental synapses that conceived it. We always needed to make them believe it was their idea at the outset and then express how brilliant we thought it was.

Hobbs turned and headed one way, and I

walked straight ahead to the two men who'd just been in the verbal free-for-all with their boss. They were standing just outside the area that had been so loud only a minute or two previously. They were discussing the merits and attributes of their "superior," and it appeared they were in agreement with the least attractive conclusion.

I broke into their conversation and introduced myself to both individuals. The tall, thin red-headed one turned out to be Stan, and he was happy to help me after I told him Hobbs had given it his blessing. I asked them what all the big fuss was about as I arrived and they explained that Hobbs had told them that one of them might be laid off as there wasn't enough work to keep them both busy. They expressed their opinion that Hobbs should be the one let go as he was the biggest goldbricker in the entire county. It was right after that statement that the fireworks started in earnest.

Stan, who turned out to have a last name, Gross, was a bright, good-natured young fellow who really ran the shipping department, but received very little credit. He was still coming down from his major tête-à-tête with his boss. They were instructed to release at least one employee, and Stan believed it might be him, as Ken Hobbs didn't care to have some good competition around to outshine him. Bob, the other fellow in Shipping, was a hard worker, but usually needed direction to organize and accomplish his tasks. Stan, on the other hand, was the one who did most of the planning and work allocation, with

Hobbs plagiarizing and falsely taking credit for all the management and some of the physical labor.

We did most of the interview on our feet, which was fine with me as my waist needed some trimming fairly soon. Gross literally walked me through the shipping operation in the space of fifteen minutes, and then we headed for the office. After that short time, I hoped he would be the one who would be released as he could easily obtain a foreman's position at many other small firms in the metro area. It truly bothered me to see such a competent individual in such a menial slot with little chance of recognition or advancement. I also discovered that David Rogers knew all of this, but for some unexplained reason, not only allowed it to occur, but encouraged the strange behavior. It was just one more anomaly which begged for some reason.

Gross and I poured through several volumes of shipping and receiving logs when something else appeared that I couldn't understand. My creative accounting lessons on my expense vouchers were no help. Sure, the numbers agreed with Evans' figures for volume, but that was only for the outgoing shipments. Stan Gross displayed the entire picture of the volume by showing me the receiving volume as well as the out-going shipments.

"What the heck are these?" I said, scratching my head with some wonderment and confusion.

"Nothing special, Mr. Hale," he answered with an honest smile and a genuine willingness to be helpful. "Almost every manufacturer has material it uses for its product. Even software manufacturers need blank diskettes or CDs to write the software games on so the people who purchase them can get it properly installed on their computers."

"I understand that much," I indicated, "but what are these figures over here?"

"Oh, that's packaging and packing material. We send most of that work out to packaging suppliers and printers. They do a fairly good job of it too, and we don't have many shortages or damaged material other than what the shipper messes-up or loses en route."

We stopped a minute or two and then began discussing personnel at the company. Gross seemed to be about on target with most of the people whom I'd already met or heard something about. If that were the case, then I reasoned that he would be a good source with others whom I didn't have time to meet. I tried not to be too anxious to draw him out, but rather, to agree with him and tell him others had the same opinion. He asked if I would like a cup of coffee, and I was ready for a break anyway. We just sat there with our feet up and kibitzed for an hour. I was about ready to wind everything up there, but decided to get a quick review of what I'd just learned and write down a few notes in the process. It was then that I saw another set of figures in an offset column and asked about them.

"These figures don't seem to be totaled into anything else?" I said with a confusing, questioning tone as I scratched my head and looked to him for an explanation.

"I'm not sure what they do with these numbers, but I can tell you what they are," he answered confidently with a knowing smile of someone who could really be helpful and was happy to have the opportunity.

"Sure, but remember who you're talking to and keep it as simple as you can," I pleaded.

"Well, Mr. Hale, it's really not too complicated, so I believe you're in luck."

"Okay, shoot."

"Well, you see, we're in the computer software business, but we aren't all that different than other businesses in some aspects."

"Uh, huh," I mumbled, just to keep him rolling with some feedback.

"Some manufacturers sell their products to retailers or wholesalers who are middlemen in the merchandising process. These businesses may buy from the manufacturer with an agreement to repair defective material that was made with that defect at the time of manufacture or was later damaged in shipment. They might also agree to service some better customers first or give them some kind of preference."

"Still with you, Stan, but I don't see how this fits into the situation here." I was beginning to feel impatient and thought this entire line of inquiry wasn't going anywhere at all.

"Hold on a minute, Mr. Hale; have a little patience and I'll get there," he said with a smile. "I only wanted to lay the groundwork for what I was about to tell you to let you know that it wasn't something out of the ordinary."

"Well, then you're saying that these figures are only normal, and there isn't anything out of the ordinary?" I asked in an easy tone as I didn't wish to irritate a fellow who was genuinely trying to be helpful.

"Sure, I think these are all normal figures for the unsold come backs."

"The what?"

"The unsold comebacks," he reiterated.

"Now I am confused. What in the devil are unsold comebacks?" I stated with an apparent bewildered inflection that brought a grin to his face.

"That's the name we give to the products that the middlemen or retailers don't sell," he answered with a smile.

"Do you mean the returns?"

"Some companies might call them that, but we don't."

"Maybe that's because they aren't defective, but only unsold," I voiced out-loud what I was thinking.

"Correct," Gross said with an air of satisfaction.

"So none of these numbers reflects anything other than unsold comebacks?" I said.

"Right," he answered as he nodded his head, "the other numbers for the defects are so small that we just combine them in the damaged amounts which

197

are also very small. The two of those added together don't amount to much. I wouldn't even keep score of any of them except we do make claims to the carriers and trucking companies for the damaged ones."

"How do you keep it straight for the damaged products so you can bill the carriers for the claims?" I asked as I knew they needed accurate records or no insurance company or carrier would pay any claim for damage without those records.

"I keep those records split to a distribution on this other worksheet," he said as he pulled a recent copy of another worksheet that was a feeder into the final column on the total worksheet.

"Okay, I've got what you're saying now, but I'm still a little unclear about the unsold comebacks," I stated truthfully as I wasn't familiar with the term. "I am more used to the term 'returns,' but I understand why you wish to break them out from the damaged and defective products."

"You are right. That's why we label them unsold comebacks."

"I guess other industries have products like that?" I said as I was wondering out-loud again.

"Guess they do."

"I know that publishers ask bookstores to do something like that. I've watched them strip the covers off paperback books to send in for credit and destroy the rest of the book."

"Sure, I've seen the same thing," Gross agreed with a pleasant tone and expression.

"Does the rest of the software industry do

the same thing?" I asked.

"I don't know as I haven't had that much contact with others," he answered with a rueful tone of annoyance. "Ken Hobbs has the opportunity to get out and meet others because he's the boss. He doesn't tell us a blasted thing about the business when he comes back. He just gives orders like a drill sergeant, and we're supposed to snap to like a couple of toy soldiers."

"What's your best guess?" I asked.

"I guess it depends."

"Depends on what?"

"Whether you're the big fish or the little fish," he answered with some of that good humor returning.

"Sure, I see what you mean," I told him with a smile. "The big software developer can sometimes dictate to the retailers."

"Probably happens everyday," he agreed.

"So this company takes back software that sits on the store shelves and doesn't charge the store for those comebacks."

"Now I didn't say that," he stated emphatically.

"Why else would they ship the software back if they didn't sell it?" I wondered verbally.

"That's out of my department, Mr. Hale," Gross answered firmly. "What the other departments do and how they handle the rest of the business is their job. I don't try to tell them how to do it."

"Sure," I agreed quickly, "but I just thought

that you might know the answer to that question."

"No, I don't," he said. "But, I'll bet there are several people that can tell you what you need to know. It's not that I'm shy. It's simply that I don't know the right answer, and I don't want to mislead you."

"I appreciate that, Stan," I told him. "You're right. There are many others that simply won't say the phrase, 'I don't know.' They'll make up things they think you want to hear, and often they're inaccurate."

"Yep, find it all the time," he agreed.

"Those are some fairly significant numbers in that unsold comeback column," I told him in earnest.

"Guess so," he stated with a thoughtful expression while he slowly shook his head.

"They sure are," I said with emphasis. "I hope they get a good price for the ones they do sell."

I asked him to make a copy of the wrap-up documents that had the final figures and several other sheets that had vital data that fed into the totaling sheets. I wasn't sure if he was happy to provide the information, but it appeared that it gave him some satisfaction. I knew it wouldn't hurt his soul to slam-dunk the buzzards who discriminated against him. Why feel sorry for those who threatened to cut his job and keep the nonproductive jerk instead of the people who really worked their tails off for them?

I collected all my data and was amazed how fast the time had gone. I thanked Stan Gross for all of his insightful assistance and told him that he was probably wasting his time there anyway. This "cutback" that Hobbs was advising the two about may have been a blessing in disguise. Sometimes people like Gross benefit from some trauma that comes their way which shakes them out of their passivity and into some course of action. Maybe any action was better than the status quo.

I skittered out of the shipping department and headed directly back to the accounting department to probe Evans with a set of new questions. Just as luck would have it, he was wrapped up in a department chief's meeting with David Rogers. It seemed everyone that I wanted or needed to talk to was in that meeting, so I went over to Cassy's desk for some company until the meeting broke up. Evidently, she still wasn't too happy with me after our earlier discussion about the attributes of her companions. She sort of gave me the social heave-ho, and I headed for Evans' desk feeling like a lost little puppy with my tail between my legs.

While sitting at that desk and watching the dust settle, I decided to get Franky on the phone and leave there for an early lunch. Franky picked up on the first ring, like he was ready to pounce on the thing at the first sound it made.

"Always pick the phone up that quickly?" I asked to tease him.

"Damn thing scared me, Prich," he laughed. "I'd just called your office and left a message to call me, and the instant that I'd hung up, the blasted thing rang and scared the devil out of me. What are you trying to do, kill off one of the few remaining friends you have left on the face of this earth?"

"Right, big guy," I teased. "Sandy and I have a thing going, and she just started a big, new insurance policy on your poor soul. We'll be singing your praises while we're sunning ourselves in the Bahamas."

"I sure wish you would have told me about that insurance policy, so maybe I could have faked it and collected, too. I would've joined you and Sandy on the beach."

"Well, since we blew that one, how about doing lunch in a half hour?"

"Sounds good, but it'll have to be brunch as I just got up a short time ago. What about the club, buddy?"

We agreed to meet at the Chain Bridge Club. Franky swore he wasn't going to have anything off the menu with a side dish of slaw. I laughed and hung up just in time to see Judith Rogers walking back to her office. That was poor timing as the department supervisors' staff meeting was just ending. Judith looked over to the accounting area and gave me a wave to come over. Obedient as usual, I headed immediately to her office.

"Hi, there, good looking," came her greeting with a little mischief mixed in, "where are you taking me for lunch and don't pick one of those fast food places?"

"Oops," was the only thing that came out of

my mouth in this moment of emergency.

"What does 'oops' mean?" she quizzed me quickly. "You haven't gotten married since last night, have you?"

"Worse!"

"How can that be?" she said with a puzzled expression.

"My buddy and I already made arrangements to meet. I was about to head for the door when I saw you wave. Honest, I didn't know ..." I was saying when she closed the blinds on the glass partition behind her. She then pulled me over to her and held me closely. She slowly began rubbing her body next to mine and then kissing me with her darting tongue. I went from thinking about food and lunch to procreation in a single second. She then pulled away from me and laughed.

"What in the world was that all about?" I said, still breathless, gasping like I'd just run up five flights of stairs.

"I only wanted to let you know what you would be missing when you were having a good time at lunch with your buddy," she chuckled with a mock sinister tone.

"Good grief," I said with a laugh, "I'll have to wait in this office for another five minutes before I'll be presentable enough to leave here."

It was her turn to laugh as she surveyed what she had done to my anatomy. She then waved her eyes around and had the look of someone who'd just been told that they had won first place at something better than a Pillsbury Bake-Off. She made me promise to ask her first next time and gave me a boot out her door. I took off my suit jacket and placed it strategically in front of me until I was safely inside my car and had the door shut.

When I arrived at the club, I was able to leave my suit jacket in the car. George Wilkinson was behind the bar as usual and waved as I walked past. Suzie Q pointed to my regular table where she had already seated Franky Angelino with a glass of iced tea.

"Hi ya, Franky," I said as I pulled up my usual chair, "been waiting long?"

"Only been here a couple of minutes," he said in a good humored tone. "Where's your coat, fellow? Think it's summer already? You usually wear a suit coat or sports jacket in the middle of the day."

"Oh, it just felt a little warm today so I took it off and left it in the car," I lied with a slight blush which slowly filled in my neck and face.

Suzie Q came over to our table on the fly as she already had several orders in her pocket that she was going to take to the kitchen at one time. She appeared perky and added to our good cheer with her beaming, wide natural smile.

"What are my two guys going to have today?" she chirped in her high pitch, fast articulated technique.

"Wow, Franky, sounds like Suzie has a thing for us swingers!" I teased as I saw the corners of her mouth turn up.

"Watch it, buster," she chuckled back at me, "or I'll tell Kate that you're flirting with me again."

"Hold on there, Suzie Q," I countered. "You're the one who has a thing for us two well behaved lonely souls."

"Right-O, love," Franky chimed in, "and I'm a great witness to the highest bidder."

"Oh, my lord, Franky," I cried. "You sold me out again!"

We howled at each other. Another minute of that and I would've been happy to feast under the golden arches. Suzie finally had enough of the bantering, and both Franky and I ordered the last of the breakfast special of eggs and corn beef hash with homemade biscuits and strawberry jam.

"My mouth started to water when I was ordering that corn beef hash," Franky half yummed and spoke at the same time. "I'm glad we weren't too late for the breakfast."

"Remember what I told you about all of the left-overs from the corn beef and cabbage last week?" I asked with a big grin as I watched the expression on Franky's face change as it looked like someone just turned on a light.

"Oh, man," Franky groaned. "You shouldn't have spoiled it for me."

"You heard me order the very same thing as you, so how bad can it be?"

"Sure, but now you've taken the shine right out of the jewel," he complained with a whine.

"Want me to eat your portion of the corn

beef hash or do you want to tell Suzie to fix you an order of hash browns instead?" I suggested with a smile and wink.

"You'd like to scrape all the great chow into your plate, wouldn't you? Well, you can ditch that clever little ploy in the lost and found because I love corn beef hash under any conditions!"

"Turkey," I moaned and chuckled at my mischievous friend, "really had me going with a guilt trip."

"Paybacks sure are fun!" he wailed with laughter.

"Well, maybe you're right," I added with a get-even mentality. "Here I thought that I had some special work for you in my investigation, but maybe I'd better go with a pro as it could be a little nasty. You know, the last thing that I'd ever want is to have my good buddy involved in something really messy where he might get hurt."

"Bull!" yipped Franky Angelino with a moanful howl. "Don't you start that nonsense with me, bunkie! You don't want to jeopardize the only friendship that you probably have left in this entire universe, do you?"

"Well, let me think it over while you share some of that great corn beef hash with me," I chuckled and then almost choked when I took a sip of coffee that Suzie had brought somewhere during our little melee.

"So, what do you have in mind with that case you've been working with?

"Not completely sure yet, Franky. Pops wants me to get out of it pronto, but I'm trying to drag things out until they're resolved. I'm not sure where it's leading me at the moment or how long I can stall pops."

"Sounds like you need something fast."

"Right."

"Well, you'd better not stall with me too long either. Your dad might pull the rug out from under you, and you won't be anywhere near the truth."

Suzie appeared with the steaming dishes. She took one look at our faces with our ravenous expressions and broke out laughing. I stood up to steady her tray as I surely didn't wish to see all the wonderful chow hit the floor. We dug into the tasty feast, but Franky kept trying to interrupt long enough to get a better idea of what I had in mind for him. I finally had to stop chewing as Franky appeared ready to shove some of his remaining corn beef hash my way.

"Well, Prich, how do you see my part in this little melodrama?" he asked with a mouth full and his eyes wide open.

"First, and most important," I started, "I'll need some good background on the Rogers family, especially the son David. I'd also like some background on a fellow named Ken Hobbs."

"What's the Hobbs guy got to do with it?"

"I'm not sure, but I know he's diddling David Rogers' wife, and I just have a funny feeling about him."

"You mean that you don't like him?" said Franky with one eyebrow raised.

"That's for sure!"

"What do you want to know about him?"

"Primarily, his habits. Where does he go and what does he like, and most importantly, does he have a police record?"

"You can probably get the police record from Freyer, can't you?"

"Sure, but he isn't feeding me anything, so why should I put him onto anyone's trail?"

"Okay, but I can't promise that he won't find out. My source might get the word back to him as those cops always have their back channels working."

"No problem," I told him to get my friend off the hook. "If Freyer finds out, I'll just tell him the truth. That guy Hobbs is making it with the boss's wife, and that isn't a crime in most places."

"Swell, so what else have you got in mind?"

"I understand that you and Sandy have several friends in the financial markets?" I took a bite of toast with the strawberry jam and dribbled some right down my chin. "Maybe they can find out something about the Rogers family, like how well-healed they are. They live in a plush section of Bethesda and have a house staff. They drive a big Mercedes and own that software company. I'd like to find out how deeply their financial gold vein goes."

"I'll see what I can dig up for you, and I understand that you are under that time pressure from your father. I'll get right on it as the weekend is coming up soon, and everything comes to a brick wall until they open their doors next Monday. Is that about it or is there something else that you haven't told me yet?"

"I believe I've told you about everything, but I also have a few questions about that older partner, Joseph Emory, who died. We have most of what we need with the will and some financial records. I'd like to find out if you could dig up something else which could help us shed some more light on that problem. You might also ask around on the streets about the Rogers & Emory Company, how they might be doing in the software market."

"Sure wish you could've had me working on this some time ago. I'll get you what I can in this short amount of time, but I could probably do much better if I had a week or so more to do a little more digging. I'm just thinking that some of my contacts might not be willing to jump as fast as I might, so this could drag out a little longer than you might have hoped."

"I understand that," I told him to soothe his nerves again. "I know that I'm asking you fairly late in the game, but I haven't any choice. Usually pops stays with me to the end of an inquiry, and I'm not under a great deal of pressure to solve anything yesterday. In this instance, he wants to bail out, and I'm scrambling to get some results before I have all the doors slammed in my face. If you don't get all the info in time, it's not your fault and it's not mine either. We can't be expected to work miracles, only to turn lead into gold."

I calmed Franky's apprehensions, and he was thrilled to be off and running with a new and very complex assignment. I hoped that I could stall pops with a good portion of foot-dragging accompanied with a side order of hemming and hawing. I could always slip in the condiment of "Oh, gee, I'm really sorry" to give it just the flavor that would keep me in good graces. Franky seemed anxious to hit the road to get started with his new task, so our third and fourth cups of coffee and chit chat with Suzie Q were put on hold. I sort of felt left in the cold when Franky just dropped some cash on the table for both of us and said he needed to push off from the dock to get things started. I understood what Judith felt like as my lunch partner just left me, and I was standing there with a silly look on my face. Not the best mental portrait of me, and I hoped it wasn't permanent.

Chapter 13

Things Don't Add Up

After waving good-bye to Franky at the club's parking lot, I thought I'd better get into higher gear if I wished to keep pace with pops and the good buddy I'd just asked to help me. What good would it do for me to whine about deadlines and then slack off myself? He was right about the approaching weekend and everything shutting down, except the mandate to close our involvement with the investigation. Not being sure of what to do next was my biggest problem. As I weaved through traffic and challenged yellow lights, I decided that I'd better confirm the propriety of the numbers that I'd received from Stan Gross in shipping.

It seemed as if everyone were heading out to lunch as I was pulling into the Rogers & Emory parking lot. I'd forgotten that I'd gone to lunch early with Franky and that was the reason that we were able to order the last of the breakfast meal. I saw Judith and her brother David walking toward her car to go out. She waved as I was heading toward the building. I was hoping John Evans was still there, or this whole effort was going to be a bust.

When I stepped through the door and looked toward the Accounting Department, the only person I saw was Cassy. I thought I might spend some time with her trying to patch things up between us. I still wasn't very fond of her choice in men, but she seemed to be well worth the effort. As I passed several desks and was approaching her, I heard John Evans' voice from the rear.

"Mr. Hale," he said, "I thought that you'd already left for lunch."

"Just returning," I indicated and smiled at Cassy at the same time. I'm not sure if that did any good, but I had hopes.

"You seem surprised to see me."

"I am. I saw everyone heading out, and I thought that I missed the boat."

"I usually bring my lunch, so you can find me here at this time, most days."

Cassy looked at her boss and told him it was her turn to visit the rest room. She rose, picking up her handbag in the process, and slowly swayed away without taking a look in my direction. I guessed that I'd really made that excrement list of hers. Playing the matchmaker role again, I thought that I might mention something about Cassy's attributes.

"That Cassy is sure a fine looking gal," I started with a smile, "and she seems pretty darn bright too."

"She is very bright, and I'm not sure what I would do without her. She's always on time, hardly ever misses a day's work, and never balks at learning anything new that comes our way. She's even teaching me some of the techniques with a new accounting program we started using a short time ago. I guess I failed to tell you about that, and it's the reason that I might have seemed somewhat lost when I was asked a question about our accounting. If we would've stayed with the old program, I probably wouldn't have even come to your house and asked for any assistance. I think it's just my not understanding that new accounting program. It's kind of like speaking English one day and German the next."

"Maybe, and maybe not," I responded slowly.

"Why do you say that?"

"How about looking at some figures from the Shipping Department and some that you provided to Joe Lindsey at my firm. I need you to reconcile them, and if everything adds to the approximate same figure, then I'll agree that you're probably correct."

"What are the numbers?" he asked with a visible foreboding.

I opened my case and passed him the documents I was given by Stan Gross from Shipping and we began. He was just as mystified as I about what it is that creates the total volume number. He's also unsure about what had rolled into it or been taken out of it. I showed him the column labeled "returns" and indicated what I was told.

"Do you mean that the 'returns' are only damaged losses caused by the freight people?" he asked with an incredulous tone.

"Not completely, from what I was told."

"Then what are they?"

"You need to split the defective items which are very few, but still enough to cause you an accounting headache. They are broken out on this other worksheet that Stan Gross gave me. I pretended to understand what he was talking about, but you can see that I'm still somewhat in the dark."

"You sure are right there, Mr. Hale," he told me emphatically. "I can see this leading to an accounting nightmare."

"Let me ask you something, John," I said thoughtfully as I slowly adjusted my eyes to meet his. "Just how long has that new accounting system been in place?"

"It's only been about five weeks now," he answered with a straight face. "Why do you ask?"

"Isn't that about the same time when you started having a strange feeling about some odd figures?" I said in earnest. "It seems to me that I can recall you saying something close to that date, give or take a short time, the night that you came to our residence."

"I kept a small diary of my thoughts and concerns at that time, and I can check to verify your suspicions. That was the time when I was having some severe stress."

"Okay, now that I have us all confused," I chuckled trying to lighten the mood somewhat. I wanted most of this done before Cassy returned as the fewer the ears, the better. "Here's another column that should be brought into the total, but I'm not completely sure about it."

I pointed to the "unsold comebacks" line and watched his eyes become larger. He shook his head and raised his arms and then gave me a frustrated look.

"Notice the significant number there?" I said.

Silence was his only response while he was trying to gather his thoughts.

"These are items that I was told didn't sell and the stores were returning."

"Those figures used to be brought back into the totals automatically. Now I see they aren't and that brings other questions about our revenue. Does our revenue reflect the total gross sales or the net sales after the deductions with this comeback and damaged volume? Do we have added liabilities with our distributors, and when and how are they compensated?"

"Can you see my dilemma now?" I said. "I'm really not much of an accountant, and if you're confused, I'm left with an impossible goal."

"Sure, I can see that, but it isn't that much better for me. It's becoming more and more clear why they changed the accounting system now. I remember arguing fairly strongly at the time against it, and that's not usually characteristic for me."

"So you were telling them up front about the new accounting system?"

"Yes, I told them at that time that their new system seemed inferior, but they said they were paying exorbitant technical support costs to the developer of the old system and wouldn't need to do that with the new one."

"Were the technical support costs that high?"

"They weren't cheap, but it was billed on an 'as needed' basis. If we called, then we were billed. However, we didn't call that often, and as we became more familiar with the system, we barely called at all."

"Uh, huh," I responded to let him know that I was still with him.

"Don't feel upset. I'm confused by it all too. Maybe you can have that accountant over at your place take a look at it, and maybe he can shed some new light. I could use some independent help from the outside."

About that time, Cassy returned from the restroom, and we needed to become more careful. I believed she was a faithful subordinate to John Evans, but she might very well have her loyalties in the Rogers' camp, and who could blame her—they were her employers.

"Well, what's the most confusing?" I said quietly and tried to convey that same attitude to Evans.

"I just can't see where the volume relates to revenue," Evans responded, almost in a whisper. "It looks like a shell game, and I can't find the little pea."

We both arose and walked to the water cooler for a little more privacy. We could then speak in a more comfortable voice. I agreed to take the new forms to Joe Lindsey for his opinion, and Evans stated that he would continue to work with them to see if he might make some sense of the enigma. We then walked over to the copy machine where Evans made copies of the forms that he required. I walked back to the Accounting Department with Evans and replaced the forms in my case.

I decided to return to the Shipping Department to find out if there were any additional shipping or volume forms which might be of assistance to this riddle. As I passed Cassy's desk, she was just hanging up the phone on what sounded like a personal call to her hairdresser.

"How's it going, Cassy?" I said pleasantly with a big smile.

"Just fine," came her cool response with nothing else volunteered.

"Big weekend planned?" I asked, trying to make conversation. "Sounds like the weatherman had a great forecast for us this morning."

"That's personal, and I don't wish to discuss it," she retorted curtly.

She didn't look anywhere except straight ahead and then continued with the work on her desk. I thought she might continue venting her anger with another terse remark, so I remained quiet for what seemed an uncomfortable expanse of silence.

"You're right, Cassy," I told her in a soft tone. "I was only trying to make friendly conversation, so don't think I was prying or had any other motive."

"Fine."

I felt as if I were playing a straight man on a dry humored British comedy team, but no one was laughing. I looked at John Evans and wondered if he heard any of this exchange as it was in a very low tone - the volume that I found the most desirable. Evidently, he could hear what we were saying as he looked my way and gave me a palms up sign as if to say that he couldn't explain her attitude either. I gave into her persistence of not wanting to be disturbed and quietly bade her a good day and walked toward the Shipping Department.

It didn't appear as if I were having much luck there either. Stan Gross came out of a small lunch room where he'd been playing cards with several individuals from other departments. I gave him a friendly wave as he walked over in my direction to meet me half-way.

"Stan," I called from a short distance as he approached, "those forms you provided have really stirred a few questions, but I know you've told me about everything you know."

"That's right, Mr. Hale," he responded with a friendly smile.

"I was wondering if you might have any other forms with data that's similar?"

"I gave you everything that I know we have other than the waybills and shipping vouchers. I don't think you'd want all the 'eaches' as you already have the totals on those forms I gave you this morning."

"Guess you're right," I told him after some thought. "Oh, also wondering if you knew where I could find Ken Hobbs a little later. I wanted to speak with him for a few minutes, but he seems to have disappeared."

"He often goes out to the horse farm on

Thursdays if needed," Gross indicated as he rolled his eyes upward.

"Well, I don't want to disturb him out there again, so maybe I can catch him later."

"He often hangs out at a dive on the edge of Georgetown on Thursdays because it's ladies night, and the pickings are supposed to be easy."

"Know the name of the place?"

"I've heard him mention the name, The Blue Bull, but don't hold me to that one."

"Thanks," I said as I left the shipping area for the second time. I was hoping some of the lunch crowd might begin drifting back, and I saw a few of them as I walked over to accounting again, hoping my welcome from Cassy might have warmed. Alas, it was not to be so. I saw those lovely dark eyes give me one piercing stab as I decided to ply my ambiance elsewhere.

As I headed to the coffee pot with my quarter in my hand, John Evans was already pouring me a cup and dropped a coin in the dish for me. I thanked him and tried to repay his kindness, but he wouldn't have any part of it, even after I explained that I would be reimbursed with my expense voucher.

He asked if I'd found any additional information in shipping, but I passed along what Gross had told me. He agreed that I probably didn't need anything additional at that time.

I decided that I needed more expertise with accounting and should take the shipping forms back to my firm before any further discussions with David

Rogers. Just at that moment, I saw all of the Rogers walk into the office and thought it would've been an excellent opportunity for a family album photo.

I picked up the phone receiver on John Evans' desk and was dialing Joe Lindsey at my office when I saw Judith give me the high sign to come over her way. I held up my hand with one finger indicating I'd be with her in a minute.

Lindsey answered on the second ring, and I explained to him my situation of expedience and the need to get an answer with the shipping forms. He agreed to get me an answer to my questions by close of business that day if I managed to have those forms in his hands within the hour. I promised on the head of my non-conceived son that I was on my way that very second. I didn't mention that I had my fingers crossed and was heading to see Judith Rogers first.

Judith was on the phone when I walked into her office, and it was her turn to hold her finger in the air. I pulled a chair over to the side of her desk and waited patiently as she finished her conversation. She then was nice enough to ask how everything was progressing, and I answered that I thought I would finish very shortly. She shoved out her lower lip in a disappointing expression and told me that she wished that I would be around longer. She then asked if there was anything that she might do to assist me with my work, but I couldn't think of anything.

She told me that she was occupied that evening with a family function. She and her brother were going to their club as there was a larger gathering of family from out of state in town for an unofficial reunion. She indicated that she was going to be tied up with the chores of tour guide in the Capitol city and along the mall at the Smithsonian museum with several of her relatives. She wanted to be with me tomorrow evening to see a play at the Arena Stage that had finally made it to town. Judith knew what a grand time I had with her during our last cultural outing, and I was her natural target for an escort. I was happy to accept and even happier after I announced it to her. She walked over to the shades at her glass wall as she'd done before. Again, I had to use my suit coat to conceal my anatomy. There was no other way to beat a quick path to the trusty old Mustang to make a speedy exit.

I needed to see Joe Lindsey before he broke with me and started another hot project. Joe seemed pleased to see me, and we got right to the crux of the problem. I also told him about a new accounting program in the last several weeks. Lindsey shook his head and suggested a few creative things were going on, and it was too much of a coincidence.

Walking back up the steps to my small cubicle, I found several messages lying in the seat of my chair. Naturally, one had to be from the old snoop, Amos Freyer with the Montgomery County Police Department. He would have to wait as I became a little creative again with my weekly expense voucher with pop's secretary. Mildred McCarthy would be asking for it anyway in the morning. I figured, what the heck, if the Rogers could fudge a little with their major accounting, my creativity was merely incidental. I was hoping that Joe Lindsey was having as much luck as I with that accounting project. I was about to walk my completed creation over to Mildred when the intercom buzzed to alert me to an incoming call.

"Freyer here" is what I heard right after my cordial hello. "Don't you ever return your calls? I've been trying to reach you at that Rogers' place and also your office. Where in the devil have you been hiding?"

"Which question do you want answered first?" I casually replied which only made him hotter.

"So, it's going to be one of those conversations, is it?" came the angry response.

"Look, sweetie, cool down would you?" I answered lightly which could push the cop in either direction. "I just got back from Rogers, and I didn't receive any word you tried to reach me until a minute ago when I arrived. Now I had a choice of doing my expense voucher or calling you first. Guess which one won?"

"I'm not sure who you lie to more, your office or me," the sully cop groaned.

"Who cares if it all works out well in the end?" I laughed.

"What came over you today with this fit of honesty?" he said in surprise.

"I think they slipped me a mickey of some type of truth serum at the club today. Hey, what's shaking out there that's got you so hot to reach me?

If you made any progress, I can't picture your calling to tell me anything. You must need something from me, right?"

"Wish I could find out what it was they gave you. I think you could use a constant drip. The reason I called was to give you some news for a change."

"Oh, really!"

"Really. Lab results from the state and the coroner indicated the old man Emory did a little damage before he went down. It may have been out of reflex or it could have been intentional. I'm not sure which, but there was some tissue under his one fingernail."

"Oh, ho!" I yelled.

"Right-O. My sentiments exactly."

"Was there much tissue, or were there other fingers involved? I'm wondering how much damage he did?"

"Hard to tell how much damage. However, I don't believe there was too much. There was only one finger with the tissue and we can't say for certain if it belonged to the perp. He may have gotten it from someone else sometime before he was killed, but after he last washed his hands."

"Baloney!" I yipped. "You're beginning to sound like a defense lawyer, and I can't see any jury letting the killer walk if they got a positive DNA match."

"Hey, Bub, you're the lawyer, so don't complain to me about one of your profession's tricks."

"Might be a professional trick, but I certainly

wouldn't want to be the poor slob looking at the jury if they had my DNA under their microscope."

"Got that right, fellow. Now what have you nosed out from some rock? Now come on, Bub; get a little, give a little."

"Can't say much now for certain, but I can tell you the shipping foreman is having a good time with the boss's wife while the boss is off on some other funny mission."

"Know that for sure?"

"This isn't hearsay. I literally walked right in on them, but they weren't aware of me at the time."

"Good thing for you," he laughed.

"You're right about that. Let the jerk find out for himself. I don't want any part of that mess. I wish that I had more for you, but pops has put me on notice with a short string. He wants me out of this honey pot and the firm too. He's in the process of pulling the plug now, and I expect he'll send Rogers the final invoice in a day or so."

"What put a bee under his tail?"

"He's concerned about me with Emory's murder and then add all of the funny stuff we suspect."

"What funny stuff?" he said, and I knew what was coming the second I opened my big flap.

"It's like I've been telling you, Amos," I back peddled. "That David Rogers has been letting his wife get it on with his shipping foreman which I think he probably knows about."

"Oh, I see," he said with an air of skepticism. "Well, if you hear any more news or see anyone with a nice scratch, remember the hand that just washed yours."

"I'll get right on the horn to you, Amos," I winded down the conversation. "Just remember that I also fed the funny playing around news to you. Your hand's also washed, and now mine's becoming soiled again."

Our line went silent at about the same time as I replaced the receiver in the holder. I thought it was wise to get the expense voucher submitted now as I wasn't sure what my schedule would be for the balance of the week. I was still mulling the news in my mind about the tissue discovered in the Emory slaying. If they could find the source, it was better than fingerprints. The problem was that they needed to match the sample with everyone in the world, and no one had a data base like they did with finger prints.

I was wondering who could be a suspect or had a motive. David Rogers looked extremely good from where I was sitting. Now all I had to do was prove it. I also wondered why I cared at all. I was only asked to help John Evans and check out Rogers and Emory as a possible client. I was already doing that and was just about finished. It didn't make sense to carry on with my little crusade, and I was coming around to pops' line of thinking very quickly. I thought I might give it one more day and have a great weekend at the beach with Kate. I owed her at least that much, and it sure wouldn't hurt me either. I had better be careful about tomorrow night and keep Judith completely separated.

I skittered off with my voucher and quickly deposited it in Mildred's inbox. She gave me her usual warm grandmotherly smile, and I remembered why pop always made sure she remained at that desk. Some kind of great combination, a wonderful employee whom everyone could always rely on and a great boss who truly appreciated her. I thought they were both lucky.

One chore done and I was off to accounting to see where Joe Lindsey was with that wonderful project. When I pushed through the corridor entrance, I saw him in his corner using the phone. He looked up and waved me over as he was placing the receiver down.

"Good timing, Prich," the young accountant said as he was shaking his head sideways and displaying a frown on his face. "I was just on the phone with John Evans, and we've come to the same conclusion."

"I'm happy to hear that someone knows what he's doing," I groaned.

"I didn't say that I knew what was going on," he qualified his statement. "All I'm saying is I am sure this isn't the proper way to do business."

"Oh," I mumbled. "Do tell, my man."

"Well, Prich, a company like Rogers & Emory just can't ignore a product that's returned and can't ignore customers who want credit for these returns."

"Is this common in that industry?" I said with interest.

"It's common for the wholesalers and retailers to pay only for the items they sell. John Evans stated that was always their policy, and it was always the industry's policy."

"That's a significant amount of money?" I said as I shook my head and tried to give it some reason. "Why would they intentionally withhold payment if they knew there would be a clamor at their door by all of their customers just a short time later?"

"Beats me," came Lindsey's response.

As soon as Joe Lindsey uttered his response, a light went on in my noggin. Ho, ho, I thought and wondered if it were possible. Sure, it could be, but I wondered if it truly was what I contemplated. But then again, I was puzzled about how this all might fit together.

"Joe," I began slowly, "could you do a little checking around the block and down the street? Find out if there are any rumors of a possible sale of a software company. I've got another source, and I'll also ask him to do a little snooping. I'm under a time constraint, and I need as many sources working this process as possible."

I watched Joe Lindsey's eyes slowly light into a smile with his entire face following closely behind. He nodded his head and slapped his knee and then gave one loud laugh.

Chapter 14

Human Punching Bag

My mind was still whirring all the way home as I continued to give meaning to the twisted labyrinth. I was so preoccupied; I almost ran through a red light. Who was involved and what was their motive? It was still a maze, but it was beginning to unravel. My question and primary concern was could I get it unraveled before my father shutdown the operation.

As I entered the house, I saw Romney nearing the kitchen area. He was in and out as he moved several cleaning and polishing products around. A cup of coffee sounded good. Pouring a sizable mug of the magic black elixir, I caught his attention as he returned to replace a container of cleanser under the kitchen cabinet.

"There's some coffee cake in the cabinet if you're a little hungry before dinner," Romney commented in his usual pleasant voice.

I thanked our houseman and willingly took a well endowed portion for a snack, but that wasn't my main purpose. I needed information quickly, and it was collection time for anybody and everybody.

"Romney," I began to make sure I had his attention drawn away from his task at hand, "you indicated that you could maybe find something more about the Rogers' family if the household staff would be forthcoming."

"Right, I was meaning to talk to you about that and guess this is as good of time as any."

"If you have a few minutes," I said for him to know that I also truly appreciated his work, "maybe we can discuss what you've already discovered."

"I've got an earful to discuss with you."

"Do tell," I said in mock-exaggerated surprise that brought a grin on his face.

"I've heard they have a pretty kinky family for starters."

"How kinky?"

"The old man does more than play golf - you could say his game sings both ways."

"He's AC/DC?"

"That's what I'm saying. He's sometimes seen in the company of a younger fellow who they think might be a male model. They even have a quartet of them that play a foursome out on the golf course."

I didn't want to tell Romney that it wasn't any big deal in today's society to be gay or swing both ways. Some of our most creative people and superb artists were gay. I gave him a big visual show of surprise to reinforce his notion of a great discovery as one negative remark could nix this wonderful source of information which truly was of great assistance.

"Do you believe that he was the catalyst for some other strange behavior in the family?" I said.

"The son encourages his wife to have an

affair with a fellow at their company. He sits around and watches and then may jump in the middle to swing both ways just like his father does."

Now that was news, and my surprise was genuine. Romney smiled as he knew he was on a roll. His weekly income would have a healthy supplement.

"What about the daughters?"

"There's one that sometimes gets it on with the son, while the wife gets it on with the company employee."

"Which daughter does that?" I said while holding my breath and dreading the answer.

"The super looking one is kinky. The other one's had some very bad luck with a few shady characters."

"What kind of bad luck?" I said with some relief, but I wasn't sure what was coming next.

"I heard that she was beaten very badly once, and they had to pay another guy off to hand over some pictures he'd taken when she wasn't aware of what was happening. They bought all the pictures and negatives and that thing ended. At least they think it's ended. He hasn't returned yet, but maybe he will when the money runs out. It's been about six months since that episode happened."

It wasn't good, but it wasn't as bad as it might have been. I sighed a breath of relief. I didn't think that I had Judith pegged too far off, and this sort of confirmed that much. She was probably basically a good person, who'd been caught up in a foolish mistake. She may have been somewhat unlucky. None of that would've occurred if she'd met a decent guy first, rather than that leech.

"That about it with the better looking daughter?"

"She also swings both ways as she works out with the son's wife when the son swings the other way with the company employee. I tell you, Prich, it's a real funny farm over there, and I'm feeling very fortunate that I'm with you folks."

"Thanks, Romney. That works both ways," I told him as he beamed a big smile. "Anything else that you can think of which might add a clue about them?"

"Just that they aren't in the best financial shape recently."

"Oh?" I voiced with my tone rising and curiosity stirred.

"I was told that some of the house staff had their payroll checks bounce several times in the last year. They always made it good and made excuses about their accountant having deposited the funds in the wrong account, but the staff knew the real story. They also said they may have gone to some very shady people for a temporary loan since they saw some very strange people hanging around. When they asked the family about them, they were just told that it wasn't any problem and not to mind them."

Bells started going off about this time. I was remembering the Chevy which had chased us and the fact it appeared to be a professional. It was probably a very good thing that it never caught up with us that evening.

Romney indicated that was about all he could find out in that short time, but I was amazed that he had found more than most private investigators might have after a considerably longer time. Nothing beats the family staff for the most reliable, detailed information.

I thanked him for his quick and precise work and then slipped him another couple of fifties. The more I greased the skids, the more good info always seemed to slide my way. I knew that he probably invested one of those fifties in a well placed position with the Rogers' staff. The other fifty would help with his own budget when he and Renate went out on the town on their day off. He smiled and thanked me for the cash, but I just shook my head.

"That always comes out of the expense account, so I'm not putting myself in the poor house," I told him with a pat on his back.

"Well, it was too easy this time," he said with a grin. "The staff at Rogers was more than willing to say anything they could about them because the son and that kinky pretty daughter were evidently somewhat ugly and abusive with them. It's always easy for a staff to find a way to get even, and this was probably just one of them."

I thanked him again and headed upstairs to my room, when I saw mother's door open and heard a soap opera just ending. She appeared in the doorway looking somewhat upset and wanted to explain how all the characters in her show were cheating and lying to each other. I smiled and told her it would come out all right soon, then gave her a hug. As I was continuing to my room, I thought that I had a real life soap opera happening in front of me, and people were really being hurt.

While dressing for the evening, I sat down for another spin with my diary. I also updated and added to my card file and reshuffled them several ways to fit my new possibilities. It helped to visualize the various scenarios to see what might be more possible or less likely. I could more efficiently allocate my time which helped a great deal now that pop had pulled the rug out from under the entire schbang. I dressed in my "get down roughing it apparel" for my excursion that evening, but wasn't sure how I would be received at the dinner table with my family first. Father had his standards, and it might have been wiser to do this after dinner, but why change now?

I was beginning to wonder why I wasn't smelling some of those wonderful aromas drifting up my way when it occurred to me that it was Romney and Renate's evening off. They usually had Thursday evenings off while we fended for ourselves on those nights. I couldn't keep up with their schedule as I knew they sometimes accumulated time off and then took an extended trip. Not a bad deal for a less stressful life if you could only get with the right family. I don't believe too many envied the staff at the Rogers family though.

I was almost ready to head down stairs when the intercom buzzed, and father wanted to know how Chinese take-out sounded for dinner. You never needed to ask me twice about Chinese food. Yet, I always knew that I would be expected to drive over to the restaurant in about fifteen minutes to pick it up. I heard they were getting a delivery service soon. I only hoped that we didn't change restaurants about that time.

I scampered down to the kitchen as father was wrestling with the food selections on the take-home menu. I always opted for the "Shrimp in Garlic Sauce" that had the star in front of the name indicating it was hot and spicy. Some nights the hot received top billing over the spicy, and my tongue paid the price for some time to come. I certainly wouldn't try to repeat the mistake that I made with the hot mustard on my egg roll where I took too big a bite of that mustard and then breathed in my nose at the same time. It sure beat any medication for opening up clogged sinuses. I thought I came out ahead with my fortune cookie, though, as it seemed the most prophetic in my existence: "Enjoy life! It is better to be happy than wise."

There were a few strange looks in my direction with my dress down ensemble. They really gave me the once-over when I was leaving for Georgetown wearing my new chapeau as I didn't wish to be blown all over the place with the Mustang's top down. My trip to the inner city was faster than normal as it was still the work week, and it wasn't rush hour.

I'd waited until around nine as I didn't want to be the first lonely soul in any bar that evening. The Georgetown main drag down M street was as busy as usual, becoming impossible during the weekend. I took my time cruising the strip like a teenager wanting to be noticed and received several good look overs in the Mustang with the top down. There were Mercedes and Jaguars and other spiffy cars all around, including a Rolls or two, but they didn't have my classic.

The Blue Bull was near the end of the strip, and I still had difficulty finding a place to park. Even though my classy beauty was parked in a lot with an attendant on duty, I was still uncomfortable leaving the Mustang where many similar classics disappeared every day.

As soon as I walked into the night club, I was at once blinded by the dark, deafened by the loud country music, and smothered by the thick layer of cigarette smoke. I thought I might need a white cane, a hearing aid, and an oxygen bottle after I finally got out of that joint, and I wasn't sure if my liver would make it either.

I walked over to the bar, which was almost filled as it was nearing ten, and found an available stool. The Blue Bull was something akin to what historical architects would call a single-barreled shotgun design which had been modified with over a century's worth of commerce. The revised area was likely a previous short order kitchen and the remaining all important requisite lavatories for both genders. There were several dozen tables for four which often accommodated three or four times that number when the place got into high gear. Budding romances must have been enhanced with severely dimmed light which might assure quite a surprise after leaving the establishment unless the alcohol dimmed the senses to the same level as the available illumination. The long bar, running two-thirds of the establishment, was a treasure of gorgeous polished hardwoods with the accompanying gleaming brass foot and hand rails.

A large mirror running the length behind the bar allowed a customer to peek-a-boo anyone else sitting along its length. It appeared as if the fellow sitting next to me was making a pass at a gal about ten stools down, and she was giving him the big come-on smile in return. A huge pair of steer horns was centered over the bar which must have provided the bull part of the name. I was still mystified about the blue part of the name as the walls appeared to be a dark green. Paddle fans hanging from the high ceiling turned ever so slowly, barely disturbing the heavy layers of smoke, as thick as fog.

I observed two individuals behind the bar, one male and the other female. The country rock band at the opposite end of the long room was mercifully on break at the time, but I doubted it would be any louder than the wailing jukebox and the undulating roar of laughter and conversation. Everyone needed to shout to the person next to him and still be an accomplished lip reader to comprehend a simple phrase.

The bar maid didn't waste any time putting

a small drink napkin in front of me on the bar and slipping me her best customer worn out smile. She was a cute twenty-fourish bleached blonde with shining blue eyes and a twang in her voice. She moved as if she had the energy of a teenager, but I doubted the innocence was still there. I didn't believe that I had the scales of lady justice tattooed on my exterior, but she had me pegged from the get-go.

"I think a good lawyer's drink would be a Vodka Collins, wouldn't you?" came her flip inquiry with a wide grin. "What's your pleasure after a hard day in court?"

"No court today, love," I came back in a somewhat startled voice and then asked for a glass of white wine. It was probably odd in a honky tonk place like that.

She left for a brief minute or two while she served several others at the bar. Another bartender served the floor waitresses with orders from the tables. She returned with a glass of draft beer and sat it on the napkin which she'd placed there earlier.

"Name's Jackie and why no court today?" she said in her perky voice. "Oh, this place is death on wine drinkers so I thought this might get you by for a while. You never mentioned your name."

"Cause the flippin' cops missed giving me a ticket again," I joked right back at her. "Prich Hale and thanks for the beer. You're probably right about the wine."

"Prich?" she yipped with a laugh. "What kind of name is Prich, anyway?"

"I was told that I kicked and behaved badly before I was born, and that was one way my parents found to teach me a lesson."

"You have to be a lawyer," she laughed. "You've got too good of a sense of humor to be a doctor, and you walked in here like you were looking for someone to sue."

"Well, I am looking for someone, but didn't see him," I confessed. "You know a guy named Ken Hobbs? He's about my height with dark wavy hair. He's a fairly handsome fellow."

"You didn't mention that he was mean as the devil also," she stated with a laugh that was almost drowned out with a loud burst of noise.

"How would I know?" I chuckled back. "We don't date much. He's not my type."

"Didn't figure he was," she laughed. "He usually gets by here a couple nights a week and raises high heaven from time to time. My roommate dated him a couple of times and she said he tried some wild kinky stuff. She ditched him really fast, but it wasn't before he knocked her around some. She had some black and blue marks for a couple of weeks on places you wouldn't normally see."

"Bad temperament, huh?"

"At least that and more if you ask me!" she said emphatically. "Hope you don't get him going here tonight!"

I agreed with her and thanked her for her concern. The last thing I needed to do was mix it up with a knuckle dragger who was in great physical shape. I still had a somewhat injured and tender paw. Jackie served several others and returned minutes later with a napkin which had her phone number written on it.

"I didn't see any rings on the left hand," she mused as her eyes twinkled in the dim lights. "You don't pull a gold band out of your pocket when you leave a place like this, do you?"

"I haven't yet," I laughed as my ego soared several notches.

I started to say something else to Jackie, but she looked at the door and then touched my arm. Ken Hobbs had just swaggered in like a lost sailor who'd just come home from the raging sea. He stood off to the side for several seconds as his eyes adjusted to the diminished light. I turned and held up my hand to attract his attention. He appeared to have identified me, but I didn't see any smile spring on his big square jaw.

"You seem to pop up everywhere," he moaned loudly as he approached.

"I was down here in the area and remembered someone saying this was one of your haunts," I lied, but didn't know how skillfully.

"Well, maybe I can help dry up some of the wetness behind your ears," he roared with a sinister bellowing voice that even stopped two patrons momentarily from talking who were sitting half a dozen stools away.

"You're right," I conceded. "This is a new experience for me."

"This might be a night for you to remember," he chuckled as he leaned against the bar with one hand and waved at Jackie while shouting that he wanted a beer.

She held up one finger, and he waved his hand and displayed two fingers to signify that he was buying me another round. I thought that I was going to need to go slowly because I had a very limited tolerance with booze. I was planning to nurse my remaining three quarters of a bottle as I was likely to be out in the street directing traffic after two or three beers. To term me as a light hitter on the drinkers' circuit was a gross understatement.

Hobbs was surveying the place as Jackie brought over two more beers for us. As he reached out with his right hand for his beer, I saw that he had a fairly good scratch on his right forearm which already was in the healing process. It was approximately three inches long but didn't appear too severe.

"Looks like you had a dandy little scrape like me," I stated with a joking laugh as I pointed to my small bandage on my hand.

"I'm always getting some sort of scratch or bruise in that damned warehouse. Sure'll be a lot happier when the boss moves me out of there," he said, surprising me.

I thought he had found his niche in the warehouse as he didn't need to do much of anything except take credit for the efforts of others. Why in the world would he ever want to leave a situation like he had there unless he didn't feel as if he were intellectually challenged. That was an oxymoron if there ever was one - Hobbs being intellectually challenged! He spotted one table, which held his interest for some length of time and then he turned to take a drink of his beer directly from the bottle. I was about to pour a little more from my first bottle into my glass when Hobbs made a suggestion.

"Hey," he said turning to face me and then pointing further down the narrow passage, "I thought that I saw some friends over at that table across the way."

I wasn't sure where he was indicating so I nodded my head in agreement to keep him in decent spirits. I was hoping to ask him several questions about how he envisioned his position evolving with the company and what he thought would happen if the ownership transferred. He didn't appear to have any question and answer scenario operating in his scheme of events, but rather a lively free-for-all slamming good blast. He nudged me on the shoulder and told me to follow him to a table. I gathered my two beers and a glass and walked down to the table where he'd just arrived. There were two young women sitting with one fellow who didn't appear too overjoyed to see Hobbs.

"You've got some nerve showing up here after your stupid stunt last week!" the fellow at the table growled at Hobbs.

"Thought these great looking gals might want to meet some real men rather than screw around with a wimp like you," Hobbs growled in return and then displayed a toothy grin at the females. "What in the hell did you feed them, a mickey in their drink or are they blind?"

"You're not sucker punching me again, you jerk!" the fellow yelled back as he was becoming red in the face. "I turned my back on you once, and you nailed me from behind. You're not man enough to face anyone heads up when he's healthy. You're here right now just because you think I'm still broken up from last week. Well, you can go straight to ..."

Hobbs kicked the chair legs out from under the young man's chair which sent it spinning and the fellow flying backwards. His head hit the floor with a thud as I saw his eyes turn up dazed all at one time. Hobbs was on the poor fellow in one swoop and had the man by the hair while pounding his head continually against the floor.

I jumped backwards and sat the drinks on an adjoining table to get my hands free and my feet ready to go. I was in the fight or flight mode at that moment, and the latter seemed the most appropriate thing for my survival. I was just ready to initiate the "come on, feet, don't fail me now" when two very large men picked Hobbs off of the young fellow on the floor and stood him straight on his feet. One of the young ladies who was with the fellow leaped to the floor to assist him. I stood paralyzed in the midst of the high drama with my mouth open, but nothing came out.

"Let me get him out of here, and I promise

there won't be any more trouble," I pleaded with the two huge men who were also very well dressed in high priced business suits.

"Shut up and keep outta this," the one big man closest to me growled in my direction.

I was confused, but certainly wasn't going to argue with two man-mountain types who could pick a fellow like Hobbs off the floor like he was just so many ounces of feathers. The gal on the floor looked up with a bewildered expression as if to ask what was happening, but I could only be a spectator in the event. The other big man said that he thought they should take Hobbs out back while the one nearer me growled his approval. He then stared at Hobbs and began speaking with an ominous tone.

"We warned you once; you don't get any second chances!" the big assailant nearest me said in his menacing tone.

Hobbs jerked, grunted, and kicked, but it didn't help. They dragged Hobbs towards the back of the establishment while I skittered back over to the bar. Jackie was about ten feet away as I called and waved to get her attention. She was also watching Hobbs being dragged out the back way. The other bartender and Jackie appeared as if they were uncertain about what to do next. Another well built fellow came hesitantly over to the bar and leaned over to speak to Jackie and the bartender. Jackie appeared to listen intensely to the man on the other side of the bar and then tossed her hands into the air as if she were completely confused. I motioned to her again as she looked my way, and she reluctantly walked over to me.

"What in the world is going on here?" I said with my mouth still open in bewildered amazement.

"I wish you'd tell me!" she exclaimed as if I were the one who stirred up this mess. "What in the devil started it all?"

She appeared as if she already knew the answer I was about to give her. She probably asked that same question several previous times when Hobbs started mixing trouble with booze.

"Well, you know Ken Hobbs, I guess?" I said and watched her shake her head in acknowledgment. "He's a jerk who's likely to do anything."

"You've got him pegged right!" came her reply. "What was all that over at the table?"

"He wanted to hit on those gals and bully that fellow after he knew he wasn't a hundred percent, I guess."

"Right, we saw all that, but what was all that other stuff with those two big guys?"

"Aren't they the bouncers?" I asked as I was really confused now.

"Hell, no, they're not our bouncers!" she wailed over the noise. "We only have one bouncer, and that was the fellow who just came over and talked to us."

"What did he tell you?"

"He wanted to know who those big guys

were," she answered with some steam.

"Well, that's just great!" I broke out in a lather. "What in the world was your guy doing when all that was taking place?"

"He was told in no uncertain terms to shut up and sit right where he was."

"Some bouncer he turned out to be!" I yipped now.

"Well, what would you do if one of those guys was holding you down in your chair while the other one told you what to do?" she responded partially.

"So what?" I came back. "He still should've behaved better than he did."

"What if when those guys were telling you just to sit there, you could see a big gun bulging under their coats?" she countered promptly. "Seems like you aren't too quick with an answer now, smart guy."

"I guess you're right on the button, Jackie," I admitted, but not without a wince. "Knowing which conflicts to get involved with is often a very smart lesson to learn. You can often live to fight another day."

"Well, what do we do now?" she said as if I had all the answers, which I certainly didn't.

"Would you laugh if I told you to call 911 or the cops?" I volunteered reluctantly for a change.

"Do you want to go out back and see what's going on first?" she said, but then probably saw my face and knew that she had asked a silly question.

"You're not serious?" I answered anyway.

She no sooner asked me that question and I answered when several patrons of the bar started opening the rear door and poking their heads outside. One of those young men came running back to the bar and shouting something about an ambulance. The other bartender picked up the phone from under the bar and dialed 911 and then came over to Jackie and related the news. I couldn't stand it any longer and hauled my frightened tail in the direction of the rear door. I also poked my head outside, but several others were already standing there in that dark alley over a crumpled heap on the cold ground.

"Is he still alive?" asked the barmaid, who'd ventured out behind me.

"I think so," said one of the people standing around him now. "We just heard him moan, and he also twitched just now."

"The ambulance and cops should be here in a few minutes, if there are any cops still on duty in this town after all the budget cuts," Jackie grumbled.

"Hope they hurry," I wished out-loud, "because he sure doesn't look too good."

I'd just said that he didn't look good when I heard a siren in the background that was sounding louder all the time. I'm not sure why I was doing what I was doing, but I could hear myself praying for that rotten jerk all crumpled in a heap, even though he probably deserved everything that he had gotten out there on that dreary night.

The paramedics arrived in less than a minute, and two of those wonderful young people worked like it was one of their relatives lying on the ground, rather than a total stranger. They must have labored over him for ten minutes with a respirator and IV's before they had him stabilized where they felt confident enough to transport him to the hospital.

I didn't even walk back into the bar, but rather out the end of the alley and down the street to the parking lot. I imagine there was quite a hassle and a plethora of chatter abounding from within, but I just wanted to call it a night and try to work it out in the morning with a clear head and rested body.

Chapter 15

Sleep Didn't Come Easy

I was just beginning to feel the weariness of the entire day as I had been on an adrenaline high while at the Georgetown bar. My emotions were still in a turmoil when I pulled into our driveway. However, I was very happy to breathe the mild evening air and hear the peaceful chirping of the crickets with the sounds of the night. Although it was still before midnight, the entire household had judiciously called it a day, so I behaved accordingly by stumbling and banging my way to my room.

I wanted to hit the sack without undressing, and I grudgingly began unbuttoning my shirt. When I saw my answering machine blinking with a message, I carefully bumped my way across my small room to the contraption after running into my bed twice. I pushed the play-back button and heard Amos Freyer's voice almost commanding me to call him at the police station. He indicated the time which was about fifteen minutes before I had arrived home. I wondered which royal family was deposed and left him king. Here he was calling me with his first royal edict.

It took a minute or two to get Freyer on the line, and he was breathing hard as if he'd been running.

"Where have you been all night?" came the challenging voice sounding as weary as I felt. "I've been trying to reach you for several hours while you were out carousing and playing the field."

"I've been out working," I returned the fire in my defense. "That's a lot better than some others that I can think of right now."

"Out working?"

"Right, and have I got a story to tell you," I told the cop with an attitude matching his own.

"Well, it's about time you provided some input into this investigation. I thought you were out on Mars or some other part of this universe."

"What in the world are you doing at this time of night?" I said as it just occurred to me that Freyer usually worked an eight-hour day. "You shooting for the cop of the month award or just nailing us taxpayers with a ton of overtime?"

"You'll hear about it soon enough, wise guy," the cop snapped. "Just tell me what was so important with you tonight."

I sat back on my bed and didn't know if I should continue undressing or wait and talk with Freyer first. I gave the cop the benefit of the doubt and began filling him in on my evening.

"So you say that you were out working in the yuppie bars in Georgetown, right?" Freyer laughed. "I need a job like that!"

I continued with my story and ignored Freyer's ribbing and verbal insults. When I reached the part where the two huge Neanderthals in business suits with bulging shoulder holsters showed up, Freyer became all ears. He was down to business and had considerably less wise cracking.

"Where'd they take him?"

"You know, I never asked that question," I replied feeling somewhat numb and ready to hit the hay. "But, I think that I heard one of them say something about D.C. General Hospital."

"Right, I know they have a very experienced trauma center there with drug shootings showing up on their doorstep hourly."

"Well, he really looked terrible, but I believe those paramedics thought he'd make it," I told the hard-working cop. "They had him breathing and he was semi-conscious the last I saw of him. Looked like they had him stabilized when they shoveled him in the rear of that emergency meat-wagon."

"What can you tell me about those two big guys who dragged Hobbs out of the place? Remember anything at all about them?"

"I'm not sure."

"Did they say or do anything while you were near enough to them?"

"I believe that I heard one of them say something like 'We warned you and you don't get any second chances!' but I'm paraphrasing. I can tell you these guys were very big and could be professional wrestlers if they lost their current jobs. The one fellow that I heard nearest me surely had a dandy, menacing tone."

"Could you ID them if you went through the mug shots down here?" I didn't want to hear what he had to say at that time of night.

"Oh, Amos," I pleaded with the most sorrowful voice I could conjure. "Can't we possibly put this off until tomorrow?"

"I feel the same way as you, Prich. Remember, I was up and at em earlier than you this morning. Listen, buddy, I need you down here anyway, and I'll get our crew to cut out most of the nonsense and show you a few of the likely ones from the description you already provided."

"What's this buddy stuff?" I moaned back. "There were others there who saw everything, and I've got the name and phone number of the gal who was the bartender. She saw it all and has all the names of the others who were there."

"Great," came Freyer's enthusiastic reply, "bring that with you too when you come down. We need everything that we can get."

"You mean that I still need to come down to the station tonight?"

"Right, I still need to talk to you."

"Well, what in the devil do you think we are doing right now?"

"I still need you here."

"Really?"

"Really," he replied with more emphasis. "There are just some things that I have a great deal of difficulty trying to communicate over the phone. This happens to be one of those times, and I can't think of any other way. Please bear with me on this, would you, Prich?"

"Okay, sport," I growled, "but this better

be worth it or I'll put the worst curse on you that you could imagine."

"What would that be?"

"You don't want to know!" I said with a groan and then told him that I'd be there in a couple of minutes after I threw some water on my face and struggled back to my car. The water seemed to help, and the cool night air was refreshing. I arrived at the station in good time as the roads were uncharacteristically empty. I was about to park when I noticed a small group of young thugs leave the station and kick a police cruiser sitting in front. I wondered what chance my classic would have if a cop car wasn't safe right under their noses. I pulled away from the curb and motored right into their own parking lot on the side of the building, which contained a mixture of police vehicles and their own personal cars. I slid conveniently into a slot next to Freyer's car.

Freyer was at his desk and smiled pleasantly when he saw me approaching. He rose from his chair, walked several steps to meet me, and then offered me a chair beside his desk. The offices which were reserved for the higher-ranking individuals were around the perimeter of the room. The desks for the working stiffs were sparsely occupied at that late hour. It would be quite different twelve hours later with the first shift of society's mischief-makers wide awake.

I was surprised to find how outdated the furniture appeared with some old scarred wooden desks intermixed with the ugly gray metal ones of the fifties. I expected to see considerably more automation also, but the old IBM Selectrics typewriters outnumbered the personal computers. I didn't even see a PC on Freyer's desk and wondered if that was his own choice as I remembered him groaning about automation previously.

I saw two or three cops I'd become acquainted with over the past several years and even received a pleasant greeting and friendly wave a time or two. Freyer motioned to another cop across the room and asked him to bring over the couple of mug books they had constructed for me.

"Got some pictures here of a few local talents which fit the general category which you described on the phone," Freyer stated with a congenial tone which seemed somewhat odd and out of character. "Maybe you could spend a couple of minutes perusing these handsome portraits for a match of your newest friendly admirers."

"You didn't bring out every living soul in the universe, I see," I told him as I looked at only two books.

"Our guys narrowed it down to the most likely files that would fit your description."

"I didn't know they could do that," I stated with a questioning tone and puzzled face.

"It's something new we're trying and thought we might give it a try with you to prove some future value."

"Only if it works," I said with a smile and opened the first book. As I was turning the pages fairly rapidly, I wondered why all the fuss to get me there at that late hour.

"What else do you have up your sleeve, Amos?" I said as I continued flipping pages in their mug book. "Did you really drag me out of bed for this right now?"

"Not sure what to tell you," replied the hesitant cop who didn't seem very sure of himself even on his own turf.

I just shook my head and continued turning the pages. I looked up from time to time and caught Freyer studying me for some unclear reason. I was about to close the cover on the mug book and pick up the last book when I turned the page to a figure that caught my eye. I flipped back the page and began shaking my head. I guess that I also had a smile on my face and probably even said something as I caught Freyer's attention while he'd been diverted with some other task for only a moment.

"Find somebody?" he asked eagerly

"I think so," I replied with some certainty. "This photo looks somewhat younger, but I could almost swear that he's the fellow who growled to Hobbs when they were dragging him out of the place."

"Let me see that," Freyer said as he reached across to receive the book that I was handing him.

"Know that guy?" I asked in anticipation.

"William Leads," Freyer stated slowly as he was reading the abbreviated rap sheet with the photo. "Oh, yes, a real fine upstanding gentleman of our community."

"What else?" I said quickly as if Freyer had all the answers to the zillion questions that I was about to ask.

"Let me get a complete rap sheet and bio on the guy, Prich, before you start throwing every question in the book at me," the cop laughed.

"I'm still not clear about what this will do for you, Amos," I said with a puzzled tone. "That happened out of your jurisdiction, so what good will it do you?"

"Yeah, I know that," he responded with his evasive answer as he diverted his eyes.

"Come on, will you?" I moaned as I was becoming frustrated with his concealment and strange behavior.

"I know it's out of our jurisdiction," Freyer stated with a concerned expression, "but it'll probably help tie our investigation together."

"Sure, that makes sense," I said with some annoyance, "or I wouldn't have been there in the first place."

"Right," the cop stated, "and we get along with the surrounding jurisdictions fairly well. Many of the criminal cases cross state and municipal lines, but we wouldn't get anything done if we didn't cooperate with each other."

Freyer walked away with the mug book and asked me to continue with the second one. He also asked for the friendly female bartender's phone number. I provided the number, but told him that was all I was sharing. I suggested that he keep his conversation with her strictly business.

He indicated that he'd return in a minute. First, he had to put in an inquiry for the complete rap sheet on the fellow I'd fingered. I clumsily plodded though the remaining book with my bandaged hand with no success. I didn't necessarily get the best look at the second thug, but I didn't see anyone in the books that even closely resembled the fellow. Freyer was true to his word and walked back over to his desk just as I was closing the last book.

"Find anyone else?" he asked hopefully.

"Nope."

"Nothing even close?"

"Nada, zilch, zippo," I answered wearily as I found myself sagging in the chair. "Also amigo, I think I'm finito too."

"I need to talk to you, Prich," the cop said with a stern look on his face, "and it's about the reason I first called you tonight."

"Gee," I stammered with a smile, "and here I thought that you were going to give me a ticket for parking the Mustang in your personal parking lot outside."

I didn't get a moan or smile or anything from Freyer, and that was strange, to say the least. I could usually get some type of reaction from the good-natured cop as even his grumbles were funny.

"While you were out with your little escapade, I was involved with one of my own," Freyer said slowly as he stood and moved from side to side, appearing uncomfortable.

"We talked about that earlier," I replied to keep the conversation moving. "I believe that you were somewhat evasive when the question last came up."

"I wasn't sure how to broach the subject, but I guess the direct method is the best," the cop said thoughtfully as he watched me closely.

"Okay, let's be direct and see where that gets us," I stated in a joking tone.

"The word is out that you've been seeing that Rogers lady," Freyer stated slowly with a small questioning intonation.

"Right, Judith Rogers, to be exact," I responded promptly. "There are two of them, you know."

"That's who I meant to say, Judith Rogers."

"Okay, now that we've got that straight, so what?" I said grumpily. I was beginning to let my weariness creep into my personality.

"Judith Rogers and her brother, David Rogers, were in an auto accident this evening as they were traveling to some family function."

"What happened?" I asked with some foreboding creeping into my brain. I wasn't sure if I wanted to ask the other question, but I knew that I was going to be told one way or the other. Maybe a little later was my thought.

"It seemed so similar to the chase you had the other day with Judith Rogers in the same car," Freyer stated somewhat analytically.

"How could I forget?"

"Well, Prich," Freyer said very deliberately, "you weren't driving this time. David Rogers was at the wheel tonight, and he didn't get away like you."

"Was anyone hurt?" I said.

"She was thrown from the car after it hit a very large tree and spun into another oncoming car," the sympathetic cop replied. "Rogers lost control at high speed, and it was all over."

"What about Judith?" I asked very slowly almost as a sigh rather than vocalizing any language.

"She was killed instantly, Prich," Freyer said reluctantly. "She never had a chance with her massive injuries."

"Damn!" was all I could say at the moment.

"Looked like a broken neck that did it; she probably didn't have time to suffer. It was all over for her very quickly."

"Wasn't she in a seat belt?" I asked automatically as if to put all else out of my mind.

"They both were, but hers broke; she was thrown out of the car probably as it was spinning or when the collision with the other car occurred."

"And him?"

"He didn't even have a scratch," the cop said as he shook his head. "I think the air bag saved him. The major impact was on her side, and the door was wrenched open. It appeared as if she was thrown clear."

"Did you get anything on who was chasing them?" I said, still numb.

"Not a thing," Freyer indicated with a frown.

"We got less this time than when they chased you."

"What did David Rogers have to say?" I said with a growing feeling of rage.

"Not much at all," the cop answered, as he was shaking his head. "He said that he thought that the chase car may have hit them in the rear, and that's what sent them out of control. The rear of his car did have some damage to it; our lab guys are checking that out."

"I'm not so sure that'll be much help to you," I told him. "The chase car was stolen the last time, and it's likely to be the same this time."

"You're probably right," Freyer conceded. "We already thought of that."

"Didn't he say anything to help?" I asked.

"He seemed upset and concerned for his sister," Freyer told me. "We tried to press him more about some type of motive, but he only continued babbling about his sister. We understood his grief and thought he wasn't any good to us right then."

"What better time would you ever have," I argued strongly. "Give him any longer, and it'll just be more time to concoct some kind of phony explanation."

"You really don't like that guy, do you?"

"You're beginning to get the idea. He's a slick one. I wouldn't trust anything he might like to tell me. I think he's got to be involved in this thing in some manner, and I'd love to prove it!"

"Well, I saw his grief, and I don't think he was faking that."

"He probably wasn't faking or trying to do a con job then," I argued. "It was later when you asked him about the motive of that whole affair. I think he knew what was happening, and I believe he knew something when I was chased by that Chevy. He's involved in something, and he's doing a good job of concealing it from us."

"How do you figure?"

"There's just too much happening, and you know it!" I said strongly. "What're the chances that one of the founders of the company gets murdered, and then all the rest of this happens? It's too much of a coincidence; you know it as well as I do! I'm not even sure that my experience tonight with Hobbs wasn't tied into this entire affair!"

"Sure makes sense," the cop volunteered.

"What makes you say that?" I said with an inquisitive inflection. "Is there something else that you haven't told me yet, or do I have to drag everything out of you bit by bit?"

"The rap sheet on the fellow you picked out tonight indicated that he had some ties to some very mean people."

"What does that mean exactly?"

"I'm not necessarily saying the New York mob," stated the overworked cop as he pushed back the hair on his head and scratched his face as if to keep alert, "but I'm talking about people who have their fingers into almost all of the rackets around this entire metro."

"Organized criminals!" I yipped loudly and

drew the quick attention of several other cops sitting completely across the other side of the immense room. "You're saying we're involved with the Mafia?"

"No, I'm not saying that at all," Freyer groaned as he was holding both of his hands palms down, suggesting that I keep my voice lowered.

"Then what?" I moaned a bit quieter.

"I'm not sure how these guys are connected today," answered the weary cop. "I do know they're mean as hell, but they aren't any worse than the drug gangs. Hell, they'll put holes in you today if you just look at them wrong."

"Yeah, I hear about that all the time," I said as I was shaking my head in agreement.

"Well, remember how you described the first encounter with that Chevy, Prich?"

"Right," I replied as it was also making sense to me too. "That Chevy driver wasn't any amateur and that's for sure! He handled that car like a real pro. I'm not sure if I could have gotten away from him, if he hadn't peeled away from us when I was heading here. Everything about that episode seemed very professional ... a stolen car and the driver disappearing into thin air as soon as he stopped the chase."

"And what about tonight with that Hobbs fellow?" said Freyer as he sat down on the edge of his desk.

"Yep," I answered, "they had all the earmarks of a couple of pros. It happened so quickly. Rogers is tied to Hobbs, and they're both catching the devil from people who are pros. We both might be a little slow, Amos, but things are certainly beginning to smell a lot stronger than they did a short time ago."

"You're right about the smell," added the cop with a smile.

"Also, good buddy," I added as something else came to mind, "I don't believe either of those car events or the Hobbs affair was meant to kill anybody. I think they're trying to send a warning or frighten the devil out of someone."

"Think so?" asked the cop.

"Well, look at it this way," I continued as I slapped his knee to make sure I kept his attention; "they beat and kicked the living stuffing out of Hobbs tonight, but they didn't kill him outright as they could have done very easily. All they had to do was take him outside in the back and pump a couple of slugs into that thick head of his. That would have ended it all and very quickly indeed. No, they were sending him a message, a very strong and not very subtle message that they wanted him to understand the very first time."

"I see what you're talking about, Prich," Freyer said as he nodded his head in agreement. "They probably didn't want to kill anyone tonight either, but it just worked out that way with a lot of bad luck for that poor lady thrown in. They didn't bomb the car or run over anyone. Could've easily put a couple of slugs in their heads also, but all they did was chase their car and give it a good bump to add to their fright. I guess it really did the job, but more than they bargained for."

"What a terrible shame for Judith," I said with tears welling up in eyes. "You sure that her seat belt broke?"

"No," confessed the cop. "I'm not really certain if she even had it on."

"I'm not sure if it really makes too much difference for your police work," I stated with a sniffle as I wiped my eyes and blew my nose with my hanky, "but maybe it would for the insurance. They might say it was some contributory negligence on her part that caused her death. That would considerably reduce the insurance company's monetary responsibility which would certainly please them to no end."

"Right about that, Prich," conceded Freyer as he frowned and shook his head. "Better get that police report straight and accurate. It'll likely be used in civil litigation as well as criminal. I didn't write it, but I'll be nailed for sure if it causes any problems later on."

"You might think that the criminal part of this case is the most important," I stated with some authority in my voice, "and you're probably right at the present time. It's later, when all the smoke clears, that the really big aspects of money come to bear with the civil portion. It's the most important part of any case. Right now, I want someone to pay for her death in something more than dollars. I want them to lose something much more precious than their money!"

"We're in agreement there, friend!" asserted the cop with a stern expression. "I believe we're getting close too. Something is going to break soon. I can feel it in my bones. Just be careful you don't become a casualty too."

"Now, don't start on me," I groaned as I rose and patted the good-natured cop on the back. "You're beginning to sound like my father, and one is enough, thank you."

There wasn't much else that I could do that sad evening except go home and get some sleep if that were possible. I had some quick work that I needed to do, and I wanted to be rested and alert. Freyer walked with me out to my car and ribbed me a little about parking in their official parking lot. I told him that I would have used the police chief's slot if I would've found it. He laughed and said he would get back to me as soon as he had any more information on Hobbs.

He waved as I pulled out of the parking lot and thanked me for coming by his office. I knew now why he'd insisted on my coming by the police station rather than just having a phone conversation. He simply didn't wish to tell me over the phone that Judith Rogers had been killed. That was very considerate of my friend. It wouldn't be forgotten.

I slowly drove home much sadder than I'd arrived. I'm not sure what I felt for Judith Rogers, but it was something more than I'd been willing to admit to myself or anyone else. I'm not sure if anything more would've developed with her, but I surely would never get another chance to find that out. It made me very angry and deeply hurt. I believe that I was mostly disturbed because I felt impotent. I needed to do more than just sit around and gnash my teeth with no useful information. I wanted someone to pay, but I knew that I couldn't just go around swinging wildly. I needed to be controlled to be effective with that sinister crowd. I also needed more pertinent information— information that could expose the guilty individuals and extract the painful payments for their crimes.

Who would speak for the dead? Judith needed to have some person speak for her. I wanted to be there as her advocate, as she surely wouldn't be available. She had to have someone like me to act for her now. I was volunteering to do whatever I might with my limited power and authority. I wasn't sure if it were more out of a feeling of revenge or a need to help Judith in some way, since she could no longer help herself. Maybe I simply needed to end that feeling of helplessness or ineptness.

Sleep didn't come easily that night. My mind raced from one possibility to another. Was there something that I was overlooking or any path that would provide a better solution? I finally succumbed to the blessed sleep more out of frustration than fatigue.

Chapter 16

Loans

Somehow I made it through the night, but wasn't sure how much rest my body received. My mind and emotions were still in high gear. I once found myself walking around doing strange things with no meaning. I noticed that I was standing in front of my closet before I'd showered. I picked up my toothbrush in the bathroom first, when brushing my teeth was the last thing I usually did after showering and shaving. My mind was out of sync, along with my physical being.

Eventually, I put my act together somewhat and plodded down stairs to breakfast. Everyone seemed preoccupied with his own life and only acknowledged me out of simple family courtesy. I poured myself a cup of coffee and settled on a nut Danish instead of my usual corn flakes and banana. That finally drew a comment from mother, as she always wanted her only son to be well nourished, which meant one banana daily. When I mumbled my agreement to her instructions, father asked if everything was all right with me. He unhappily noted that I'd arrived home late, which meant that I was my klutzy self and had awakened most of the family and inhabitants of this old structure.

"Was there something important happening last night, Prich?" father said more as a courtesy rather than a true interest.

"I only wish that I didn't need to find out," I answered with an unintended mysterious phrase.

"I'm not sure that I understand what you're trying to tell me," father replied with some growing interest. "Could you please be more specific?"

"Remember the Rogers daughter that I attended the Kennedy Center with last week?" I said with some hesitation and foreboding that I didn't wish to be the bearer of more extremely bad news.

"Yes, I do," he stated as mother also nodded in the affirmative.

"She died last night in an auto accident," I stated as calmly as I could without interjecting any inference of possible criminal activity.

I'm not sure if that approach worked as father became intensely suspicious after that point. His questions became much more specific. Mother caught my emotions first, and she could see the dampness in my eyes after a short time. She came to my defense as father was very interested in the immediate cessation of our firm's activity with the Rogers & Emory Company. I came around to father's position and admitted that his thinking was probably the best for everyone, but I was going to stay as Judith's only living advocate, even if everyone else deserted her.

"Father, I agree that the firm should conclude its business with the company and submit an invoice promptly," I said with emphasis in my voice.

"That'll mean that you'll stop your activity

also," he added with his natural firmness.

"That isn't what I said," I told him.

"What exactly do you mean?"

"I only want you to terminate our firm's business with them," I replied.

"Doesn't that indicate that you'll also terminate your activity there?"

"Normally, yes," I continued, "but not in this instance. I want to continue with this until there's a natural conclusion or I believe I've done all that I can reasonably do. I concur that we should bill them for our charges up to this current date, but I want to find out what's happening at Rogers & Emory. I also need to find out why Judith Rogers died."

"I'll instruct our staff to do what you wish, Prich, but I want you to reconsider your continued involvement with that company. All the violence could easily spill over to you, especially if you threaten them with exposure."

I told them both that I understood and appreciated their concern for me. I still needed to continue my efforts until I was satisfied that I'd done my full measure. I wasn't hoping to become a martyr, but rather I wasn't backing down just because they weren't using civilized rules. I planned to use every resource that I could think of and keep my head down in the process. Whoever these people were, they certainly had my attention. No one could ever claim that I didn't have my full share of that sense of self-preservation. I even felt like jumping behind something when a kid popped a balloon. It wasn't in my nature to be a foolish hero. Those wonderful character types never seem to have too much longevity in this dangerous world.

As I was tidying my small hamlet, about to leave for the office, the phone rang with an annoyed Kate ready to start our beach weekend. We'd put this weekend off several times already, and I wasn't looking forward to this discussion.

"I'll never rely on your promises again," came the first salvo from Kate.

"You've got me confused, love," I responded with all the charm that I could muster under the circumstances. "What promises are you talking about?"

"You promised to call me last night," she growled. "Don't tell me you forgot me that soon. We were going to make some plans for this weekend, remember?"

"Oh, yes, I remember now."

That evidently was the wrong response as she understood it to mean that she was something like priority number ninety-nine. I could tell it was all downhill from there.

"When you get around to remembering me," she continued, "what do you have in mind?"

"This weekend has been overcome by other events," I told her without glossing over the truth. "I was involved in an incident last night where there might have been several professional muscle men."

"My God!" Kate exclaimed. "Are you all right?"

269

"I'm okay, but the fellow that I was meeting is in the hospital right now."

"So how does that change our weekend?" she said with some uncertainty.

"Someone was killed about the same time at another location," I answered.

"Who was the fellow who was killed?"

"It wasn't a fellow," I answered with some intonation that carried through to Kate. "Her name was Judith Rogers; she was involved on this same case that I'm currently working on."

"You sound very upset," she stated.

"I am very upset," I answered truthfully again. "I believe that I'm more stunned right now, and it hasn't sunk in yet."

"It sounds as if she were something more than just an acquaintance with you, Prich," Kate stated with almost a questioning tone. "You really sound hurt."

"Let's just say that she was a special friend and leave it there," I said as I hoped that she would drop the subject where it stood at the time.

"All right," she agreed.

"So, I don't know what else that I can tell you now."

"Does that mean our weekend is off again?" she asked, but I thought she already knew the answer.

"I believe it does unless something gets resolved today," I told her.

"Isn't that police work?" she said with some faint hope that I might come around to her way of thinking.

I explained my current intentions to continue the investigation even though our firm was now out of the picture. She raised her objections again. However, I believe that she heard the determination in my voice, though, and understood that I would do what I wanted at that point, no matter what anyone else suggested. She also became less disappointed after I relayed the latest weather forecast. I promised to call her during the weekend at least to keep her up to date with my world. She didn't seem too confident about the prospects of my calling, but I did have the best intentions, which should have counted for something. We parted on a reasonable tone, for which I was very thankful. I had enough enemies to deal with at that time and didn't want or need to add anyone to that list.

I scurried out of the house before anything else happened to delay me. I wanted to go by the office quickly and be at the Rogers & Emory offices before my official status had changed. The drive to our offices was uneventful, but I could begin to see what the weatherman had been foretelling. As I parked at the office, I put the Mustang's convertible top up before I had a mobile swimming pool to show for all my troubles.

I scampered upstairs and found several phone messages strewn all over my desk and chair. The most important messages were from Franky and Joe Lindsey in our Accounting Department, and I planned to called them both in that order. The others could wait awhile until my effort had become considerably more stabilized. I was about to push most of the clutter aside and organize my thoughts when the intercom buzzed to tell me that Franky was on the line again.

I thought, "Okay, big guy, it's your dime, so you go right ahead and do the mental organization, and I'll do the mumbling to indicate that I'm paying attention on the other end."

"Hey, Prich," came the friendly voice booming out of the receiver, "I've been out and about with my contacts, but I haven't got too much to tell you yet."

"At least you say that you have something, right?"

"Right," he answered.

"Well, buddy, have I got a story to tell you too," I said with some emphasis. "There's another person dead and one in the hospital. This isn't a good place to be for anyone with half a brain in his head. It's looking like it's becoming a whole lot easier to become a statistic if you hang around here."

"Well, let me tell you what I've heard first," Franky told me with some concern coming through in his voice. "Scuttlebutt on the street says Rogers & Emory must be very shaky financially, as they've been out and about with feelers some time back looking for contacts."

"I'm not sure what you're telling me," I stated honestly as I didn't want to miss any information which I thought might help the cause.

"You're saying that they let it be known in financial markets that they needed a loan?"

"Something like that," answered Franky.

"Well?"

"I'm not sure if they hooked up with any money institution or not," he indicated.

"What's your best guess, and how long before you could find out more about this?" I said promptly and maybe a little strongly.

"I'm working on it," Franky responded quickly with a little defense coming through. "I only started on this full-time yesterday, and I've been working my head off."

"I know you have," I said apologetically. "I'm just not quite myself these past few days, and this death sort of threw me for a loop. I was also at the police station late with Freyer, so I'm really whipped right now. If I sound like a growly old bear, just tell me to get lost and I'll get the idea soon enough."

"Okay then, get lost!" laughed Franky with his constant good humor always shining through to give me a needed boost. "Hey, Prich, I still have several folks that haven't gotten back to me yet, and I haven't started some others. I've got your cellular number, and I'll give it a try if I can't get you anywhere else."

I filled Franky in on the previous night's occurrences with Freyer and my experiences with Hobbs. He needed to know what he was involved in. Somebody wasn't fooling around. I also needed to explain that things could become very serious without any warning for both of us. I told him where I was likely to be throughout the day, but also said that plan could fall apart very quickly. I gave Franky my cellular number again to make sure there wasn't any problem and told him that I would carry that little flip phone with me when I was out of the car. We ended our conversation, and I promised to try to be available around lunch time so we could go over our new information and try to make some reasonable sense of it all.

I packed up my gear and started my rounds like a lone Texas Ranger heading out on the prairie after the bad guys. First on the agenda was pop's office to be sure that everyone was on the right track to terminate our association with the Rogers & Emory Development Company. No problem there as father had already given the instructions for the final billing that morning. Evidently, he wasn't taking any chances since he had already billed them for most of my efforts, and we had already received payment earlier in the week. I wasn't holding my breath about how well that check would clear, but maybe David Rogers wanted to make sure that he had a lawyer, even if he didn't have anything else. That wasn't an altogether bad personal or business plan, but he'd need to look elsewhere for legal representation. Our firm wasn't a prude who believed in a utopia where all clients told their legal counsel the truth all the time. However, we usually didn't feel that we should be literally wearing a bullet proof flak jacket either.

I scampered down to accounting where I found Joe Lindsey busy with another fellow in the department. When he saw me heading his way, he waved and told the other young man that he would see him later.

"Hi, Joe," I said as I easily tapped the good natured accountant on his shoulder, "what's up with the world of high finance?"

"That's just it, Prich," Lindsey stated; "there doesn't seem to be too much happening with your Rogers & Emory group. I put out a few calls to some of my contacts, and they never heard of them connecting with any financial institution."

"Do you mean that there wasn't any activity by those folks?" I said with a surprised tone.

"I never said that," Lindsey stated emphatically. "They sure had a lot of activity going in the financial markets, but nothing seems to have connected."

"That's about the same story that I just received from a friend of mine," I told him. "He just called a couple of minutes ago, but he also said that he had a few more sources that he still needed to reach."

"Well, I'll bet he gets that same story from everyone that he speaks to because they didn't have the best prospects from what I've been hearing."

"Same here," I agreed.

"Do you know that we're probably pulling the plug on them too?"

"Right," I said promptly. "Father isn't too

thrilled with the idea of having them as a client, and I concur. There doesn't seem to be very much that anyone can find with them. Nothing seems very reliable. It seems more like a hollow organization with the same type of people running it."

"What about that Evans fellow, Prich?"

"I think he's being used; he'd better cut his ties with them as soon as he's financially able to do so."

"I had the same feeling about him. I think he's a straight shooter, even if he is a little nerdish."

"Hey, all you bean counters are nerdish, Joe," I laughed. "What's that old cliché about people in glass houses?"

"What I don't understand is how they paid their bills?" stated Lindsey after absorbing my verbal dig. "They seem to be flush with the bucks."

"What do you mean, Joe?"

"Just what I said," Lindsey continued. "They just submitted a check to us, and it cleared."

"How do you know it cleared?" I said with a growing mental dilemma as I began scratching my head and pacing from side to side. Joe had a point and I needed an answer.

"I checked their bank first," stated Joe Lindsey with a big proud smile on his face. "Then I asked the bank to put a hold on their funds for that amount until the courier arrived there to present the check. The funds are already in our account, and the problem is solved one hundred percent."

"What if I told you that we're sending out

another billing," I stated.

"Oh, brother!" complained Lindsey with a severely pained expression on his face.

"Right," I laughed again. "This one is their final billing, but don't hold your breath. It's only for a day or so, and it is also a statement of our intention to dissolve our current relationship. Father clearly doesn't want to be associated with them any longer, and this billing leaves no doubt that the association with this firm is finished."

"Then what are you still doing?" said the accountant with a puzzled look.

"You would have to ask that," I chuckled and then shook my head. "I'm going to try to make some sense out of this yet, and I'm not going to say 'if it kills me' because it just might."

I continued to tell the eager young man about the previous night's occurrences. He began to shake his head when I described my time at Freyer's office. He then told me that I might not be too bad off if I took my father's advice for a change and dropped the whole affair.

"Makes sense from your viewpoint," I continued, "but I still need to know myself that I did everything that I could to resolve this riddle. I have to explain to someone that Judith Rogers was a victim in this whole mess. I also need to feel like I'm helping her, even though I couldn't save her."

"Just be careful, Prich," cautioned Lindsey. "Those folks sound like they are really a lot meaner than the normal ones that we usually hear about."

Bingo, the light seemed to turn on, and I felt somewhat silly for missing it so long.

"Joe, you said that you couldn't find anyone that said Rogers and Emory had a sugar daddy, right?" I stated as I began a slight dance as if I needed to make it to the men's room, mucho pronto!

"Right," came his reply with a very strange look.

"Is that the end of your inquiries?" I said with great anticipation, but knowing that I probably had another source if Joe were at an end. "Have you any sources on the street?"

"That's what I've been using," answered the confused accountant.

"I've probably been saying this wrong," I stated with a big grin. "What I mean to say is, do you have any sources that are outside the normal institutions? Something like a loan shark, but not that small. Someone a business can go to if they aren't top stuff in the finance world? Some place where they might have to pay a premium over the prime lending rate?"

"I've heard of some sources like that," admitted the young accountant, "but that's all it's been. I don't know of anyone who has actually gone to any of those folks."

It was then that I saw the lights go on in his eyes too. He gave me a very big grin and slapped me on the shoulder in return. He then began nodding his head.

"What if they floated a loan and didn't make

the payments, Prich?" queried Lindsey.

"My thoughts exactly!" I boomed. "They wouldn't want to kill their golden goose, and that makes perfect sense."

"Right!" acknowledged the accountant.

"That's why they only beat Hobbs silly, but they didn't pump his head full of lead," I bleated with a charged up ego. "And that's why they were only chasing me the other night."

"It's a shame about that Rogers lady," stated Lindsey.

"Sure is," I quickly agreed. "It's probably just like Freyer thought it was. They were just trying to frighten them, but not kill anyone. Judith was accidentally killed when she was thrown from the car after it hit that tree. It's a rotten shame that she had to pay with her life for something that she probably wasn't even involved with!"

"You sure that she wasn't involved?"

"No, Joe, I can't say that I'm positive," I admitted with a frown, "but I guess that's what I'm hoping anyway."

"Well, what about the other killing?" said the accountant with a very good question.

"I've been mulling that around ever since the beginning," I stated, "and I can't put a firm handle on that one. Maybe it's because they aren't related. I have been trying to tie everything together, and maybe that's my biggest problem. Possibly they are related, but only very loosely. I might have better luck if I looked at everything in its parts, rather than trying to make every piece fit perfectly together."

"I'm not sure if I follow all of this," admitted Lindsey.

"I'm not too sure if I do either, Joe," I reluctantly admitted also, "but I do know that I need to continue for a while until I can make better sense out of it."

"What else can I do to help?" asked Lindsey with a pleasant smile.

"You've helped a lot already, Joe," I said, trying to tell him how much I truly appreciated his assistance, "by just being a sounding board and listening to me rave on. Sometimes it just helps to talk it out."

"Well, just let me know if I can help anymore."

"You might be of some assistance if you could verify what we were both thinking," I told him as I was getting up from my chair and heading back to my cubicle.

"I'll do whatever I can," Joe Lindsey promised as I was walking away. "Don't be too disappointed if my link to that type of crowd isn't as great as you might be hoping."

I was shaking my head in acknowledgment when the flip phone that I was carrying with me began ringing. Joe Lindsey had to get his parting shot as I was leaving.

"Hey, your pocket is ringing," he laughed out loud. "You'd better answer it. It might be a phone call."

I blew Joe Lindsey a big raspberry as I fumbled to retrieve the blasted cellular phone from my pocket. That blessed bandaged paw was still a great nuisance, but I finally managed to flip it open and get Franky on the line before he became tired of waiting and hung up in frustration.

"Yeah, Franky," I started before he could get a word in, "What's up, amigo?"

"Now how in the devil did you know that it was me who was calling?" Franky Angelino groaned.

"Who else has my cellular number, bub?" I answered my good-natured friend. "I'm not even sure that I should've given that number to you as it's probably costing me a fortune every time you call me. This had better be worth it, good buddy."

"Ha, with the rates that you're paying me, I should be talking to you on that thing exclusively."

"Okay, you win," I laughed. "What in the heck have you got that's so almighty important that you need to talk to me every five minutes?"

"Well, Prich," Franky yipped in return, "you're the one who said get right back to you. I'm calling to let you know that just about everyone has gotten back to me with the same answer which is no dice. What do you think of that, sport?"

"Sounds just about what I'd expected," I answered firmly. "Now I wonder how good your contacts are if I asked you to check some other sources that aren't on the official register with the White House crowd?"

"What's that mean?"

"Well, Franky, old buddy," I started, "where would a bunch of scoundrels go if they couldn't find a legitimate loan from a reputable lender?"

"Lordy me!" cried Franky in a voice so loud that I needed to pull the phone away from my ear.

"Are you with me?"

"Right on the button, bunkie!"

"What are your chances now?" I said apprehensively, hoping that he would come back with the right answer.

"What are you jabbering to me about, Prich?" came my best friend's reply. "We're wasting time right now when I could be getting a lot of very good info!"

Chapter 17

The Witness

After scurrying back to my desk to gather some notes, I headed out to stir things up. I hoped to get everything into the fastest turmoil I thought possible. I wasn't sure what opportunity I'd have with the Rogers family since they would be involved with the arrangements for Judith, but I hoped to speak with them if the time ever presented itself. At least I might speak with some others at the company without the glaring eyes of David or Evelyn Rogers. It appeared that I gathered enough attention from every other company busy-body without attracting top management's notice.

Before leaving my office, I checked with D.C. General Hospital to find out something about Ken Hobbs. It seems the song about only the good die young was right on the mark, as Hobbs had been taken off the critical list. He was listed in a serious, but stable condition. I asked if he were conscious or could receive visitors in the evening. They couldn't tell me anymore about his condition, but they did tell me the visiting hours that night. He must not have been too terribly serious since he had visiting hours that evening.

As I was just about ready to leave, I saw a new phone message near my desk lamp which I'd missed when I'd turned it on. It came in fifteen minutes

earlier and was from David Rogers at his residence.
I promptly dialed their home number, and one of their
house staff answered. David came to the phone about
thirty seconds later and thanked me for returning his
call.

"Mr. Hale," Rogers began, "the reason why
I called was to ask that you participate at the church
ceremony this evening. Judith told us all what she
felt about you, and we thought you might wish to say
a few words on her behalf."

I thought that I was a more controlled
individual with all that masculine emotional strength.
I began slobbering all over the place and told Rogers
to wait a minute while I needed to talk to someone in
our office. I went to the washroom and threw some
cold water in my face and then returned to the phone.
Some tough guy I turned out to be.

"I would be pleased to assist your family in
their hour of grief," I told him as I gritted my teeth.

"I know that she would want you there,"
Rogers continued, "and we all thank you for your
caring and understanding at this dreadful time."

"She was very special to me," I responded
as I became teary eyed again.

The conversation ended with some logistical
instructions dealing with the time and place of that
evening's ceremony. I jotted down the information
with the promise that I would be there to assist in any
way that was needed. Here I was comforting an
individual whom I was clearly intending to cause great
public harm and ridicule. The world was not clearly

so black and white, and I was having a great deal of difficulty with those in between shades of gray.

I called the Rogers & Emory company to see if they were even open for business at a time like that. A receptionist answered the phone and indicated that there was a full staff there except the Rogers family itself. I then asked to be connected to John Evans. I was told he was unavailable at that time, so I asked if Cassy or anyone else in the Accounting Department was available. I was then told everyone was in a division meeting at the moment. At least I had been able to speak to a real person rather than a computer, but the results appeared the same. That didn't seem to be my lucky day with their company as no one wanted to speak to me, not even the people I was trying to assist. You might think that I could find someone. I said the heck with it and I would just drive out there. Maybe I would have better luck in person; I wasn't doing very well the other way.

On my way out of our building, I stopped to pick up a newspaper. There was barely a half inch mention in the paper about the accident and death of Judith Rogers and the slight injury to her brother. It was too soon for the obituary, but I snipped out the small article with my pocket knife which had a tiny pair of scissors, and put it in my pocket. I had a strange feeling on my way to Rogers & Emory.

I stopped to visit an acquaintance who worked with a retail automation store and did PC consulting work on the side. I needed to verify several things that David Rogers had told me about their

285

products and could think of no one better than Freddy Wilson. I thought that maybe talking to someone else would help get me out of that sad feeling. Freddy had that wild-eyed look most of the time, and I could always see that pained expression when he saw someone as computer illiterate as me coming his way. Freddy had that "Oh, no, not him again" look when he saw me enter the shop on that bright morning.

"Freddy," I laughed when I first noticed his expression, "you don't need to run for cover. I only wanted to get a few things straight."

"Like where the on-off power switch is located?" I heard him mumble under his breath.

"Gee, it's great to meet one of these independently wealthy individuals who doesn't need any additional income. Maybe I'll hit the Lotto and be like that one of these days."

At the mention of income, I saw all traces of intellectual superiority leave his face, replaced by eagerness. The frown was immediately supplanted with a wide smile, and he even offered his outstretched hand in a warm greeting.

"Nice to see you again!" he stated enthusiastically. "I think it's been a while since I helped install that new equipment over at your law firm."

"Freddy, I'm working with a company that works in automation," I began. "They are mentioning several things which I'm not sure I understand. Would you have a minute or two to answer some questions?"

"Sure, Mr. Hale," he said with a smile.

286

"Always happy to help you folks."

"What would you think about some new software to help use the random access memory better for newer and larger game software?" I said with some apprehension that he would come back to me with some other technical question to clarify what I'd already told him.

"Sounds pretty strange to me," he answered straight forwardly to my great relief.

"Can you explain that in layman's terms?" I said with a pleading look on my face which made him break out laughing.

"Sure," he said as he continued to chuckle. "I'll give you a 'See Spot Jump' version which I believe you'll be happy and very comfortable with."

"I never read past the 'See Dick and Jane Run' chapter," I told the young nerd who was having a great mirthful time at my expense, "but give it a try, and I'll yell at the first notice of mental abyss."

"Well ...," he started with some long thought. "It's fairly simple. No software is really needed with the new operating systems or the new Windows graphical mode. Still with me at this point?"

"Sure," I told him, but wasn't altogether clear on what the Windows or operating system did. All I really understood was that my personal computer on my desk worked when I switched on the power, and it stopped when I turned it off at night.

"The operating system using the older DOS had a command that everyone could use if those games used too much memory," he said with confidence.

"The Windows graphical environment which you have on your computer manages memory automatically if the game is a Windows compatible program. Still with me?"

"You're starting to fade," I admitted to the young computer jock, "but I think that I understand. Is there anything else, because I believe you are just about at my limit?"

"No," he stated emphatically, "not unless you can tell me something other than what you have already."

"Great!" I replied with glee. "Now, it would be a whole lot easier if you wrote down what you just told me. I've got it now, but I'll probably lose it all before I reach my car."

Freddy was good enough to sit down at a PC that was up and running at the time and type out what he'd just told me. He even went beyond what he had mentioned and described the actual DOS command to activate the extra memory while working outside of Windows. I told Freddy that I would specify a minimum payment of one hour, and he would be receiving a company check from our firm soon. He only billed us fifty dollars per hour, and I thought that was very reasonable for the information that I received.

Back on the road again, I had something else to chew on. I wondered how many curves had been thrown by those folks and why they were doing all of that nonsense. Maybe I could find something more at the company if the Rogers family wasn't there. It truly might be a welcomed change. I was pulling into the parking lot in less than ten minutes and halfway expecting to see a flag at half-mast or something denoting a very sad occurrence. Everything appeared very normal except that the executive parking places were empty.

Evans was at his desk busily engaged with Cassy and two other coworkers. After getting a drink at the water cooler, I saw their small ad hoc conference breaking up and John Evans returning to his desk. Walking over in their direction, I attracted the attention of John Evans who motioned me over to his desk. Cassy even gave me a hint of a smile for a change, and I considered the old barometer theory, which says if the barometer is rising, so are the human spirits. I heard that inmates in mental institutions literally climbed the walls when the barometer was falling.

"I guess you heard about Judith?" said Evans as I approached.

"Yes, I did," I answered, my spirits diminishing. "I'm still trying to adjust to it, but it's very difficult."

Cassy was obviously listening to our conversation as she turned around in her chair to add her shocked sentiments. That brought two thoughts to bear, since I could now see Cassy mellowing with her emotions toward me if she would convey her sincere feelings as she did. However, it also showed the lack of privacy John Evans and I had with our conversation. I leaned over and quietly asked Evans if he'd like to stretch his legs for a time, and he gave me a knowing smile. He then asked me in a louder voice if I might like to see the new business plan which the company was developing. We both stood and Evans told Cassy that we would be nearby if any urgent call came in.

"What business plan were you talking about?" I said with some interest. "Usually a business plan is developed when there's a new start for a company."

"You're right, Mr. Hale," Evans conceded with a smile, "but there are instances when a company may expand with a new development and would wish to have a new business plan."

"Makes perfect sense," I told Evans as I shook my head in agreement. "I could see that happening if the company went to any financial institution for development funding or resources to expand."

"Exactly."

"Well," I stated with some exasperation, "I sure don't see this company in any legitimate financial market."

"Really!" said the shocked accountant. "Then what in the world's going on?"

"That's what I'm trying to find out, John," I answered in the most diplomatic way that I knew how. "The checking that I've done so far has not revealed any known legitimate financial arrangements."

"Well, what's happening if you can't find any legitimate contact with lending institutions?"

"I didn't say there wasn't any contact," I carefully stated. "All I know so far is that they contacted just about everybody under the sun and were turned down flat. I can't find anybody who accepted their financial condition as stable."

"But there was a great deal of influx of funds," Evans added with his eyes growing wider. "How did they get all that revenue, Mr. Hale? That's why I came to you in the first place, remember? I couldn't figure out where all the extra funds came from. Then you also found that area from shipping which seemed to balance the numbers due to some kind of returns of unsold products. It's all an accounting fantasy land."

"Maybe you folks had a new product?" I wondered out loud. "That would provide some explanation."

"Only what you already know about," Evans stated flatly with an immense frown. That fellow would never be a great poker player with a face like that. A newborn baby could read his entire life story with one look at his expression. I let it all sink in for a very long half-minute while Evans finally came to a decision.

"I believe that you just helped me make up my mind, Mr. Hale," he said with a remarkably different expression. It almost appeared as if all the stress in the world were lifted off his back, and he seemed satisfied with his life.

"Mind telling me what you've decided?" I said with some anticipation of what was coming.

"I'll start looking in the paper today and put out some feelers to several friends of mine around this area," he commented as easily as he might tell anyone that he was just leaving for lunch. "I'm going to start updating my resume' as soon as I return to my desk."

"I'll also put the word out about you, John," I told him. "After what I've learned about you, I would be doing any other firm a great favor. I've also heard Joe Lindsey brag about your ethics and abilities, and he's a hard guy to sell."

"I really appreciate what you've done for me and thanks for your kind words," he continued. "You can't believe how upset I've been with this entire episode, and I'm happy that I can make the decision now."

"Get that resume' updated," I requested with a smile, "and I want you to give me the first copy. No promises you understand, but I would lay odds you have a comparable position without missing a paycheck. I'd bet that you wouldn't need to start all over again at the bottom, John. I know that you expressed your concerns about that and also relocation. This town always needs professionals like you. Don't sell yourself short. You'll be in great demand."

"Just hate to leave Cassy in the lurch," Evans complained. "She's a fine accounting clerk who's highly intelligent. I only wished she had a degree and better credentials like some others. She's almost exactly where I was several years ago before I decided to finish my degree and continue from there."

"I'll bet that you'll always need competent personnel anywhere you go," I told him with a high degree of certainty. "She'll always be in demand if she's recommended by people like yourself. Who would you rather hire after you get to your new place: a new individual off the street that you know very little about or someone tried and true like Cassy?"

"You're exactly right, Mr. Hale."

"Well," I chuckled, "I know a lot of things that'll never put one thin farthing in my impoverished pocket."

I saw John Evans laugh for the first time that I could remember since taking on the improbable tasking. I'd just lost a person that I considered a wonderful friend at the very least and something potentially more lasting at the most. I was pleased that I wasn't so distraught that I could also still laugh and function properly. I believed Judith Rogers would've also wished that I do well if she thought as much of me.

I walked back with Evans and then moved over to Cassy's desk. She seemed surprised to see me back so soon.

"Cassy," I started with her, "I was there with your friend Hobbs the other night, and I'm very sorry that he ended up the way he did."

"My God!" she exclaimed. "What happened? I knew he liked that place, but he didn't tell me that he was going there the other night."

"I'm not sure what happened, Cassy," I told

her truthfully. "He was into a small brawl with one fellow when two other big guys came over and dragged him out the back door. I thought they were bouncers, but found out later that they were strangers to that place. We were all confused; it happened so quickly."

"What were you two doing there, anyway?" she asked, but I think she already knew the answer.

"I was trying to ask him a few questions about his function here at this company," I told her.

"I believe you, but what was he doing there, and why was he fighting with that first fellow?"

"Listen, Cassy," I said slowly and very deliberately, "the last time I mentioned anything about Ken Hobbs to you, you became really angry with me. I like you and don't wish to make you mad at me again. You had it right before when you told me that it wasn't any of my business. I'd better shut my big trap right now and not lose the friendship of a young lady that I like very much."

"You know, Mr. Hale," she laughed out loud, "I've really been a bitch, haven't I?"

"Is that a rhetorical question?" I joked. "If not, I'll take the fifth like any good lawyer."

John Evans overheard me and Cassy, and he began to howl along with the rest of us. I told her good-bye and good luck. I began packing up to see Lew Winston in the Development Division, but the remote idea struck me to ask John Evans one more question before I headed off.

"John, has anyone asked to see your

accounting records recently besides me?" I said more as an innocent question in passing rather than anything of great note.

"Well, yes," came his answer, "but only David Rogers. Any problem?"

"No. I was only curious if anyone else had access to your records."

"Oh, all right," came his response, "glad to help."

On my way to the Development Division, I stopped off in the Shipping Department and asked the same question of Stan Gross as I did with John Evans. Gross had the same answer as Evans and then turned around and asked me the same question as Evans did. It shouldn't be any great surprise that I also provided the same answer. I always hated to be so predictable, but if that were my worst fault, I guess that I could live with it.

My discussion with Lew Winston wasn't any more enlightening as it was the first time that we talked. I don't know why, but those techy types always seem to intimidate me. I usually agreed with them and nodded my head as if I understood what they were saying when I was actually completely in the dark. I had to limit my talk to what Freddy Wilson had told me, and Winston was in complete agreement. I asked if there were any new developments on the horizon which weren't widely discussed, but was answered in the negative. They were plainly in the upgrade mode with no new direction in sight.

Before I left the facility, I called D.C.

General Hospital again to ask about the status of Ken Hobbs. To my amazement, I was told that he was alert, already up, and walking a little. I asked when their visiting hours would start and was told they would begin in less than an hour and would last for only an hour. I had the later schedule, but needed the early hours now. I didn't have any time to waste and was a little put off with myself for not asking about this information sooner.

I decided it would be worth a speeding ticket to try to get there before visiting hours ended for the midday; otherwise, I'd need to wait until evening to see him. I barely had time to wave to everyone as I quickly skittered through the door and out to my car. I zipped and dodged through traffic, ran two stop signs with a hint of a rolling stop, and went flying through two traffic lights that were already turning bright pink. Remarkably, I made it there without one traffic ticket and still had thirty-five minutes left on that one hour they called visiting hours.

I was so out of breath when I arrived in Hobbs' room that I believe that I looked more like the hospital patient than he did. In fact, my gasping and red face even produced an honest laugh from Hobbs when he first saw me. He quickly grimaced and reached for his pained ribs with his one hand that wasn't enveloped in a cast. His face was a patchwork of bandages and white tape. He almost reminded me of the invisible man with all the sterile wrappings. However, I knew that he wouldn't disappear when the bandages eventually came off.

"Wow, I thought that I'd never make it here before they closed the doors," I half choked with another gasp. "I should've been more careful about the time. Sorry I didn't have enough time to pick up a magazine or something to help cheer you up."

"Well, it's good to see a familiar, friendly face," he said which really caught me off guard and took me several seconds to recover. "I'm really not any good at crossword puzzles."

"Guess I'm one of the few people who isn't here to poke or stick you," I laughed. "I don't think you could afford to give away any more blood right now, so they allowed me in for a short time."

"Thank God for small favors!" he feigned a groan. "I'm already feeling like a pin cushion."

"Sure hope you get over this soon," I said as a matter of courtesy. "Maybe we'll see you back at the shop in a limited capacity."

"That's not likely," he moaned, and I knew that he was thinking of a nice, long holiday.

"I wish that I could've helped you the other night," I said with a twinge of concealment, "but I thought that those fellows were bouncers. It looked as if they were angry that you were in a tiff with that other fellow. When I found out differently, I called 911 and got you some help as fast as possible. You really had us all worried for a time."

"Well, thanks for all you did to help," he told me which certainly surprised me as I didn't believe that "thanks" was a part of his vocabulary.

"Who in the devil were those guys?" I said

as I thought that I was beating around the bush enough by that time. "They sure were big and mean."

"I'm not sure that I know who they were," he said. I thought for sure he was lying.

"Well, they seemed to know you," I told him truly, as I didn't want my nose to grow too long today.

He seemed to be a little agitated and nervous. He understood that I probably knew he was lying, and he was trying to put a better spin on the whole concoction. He was searching for something to say which would be non-committal and yet fairly believable. He decided to test the waters with something to see how gullible I really was. Well, maybe I bought those two bridges down the street along with the big one in Brooklyn, but there's a limit to it all. He had found my limit quite some time ago.

"I was thinking about the very same thing," he began with his fairy tale, "and I believe it was simply a case of mistaken identity."

"How can that be when I heard them say your name?" I lied.

"You did?" he seemed surprised.

"You bet!" I came back quickly. "Those loan sharks knew you very well."

"How'd you know that they were loan sharks?" he snipped as his eyes became extremely wide open.

"I heard them say something about no payments, and that wasn't the first warning," I continued my story. I thought I may as well mix in a small amount of truth to make the whole story easier to sell.

"My God!" he exclaimed, but then fell silent.

I was concerned that he might have time to regroup, and then the whole ploy would be down the drain. I needed to be fast on his thought process and keep a fire lighted under him at every moment.

"You're very lucky that we scared them off when we did," I stated with emphasis. "They looked like they had all the intentions of not making a second visit."

"Thanks again," he stated trying to end the dialogue.

"Those guys are going to extract some kind of payment, or they'll kill again," I stated emphatically.

"What do you mean, 'Kill again,' Prich," he said, his face all screwed up in a painful expression. "I'm not aware of their killing anybody."

"Well, Ken, I hate to tell you," I told him while I was hoping that I wouldn't burn with the devil for all the rationalizations with the truth that I'd been using so easily, "but I believe those two guys are still after you."

"Hell are you talking about?" he growled now. "And what are you saying about someone being killed by them? You're not making any sense, and you're not answering any of my questions. Damn it, fellow, would you quit acting like a stupid-ass lawyer and tell me what the hell you're talking about?"

"Well, Ken, I didn't want to worry you," I snickered silently, "but I thought I saw those two big fellows who are the muscle men for that loan shark downstairs. I didn't know if they saw me, but I didn't want to take any chances, so I came up the stairs rather than use the elevator. That's why I was so out of breath when you first saw me a while ago. I climbed all the way up here on those blasted stairs."

"Oh, God!" he exclaimed again. "You sure it was those two?"

"No, I'm not," I answered as sincerely as I knew how, "but I didn't want to take any chances. I know what they did to you, and I couldn't take the slightest chance. They also scared the devil out of me, and I didn't want to get into any confrontation with those gorillas. They're way out of my league. Those animals are pros!"

"Christ, they could be right outside at this very moment!" he yipped with visible panic. "Prich, if they come in, you've got to do something to help me."

"What can I do?" I asked as I tried to conceal my joy at his obvious discomfort.

"Can't you negotiate something for me?" he pleaded with a grimace. "And what did you mean about someone getting killed by them already?"

"Sure, I'll try to help you," I told him as the drama rose in his eyes. "Just tell me whatever you want me to say to get those killers off your back. You know that I'll do anything that I can to help."

"Christ!" he yipped again. "Can't you level

300

with me about all those statements about someone being killed by them? You're driving me nuts, and I'm stuck in here like a sitting duck. I need to know what's happening, and I'm cut off from any news. For God's sake, tell me what you're talking about!"

"I thought you knew," I answered with a straight face as I continued to lie through my dental work. "They tried to kill David Rogers last night at the same time they got their hands on you. Well, they missed him, but killed Judith in the process."

"I don't believe you!" he yelled with his crimson face and bulging eyes. "I never heard of anyone being killed!"

"Judith was certainly murdered by them!" I cried out for the shock effect.

I then reached into my pocket and produced the newspaper article about the terrible wreck. Hobbs grabbed the small slip of paper, scouring the few phrases and mouthing the words at the same time.

"Oh, no, oh, no!" I heard him say several times.

"Now do you believe me?" I growled to keep him off balance.

I saw him shake his head to acknowledge me, but he remained silent in the process. I believed that he was about on mental overload and that was exactly where I'd hoped to have him. I needed to press him hard at that point, since I might never have him at that level of anxiety again. That mental stress was almost better than truth serum. I saw him look away with moist eyes, but I couldn't believe that he was grieving over Judith Rogers. He probably was upset that his soft living in that fine world was about over. It was very easy to see that egotistical maniac worry that it was all ending. Selfishness came easily over concern for others with his lot.

"I asked you," I growled again which startled him and made him jerk in pain, "do you believe me now?"

"Yes, I believe you," came his straight forward answer as he continued to look away.

"Well, Ken," I started with the big lie, "David Rogers was so distraught and mentally unnerved that he babbled everything to the police."

"Oh," he mumbled as if the wind were kicked out of him.

"Right," I jumped right back. "He told them everything, and they couldn't stop him from talking."

"You mean that he spilled everything?" he said with wide questioning eyes. "Even about Em—"

"He sure did," I replied very quickly while the iron was still sizzling. "He told them about getting all that money from that loan shark, and he spilled the beans about why. Then he blurted out about Joseph Emory."

"My God," he mournfully wailed, "that big mouth might get me fried in the chair!"

"Ah, ha! That sucker iced old man Emory for David Rogers to get complete control of the firm," I thought, but remained silent for a short time. I wondered what else that I could pump out of the dimwitted loud mouth and now admitted killer.

302

"How long do you think that he could've gotten away with it all?" I said and primed the pump a little more.

"He didn't need much longer," he said; "the deal was just about concluded."

"Didn't they suspect anything about what they were buying?" I primed some more. "They couldn't be that stupid."

"You can't believe what they'd swallow," he stated with an air of superior satisfaction. "Those stupid venture capitalists were so anxious to dump their money into the high tech field that they swallowed everything we fed them. It was so easy!"

Just at that moment, the door to his room swung open quickly, and we both jumped. I thought that it was the nurse who was about to tell me that visiting hours were over. Instead, I heard that announcement over the PA system, and visitors were politely asked to leave promptly at that time. At the same moment, I saw Hobbs' face and a genuine look of surprise. I turned to see Evelyn and David Rogers slowly walk in with a small vase of flowers. I looked back at Hobbs as I heard David Rogers say that he was sorry they were so late, but they'd been given permission by the head nurse. The expression on Hobbs' face slowing changed from complete surprise to open mouth bewilderment and then to anger.

"Hell's going on here?" Hobbs yelled.

"We were concerned about you," stated Evelyn in a confused tone as she looked over to her brother.

303

David Rogers shrugged his shoulders and then gave me a questioning stare. I only smiled in return and then looked at the confused, beautiful face of his sister.

"I don't mean that!" yelled the excited Hobbs. "I'm talking about this lousy creep in here with me!"

"He can't be talking about me," I chuckled loudly.

"What's he saying?" yipped Evelyn.

"Beats me," I answered with a laugh. "Sounds like maybe he became upset with you folks. I can't understand it. He was perfectly fine until you came in.

"Sure, you dirty bastard!" Hobbs yelled again loudly.

"What's he talking about?" asked the puzzled David Rogers as he walked closer to the bed.

"You want to tell him," I asked with a chuckle, "or should I?"

Everyone looked at everyone else while I stood there with a big "Cheshire Cat" grin plastered all over my face. I finally asked who wanted to go first.

"You tell me what he's talking about," David Rogers commanded Hobbs with an extremely stern expression.

Hobbs looked angrily at me while I began laughing. I turned to look at Evelyn Rogers, but she was giving her brother her full attention. David Rogers then fired his attention back in my direction.

"What's he talking about and why is he so upset?"

"I think he half-expected you to be behind bars by this time," I told him honestly. That felt good to say, and it was more than just being honest. I felt better by venting some anger at the individual who indirectly was responsible for Judith's death.

"Have you been shooting your big mouth off?" growled a very unhappy David Rogers at the bruised and battered Hobbs.

"You dirty son of a —," I heard as I whistled out the door and down the hall.

I knew that Hobbs and the two Rogers would be going at it for a time. I could hear all three of them yelling and going at it as I strolled away. As I turned the corner, I saw the head nurse coming my way in a hurry.

"What's happening down there?" she said with a very stern expression.

"I'm not sure, but I'd suggest that you simply stand outside and only intervene if you think it's becoming violent," I told her as I read Marge Havener on her name plate attached to her white blouse.

"I think you're right," she said as she scurried to the door and remained standing outside. She appeared to be listening outside the door, and I saw her shocked expression several times.

"She will make a wonderful witness," I said out loud to myself as I began singing with a wide smile on my face.

Chapter 18

The Bent Nose Crowd

The exit from the hospital was a reasonably joyous experience. I was never very fond of hospitals, anyway. The smell of those infirmary type institutions does something to the hair on the back of my neck. I've heard it called the white coat syndrome and that's fine, but I'm always stressed out with the first smell of the site before I even see any white coats. Leaving a place like that is always an uplifting experience, similar to finishing a final examination in college.

I was so high emotionally, patting myself on the back, that I almost missed the huge man standing at the reception desk and his partner looking into the gift shop window. They were the very same two "gentlemen" that politely parted Hobbs' hair so neatly in the alley behind the night club last evening. I was only using them as a ploy before, and I wondered if Hobbs would believe me now. I quickly turned my head away from the pair, but they were both distracted with other things besides me.

I made it out the front door in a hurry and walked quickly to the Mustang in the parking lot. I called information on my cellular phone and got the number for the hospital. I called Hobbs' room and got the confused, angry man on the line.

"Yes," came the growl.

"I thought you'd be happier to hear from

me," I snickered over the line.

"What in the hell do ...," he started to yell at me before I cut him off in mid sentence.

"You can take this any way you want," I started with a sobered voice and no humor, "but I just saw those two loan shark guys that put you where you are now. They're right downstairs in the lobby, and I'd suggest that you all get the heck out of there. You know, they also want to get their paws on the Rogers, and maybe that's how they found you there. They probably followed them right to your doorstep. I'm not pulling anyone's leg now, so you'd better all hit the road and I mean pronto!"

I hung up the phone and motored away very happy with myself. The drive back to the house was a pleasant experience, and I was a happy fellow as I came bouncing into the house. Romney and Renate were playing a little pinch and tickle in the kitchen, and I broke that up like a spoilsport with a pair of amorous dogs and a bucket of cold water. I guessed my day was coming, and I heard that paybacks are the devil.

I grabbed a left over jelly donut from this morning's breakfast and a diet cola and headed for the loft to get some rest and thinking done. Don't ask me about the logic of a jelly donut and a diet cola. One was good for my waist line and the other wasn't. It didn't make any more sense than many other things that I did, but it sure tasted a super-jumbo lot better.

I first called the head nurse, Marge Havener, at the hospital to find out how things went after I left.

At the time, she was busy elsewhere, and I left a message asking her to call. I began updating my diary and index cards and thought that I'd better get in touch with Franky before I did anything else. I called his home, but he was also out somewhere. I left a message with his wife, Sandy, to give me a call when he returned. I was about to return to my index cards when the phone rang, and I figured it was one of my calls being returned.

"David Rogers here," came the surprising voice over the receiver. "I was calling to make sure that you'd be attending the ceremony for Judith this evening. We didn't have a chance to speak much at the hospital today, and then Ken Hobbs went into a fury when we arrived. What was that all about, Mr. Hale? He didn't seem too perceptive when we arrived."

"I was only teasing him about the other night at the bar with those two huge muscle men," I fabricated a quick answer, thinking Hobbs didn't want to tell Rogers that he was tricked out of the terrible truth. "I told him that he appeared like a wimp compared to those fellows, and he immediately went berserk. Maybe they pounded him on the noggin' too much."

"Don't worry about it," he laughed with a piercing shrill tone that made me believe that he wasn't too despondent about the loss of his dear sister. "He's always like that about his masculinity. I thought that he was going to take a co-worker's head off once when the poor guy joked about his being a slow jogger.

You should have seen the fit he threw that day, but he was over it all in a very short time."

"Were you there when I called him back a short time later to warn him about my seeing those same two guys that worked him over?" I asked, but I already knew the right answer.

"Well, no," he replied after a short pause, "as a matter of fact, we were asked to leave a short time later by that head nurse as visiting hours were over. She didn't let anyone stay too much later. I hope that he made it okay if those thugs were coming after him."

I agreed with him about Hobbs making it out of there safely. However, we both knew that he did just fine as he was escorted by the Rogers pair, and he made it away very nicely with their help. Rogers then went on to explain in some detail about the logistics of the ceremony and my part in the eulogy. He intended that I speak as a potential partner in her life who may've been left before any full opportunity. I truly felt some loss, but I didn't think I was ready for that full commitment in life, so why now in death? I shied away from his intended theme and only promised that I would speak of Judith as a blossoming new friendship that ended prematurely. I neglected to mention in full that my association with the entire Rogers family might also be ending before it normally would.

After hanging up the phone, I went right back to organizing the index cards into what I knew, and everything fit. There was still a nagging question

about Joseph Emory, although I couldn't pin it down.
I could understand why they wanted to get Emory
out of the way, but he was only interested in helping
a friend start a small business. Emory wasn't in it for
the big bucks or the glory. He would've been happy
just to recoup his initial investment. The older Rogers,
Charles, was the same as Emory. Charles only wanted
to enjoy his elder years with golf buddies and his wife
Sarah who loved horses. Why kill Emory who was
only there to help his friend and his friend's family?
Greed and ego: Had to be because he would've had
many of the bucks one way or another. I was still
deep in thought when I was startled by the phone
sitting right next to me. Marge Havener at D.C.
General Hospital was returning my call fairly
promptly.

"Is this the gentleman who asked me to stand
outside that room today?" she said cautiously with
an uncertain voice which told me that she'd probably
heard a doozy of a tale.

"Yes, ma'am," I replied quickly, "I'm the
fellow who was in Mr. Hobbs' room when the Rogers
family entered, and then I left. I saw you in the hall
and didn't want you to walk in on them. I just wanted
you to hear their conversation. My name is Prichard
Hale and I'm an attorney. I'm conducting an
investigation of the Rogers & Emory Company, and
I needed to have some impartial individual verify their
discussion."

"I certainly wish that you hadn't asked me
to do that," she said with a firm voice.

"I can appreciate that, Ms. Havener," I told her in all earnest truth, "but someone had to hear them besides me if they're ever going to be stopped. I'm sorry that I had to involve you. However, you were the only person available at that precise moment in time."

"I know," she indicated with a woeful tone. "I just wish it would've been someone else."

"Don't we all?"

"Well, what now?" came her reply with an intonation of resignation in her voice.

"Did you hear anything that would be beneficial to the authorities?

"I sure wish that I didn't, but there was a loud argument with the two gentlemen. The lady came in later with a terrible voice which was impossible not to hear."

"Did you hear anything damaging?"

"If you call conspiring to murder an old man damaging and then to steal all the resources of the company a problem."

"Did they actually talk about killing the old gentleman?" I asked with my heart pounding.

"They certainly did, plus in great detail. Do you know that the lady distracted the old gentleman while our patient, Mr. Hobbs, killed him with a pipe?"

I almost soared right out of bed. Those arrogant fools must've felt so confident about their terrible deeds that they thought they were omnipotent. I couldn't quite fathom my good fortune, but I couldn't wait to hear what Amos Freyer would say about this.

I could hear his cheering now.

"Did they mention who they were trying to swindle with their company?" I was excited now. "Did they mention anyone by specific name?"

"Yes, they did, Mr. Hale." My heart soared again.

"They actually named names?"

"Yes, they did!" she exclaimed as if I didn't believe her, and she was trying her best to convince me that she was telling me the entire truth.

"Great!"

"But, I forgot the specifics right at the moment," she stated as my emotions went right down the proverbial toilet. I could mentally hear the flushing at that second.

"You forgot the specifics?" I moaned out loud.

"That's why I write everything down, Mr. Hale," she stated into the phone as I felt like the phoenix being resurrected out of the ashes.

"You wrote all they said down?" I asked with obvious joy in my voice.

"Well, yes, I did," she answered promptly and efficiently as a head nurse might. "I found that I need to do that with my position as a head nurse on this floor. I need to keep track of all sorts of things, not to mention all the medication. If I didn't write everything down, I would be in very big trouble really fast. It's just a way of life with me."

"Can I get by to see you in a short time to make a copy of your notes?" I said hopefully. "I suggest that you Xerox several more at your copy machine. The police will probably want your originals."

"Are you calling the police?" she said with a frightened tone in her voice.

I didn't want to scare her off now. She was the rock solid clincher to the entire conspiracy, and the last thing I wanted to do was scare her away. I wasn't sure of the exact tact that I should follow with her, but I remember the old cliché about honesty being the best policy. I wasn't sure about it here, but I thought it would be best to be forthright with her in the very beginning. I couldn't blame her for being upset, but I knew that we would all lose her if she caught me in a lie now.

"Ms. Havener, the police are already involved with this investigation," I told her, but didn't get any response. "They were involved since almost the beginning with the murder of that poor old gentleman. I've been cooperating with a Detective Amos Freyer, and I expect he'll be the individual you'll be dealing with very shortly."

"I see," was her only response.

"Where's Mr. Hobbs now?" I said. "The police will be very interested in knowing his location as soon as I speak to Detective Freyer."

"Well," she said with some strength returning to her tone. "We moved him very quickly right after he received a phone call from someone telling him that two thugs were coming up to kill him in his room. Both Rogers came running out of the room as I was pretending to enter, and we ran into each other. They said that they were moving him up one floor when I told them where a free room was. They asked me to call the police as there were some criminals in the hospital. They were the same ones that beat up Mr. Hobbs and put him in the hospital in the first place."

"My God!" I yipped without thinking. "That sounds like a wild few minutes for you!"

"It sure was! I helped get them all out of the room, but we had a time with Mr. Hobbs. He could barely move in the shape that he was in."

"What then?"

"We quickly got them down to the freight elevator," she continued with some excitement in her voice, "when the two big criminals came up in one of the passenger elevators. Those big guys asked me about Mr. Hobbs, but I told them we'd released him earlier in the day. Well, they had to see for themselves, so they poked their heads into all the rooms on the floor. When they were satisfied, they left. Right after they got onto the elevator again, I called security as soon as they were out of sight.

"Did security apprehend them before they left the area?"

"Not our security, Mr. Hale," I almost heard her laugh. "They're just rent-a-cops that'll steal you blind if you give them half a chance. Don't ask them to put themselves into anything that could be harmful."

"Ms. Havener," I said as sincerely as possible, "I hope you understand how much this all means to me. I truly don't know how to thank you properly for all your help."

"Well, Mr. Hale," she said very purposefully, "I'm relieved now that I know that this whole thing is being handled by the police too. If it wasn't, I would keep as far away as I could. If I have to become involved, I want it to be official."

"I understand and fully agree with you," I promptly told her. "Is Ken Hobbs reasonably safe in his new room?"

"Security said that they'd keep an eye on him, but you already have my opinion of security."

"I'll get in touch with Detective Freyer, as soon as I hang this phone up," I assured her. "I'll also be on my way to see you and get a copy of your notes."

I thanked her again and hung up. I was about to call Amos Freyer with the news when Franky returned my call. I told him that I was just about to leave the house, but I needed to speak with Amos Freyer first. I explained that things were popping rapidly, and I would call him back on the cellular phone as I was driving down to the hospital to see Marge Havener. Franky hung up quickly, and I was dialing Amos Freyer the next second. Freyer answered the phone, but seemed somewhat irritated that I was using some of his valuable time.

"Yeah, Prich," he began with a moody groan. "What are you looking for today? Maybe some free tickets to the policemen's ball?"

"What would you say if I told you that I know

who killed Joseph Emory and can probably prove it? I've been out and about dodging thugs and gaining some evidence. Want to tell me what your day was like, bunkie?"

"Sure you have," he responded doubtfully. "Got any prime swamp land in Florida you want to sell me too?"

"Not today, good buddy," I assured him with a chuckle, "but you'd better get a pencil and paper and take good notes because I'm out the door in sixty seconds to pick up a very damaging transcript of a conversation between three murder conspirators. Just tell me when you're ready, sweetheart, and I'll start jabbering away to your little heart's content."

Freyer said, "Okay, go."

I started relating the hospital tale. I gave him times and places and told him about the financial conspiracy with the loan sharks. Freyer told me, "Sure you did," several times and then began to believe me when I mentioned specific names.

"You mean that you've got that Hobbs fellow stowed up in that hospital still?" Freyer came back with some disbelief. "If you're on the level, that guy's life isn't worth a plug nickel with your picture on it. They're going to grind his tail up in tiny pieces and feed it to the fish in the Chesapeake Bay!"

"What can I tell you, love?" I told him with a loud laugh. "I did my part and don't you believe it's about time to start doing yours?"

"Okay, smart ass," Freyer growled as I laughed in return. "Where in the hell is he exactly, and I'll arrange for some very fast protection. Until then, I'll get the hospital security to cover his tail."

"You'd better get the real thing first, big guy!" I told him emphatically. "And you'd better get it there fast. That nurse I told you about described those rent-a-cops just one level away from an Amazon sloth. Speed and intelligence simply aren't their strong suits."

"This is all on the level, Prich?" said Freyer cautiously one last time. "If you're snowing my tail, I'll be the laughing stock of the entire department."

"Listen, darling," I whispered with a slight chuckle. "You're going to look like the sharpest cop in the world after all this breaks in the paper. Remember one thing, sweets: I don't want any notoriety or publicity out of this entire mess. You can have all the credit. Mum is the final word with our firm. When they want a hero, just stand up and push out that beautiful chest. I'll be standing in the back row cheering like the best fan you'll find in your entire life."

"You sure that's the way that you want it?" said Freyer in amazement.

"That's the way it has to be, love," I told him happily. "Have you ever known it any other way with me?"

"Well, I remember getting shafted several times before with you, fellow," Freyer moaned. "I'll get right on this with my staff here and call the D.C. Police Department to coordinate things. I'm sorry that this isn't all in one jurisdiction, but it seldom ever works out that way."

"Great," I said as I was pulling myself together to go back on the road as quickly as I could. "I'll call you after I get my hands on that signed statement. If your friends arrive before me, please tell them to let me get my job done, and I'll be out of their way very quickly. Good luck, I'll talk to you later."

I threw a couple things together and was out the door and on my way. Father saw me for a minute as he was coming home from work. I told him it was all ending very soon and that I'd brief him later. I did tell him that Detective Amos Freyer was now taking over the bulk of the investigation. I was only aiding him to bring everything together at the end. He wasn't entirely satisfied with that short explanation, but he saw the great hurry that I was in. I started motoring back downtown to the hospital and called Franky back on the cellular.

"Didn't take you long before you were back on the road," came Franky's upbeat voice. "Glad to hear you're making some headway; maybe my information will help."

"Every bit helps," I told Franky as I jammed on my brakes to avoid someone cutting me off. I'd forgotten that I had timed my departure from the house during a high traffic time, even though it wasn't rush hour.

"Most of this that I'm telling you is street talk, you understand," he qualified his statements up front, "and I'm not sure too much of it would stand very well in daylight or a court of law. I even went down into some of the seedier sides of town to get this information."

"Sometimes it's the most reliable kind, even though it can't be used legally, like you said," I told him.

"What would you say if I told you that I heard the Rogers & Emory company was probably on the sales block?" Franky said with a great deal of pride coming through.

"I'd ask which venture capitalist is it and how close is it all to final signature stage?" I replied with a question. "This is the part that could probably be used to nail those jerks in a court of law."

"How in the world did you have all that information?" Franky said disappointed. "You just asked me for this information, and you already seem to have most of the answers. Why in the devil have I been working so hard?"

"Now, Franky," I said with a calming tone, "don't get all your feathers ruffled. I just found out about the venture capitalist this afternoon, but didn't get a name. Things have been breaking so fast in different directions that I can barely keep up with it all. That's why I called on you, good friend. This thing is in the blitz stage, and I've called in Freyer to make it all legal."

"You know that turkey always takes all the credit!" Franky complained. "I can't understand why you keep going back to that cop when I know several others that would be very happy to work with you."

"We have an understanding, remember?"

"Yeah, I know about your relationship," he ruefully admitted, "but I still think it stinks."

"I do too, sometimes," I conceded, "but it can't be helped. What about the buyers? They still around and interested?"

"You had it right when you said buyers, Prich. There were actually two venture capitalist-type companies vying for the business. One only wanted a partnership type of arrangement where the current owners and managers would stay to run the firm. The other potential buyer was so thrilled with the prospects of stealing a cash cow like the Rogers & Emory company that he actually wanted to bring in his own staff for a short time and then resell it. I heard that both had hopes of doubling their money within one year. It's really a wild time of it out there in business land. It's kind of like a school of sharks swimming around in a feeding frenzy, everyone trying to get a bigger bite, and they sometimes end up biting each other."

"Right!" I said as I needed to jam on the brakes again and dropped the phone in the process. Some pedestrian tried to make himself a hood ornament on the old Mustang. I didn't think that fellow would add to the value of the old classic. What really added insult to injury was the jay-walking pedestrian sneered at me as if it were my fault. He almost had a galloping pony permanently imprinted on his overstuffed posterior. I smiled and told him that I hoped he had a good day. He was still mouthing something as I watched him in my rear view mirror.

"Sounds as if they were both throwing funds at Rogers, and he wasn't telling either firm about the other one," Franky continued after I got control of the phone again. "That Rogers fellow must really be a snake oil peddler, since he's got venture capitalists and loan sharks chasing each other's tails. It's one of those 'Who's on First' skits, and it's almost funny to watch."

"Maybe it would be," I told him, "if people weren't ending up dead. I'm going to go out to a chapel this evening to speak about another friend that I just lost because of Rogers' games. It might be funny, but I surely won't be laughing tonight."

"That's why I'm keeping a very low profile," Franky replied. "You really can't afford to lose your last friend on this wonderful Mother Earth."

"Right," I said as I drew it out. "Now, what about those two venture capitalist companies? Do you have their names yet, and do they smell anything funny?"

"Sure do, bunkie," the good humored friend chuckled. "There's Reynolds Investments and also Jenkins Technology Innovations. Reynolds seems to be the most aggressive, but Jenkins is right on their tail. I don't believe that either one of those groups know or even want to know if anything appears wrong. They seem to have put their heads down and said, 'Buy, buy, buy!' The few questions that I have put around only seem to have driven them faster. It's like they're afraid that someone else is going to beat them to the prize, and they want to have their bid accepted first and shut out all the other competition. It sort of reminds me of the last savings and loan scandal where all the S&L's fought over the bad loans to see which S&L could write the most loans in the least amount of time. Well, some of them certainly set some kind of a record, and it seems that some of those folks never learned a blasted thing."

"The way you describe it, Franky," I interjected, "I believe you're correct."

"Sure, then throw in the loan sharks."

"That's right. They got snookered into this too."

"More than that," laughed the good friend. "They were even battling over whose turf was what. Appears as if the bent nose crowd from the old established mobsters won the prize, and the street dope South American guys gave in and let them have this one. Boy, do I ever hear those guys laughing about it on the street. The bent nose crowd doesn't want to admit that they were taken by that amateur Rogers, and they're still trying to find a way to make him pay something so they can save face. It was almost funny to listen to until they started looking at me as some kind of source, and I beat a fast trail right out of there!"

"I don't blame you one bit, Franky," I half scolded my best friend and then thought that maybe he was right about being my only friend, "but you were crazy to take those kind of chances."

"'You gotta know when to hold them and

know when to fold them' so I got out of there faster than you ever saw me move before."

"Hey, big guy," I teased a little as I was now sitting in a traffic jam two blocks long before a short stop light that appeared to be malfunctioning like so many other things around here. "I've seen you move faster than high speed film when we were somewhere that hands out a check for chow. It's no wonder you're so darn wealthy. You never picked up a check in your life!"

"Yeah, well, stuff that, old sport," he laughed out-loud. "I always pay the tab when I'm with you at the Chain Bridge Club."

"Hold it, amigo," I responded quickly, as I always won points in debate class or moot court; "you know they always put the bill on the tab and send out a statement to your house at the end of the month."

"Hey, Prich, I've got some expenses already with this job, and I don't see you running my way with an expense voucher."

"Listen, love," I chuckled. "I've got enough trouble with my own expense voucher as I'm doing all this for gratis for a day or two. Now you let me in on Sandy's big inheritance, and I'll pick up everyone's expense voucher last week."

"Okay, you win, Prich."

"Ha, that might be the only thing I've won this silly week. I just want to sit in the corner and sing, 'Oh, poor me,' in my flat beer."

"What now, Prich?" he said getting back to the task at hand.

"First on the agenda is get out of this traffic jam. Next, I need to pick up the statement from that nurse at D.C. General Hospital. Then, I'm heading home and preparing for the ceremony tonight."

"Want some company when you go over to the Chapel tonight?" Franky asked, and I was tempted to give it the big macho 'No' automatically, but I hesitated and thought about it for a moment. "Franky, can you make it over to my place in about an hour and a half, and we'll go there in your car?"

"Can do," came his welcomed reply.

"Okay, good buddy, over and out."

Chapter 19

Tattered Tail

I thought that I'd need to spend an hour or more at the hospital to see Marge Havener and then pick up her statement. I called her as soon as I hung up with Franky, and she said that she would meet me in the hospital lobby. Sure enough, she was true to her word, though I was apprehensive about her fulfilling her promise.

As soon as I walked into the lobby, I saw her standing over at the reception desk. My heart took a giant leap when I didn't see anything in her hands. I just knew that she had second thoughts, or maybe some friend had told her all of the terrible things that would follow if she did sign any statement. I started to feel my head droop somewhat, but I decided to give it the old law school whuppie and thank her for all that she already had done.

"Nice of you to meet me down here," I told her with a smile. "I need to go to a memorial ceremony for a friend who passed away, and this saved me some time. The traffic tonight has been something to write about for a weekend, and I'm running a little late."

"Well, Mr. Hale," she began, "I just didn't wish to draw attention to myself and you."

"Oh," I responded with one of my famous comebacks.

325

"Let's walk over here to the gift shop, and we can talk for a minute," she said as she returned my smile.

As she began to walk away, she reached over to the reception desk and picked up a plain manila folder. She looked at me again and flashed a very wide smile and then handed me the folder.

"This is only a copy," she stated as my heart soared and my pulse nearly doubled, "but I signed it and a very close friend on the next floor witnessed my signature. Both signatures are originals. Will that be good enough? I wanted to keep the original version myself in case anyone tried any funny stuff."

"Great idea!" I told her with a stammer and a gulp. "I'd do the very same thing as you. The copies are just fine with the way you signed it, and the witnessing is a real bonus."

She beamed with pleasure as I concurred with her analysis. I wasn't pulling her leg either - I knew it was worth so much more with an original signature and a witness. This fine lady had watched too many TV law shows, but there were some things that weren't as fictional as we lawyers would want anyone to believe.

"I'm sorry that I had to be involved with this. But, once I heard what they said, I needed to speak with the authorities," she related as we were parting. "You certainly helped in that regard, and you were true to your word about promptly involving the police. They were outside Mr. Hobbs' door in less than a half-hour. They're screening everybody who even gets close to that door."

I thanked her again, and I headed out of the building to my car. As soon as I could get that file open, I leaned back and began to read. I wasn't sure if a court reporter could have been more comprehensive than nurse Havener. Hobbs really didn't tell Rogers anything about our conversation we had and that explained Rogers' attitude with me when we spoke later.

Their conversation seemed as if it were beginning to heat up when my phone call interrupted everything. Evidently, David Rogers was very upset that Hobbs had irritated the loan shark and that brought on the harsh actions. There was even one name of a venture capitalist mentioned. The most damning language was by all of the participants concerning their perfect plan to get rid of Joseph Emory. I sort of felt sorry for Evelyn until I read her dialogue. She may have been the most vicious of them all. My intuition had been correct about which Rogers female to become involved with. I didn't read one word of Judith's being implicated with their evil, nor did I read one bit of remorse that she was now gone.

Knowing that anything might happen with that small precious folder, I stopped at a small post office on the way back home. I made two copies, mailed one to my office and put the other in another folder for Freyer. I could see that little package brightening his day as well as any present he would ever hope to receive.

I was somewhat weary when I returned home. However, the wonderful aromas emanating from the kitchen raised my spirits considerably. I quickly went to my room for a quick shower and shave and a change of attire. I barely made it to dinner on time, but it probably would have appeared odd if I started a new trend. Father had his usual half-second stern look in my direction, and then we were served a luscious meal.

I was prepared to brief my father, but I wanted him to initiate the occasion. As we were all contemplating dessert, he broached the subject, and I was prepared with the folder that I was about to present to Freyer. Father opened the folder and yummed with delight as he ate a spoonful of pudding with his free hand. He sat there and continued reading and then laid down his spoon. He needed to free himself from all distractions as he grasped the importance of the document.

"The police don't have this in their hands yet?" questioned father with a statement as his eyes shined with incredulous shock.

"Freyer will be opening the very same folder as you in less than an hour," I responded with a smile of satisfaction. "What is your opinion of nurse Havener's account of the hospital visit between all the principals?"

"She actually stood directly outside their door and clearly heard them speak all those words?" he said as he shook his head in disbelief. "How did she ever come to do such a thing?"

"I simply asked her to do that as I was leaving from my visit to see Ken Hobbs," I told him as a large smile appeared on his face. "It's a wonder that she would even speak to me after her experience, but she's being extremely cooperative."

"I can see that," he continued. "How did she ever remember all of this dialogue and information and then set it down on paper later?"

"She told me that she immediately went to her work station and began writing just after it occurred. She said that she's trained to remember every important detail such as medication and doctors' instructions and to write them down immediately. It's a normal function of her profession. Evidently, she's very proficient as she's become the head nurse of that section."

"Wonderful," he said with a large smile and a nod. "I was just thinking as a defense attorney would for a second, and you provided a superb response. She will certainly make a great prosecution witness. And I can't speak highly enough about having this document signed and witnessed. It almost has the weight of a deposition. If anything should happen to that nurse, the prosecution still has this."

"Super!"

"And we are finished with it?" he said as his eyes studied me closely.

"I'm handing this off tonight," I honestly told him. "There might be a few loose ends, but I can't think of anything of any great significance."

"Please keep me informed of tonight's

developments," he instructed as he returned the damaging document to my side of the table, "and please take great care even though you believe it may be finished. Others might not share your opinion and continue to be violent."

I agreed with father as I tucked the folder under my arm and headed back up to my loft. I called Freyer and was lucky to reach him the first time. He agreed to meet me and Franky at the chapel in a short time, and I told him about the document that I was handing over to him. He wanted to arrest the Rogers' duo as soon as possible and take Hobbs into custody at the same time. I did some fast negotiations with him and persuaded him to wait until after the service for Judith. He agreed to my proposal if I would fax him a copy of the document immediately. I told him that we had a fax machine in father's study, and I would send it to him after hanging up the phone. I was true to my word and was picking up the last page from the machine when Franky appeared at the door. We were off to the races as I climbed into the passenger side of his car.

I read the statement to Franky as he drove along. At one point where they were discussing the Emory killing, Franky pulled the car over to the curb to read the document himself. I guess some people believe things just are not reality unless they are in black and white. Franky believed it when he read it.

"I can't believe they would be so foolish!" Franky exclaimed. "Didn't these people ever stop to consider the consequences of their actions?"

"Greed and arrogance," I responded. "Some people will do almost anything for that buck."

"Think it was all for the money?"

"I believe that was a good part of it," I told him thoughtfully, "but I also think that it was as much for their egos. They didn't want to admit that they failed with their business even though they were spoon fed and supported by their father and his friend."

"They were basically thieves," Franky retorted.

"I give them even less credit than that.. They thought they were businessmen and women and they failed. They thought they were thieves and crooks, but they were caught. They tried to be killers, yet they'll probably go to prison for their trouble after blabbing about it around someone willing to be a witness. After a batting average of zippo out of a thousand, the best that I could give them is incompetent losers."

"You're probably right," chuckled Franky with a twinkle in his eyes, "but you're maybe a little too kind about it all. Let's see what Freyer has to say after he gets an eyefull of this piece of paper."

"He's probably reading it about the same time as you just did."

"Wow!"

"We'll see in a minute or two," I told him as we pulled back onto the road and continued to the chapel.

As we drove into the parking lot at the chapel, Freyer was arriving with an additional police car and two uniformed officers. I handed him the folder with the document enclosed and he even thanked me. Franky made a face when he heard that surprising remark, but remained silent. I half expected that he might make a digging remark as there wasn't any great love lost between my two good friends. Several people were gathering outside and gave our group a strange look as they continued.

John Evans and Cassy pulled in the parking lot next to each other. They both stopped beside our group, and I introduced everyone. As Evans and Cassy were walking away, Franky asked Freyer if he'd made arrangements to have Hobbs arrested for Emory's murder. I saw Cassy put her hand to her mouth and turn around to return to her car. I asked if she were all right as she passed, and she told me that she felt somewhat nauseated and needed to go back home. I returned my attention to Amos Freyer as I needed to make sure to have his plan straight.

"Amos, are you going to let this service continue without interrupting?" I said quietly.

"It's against my better judgment, but I'm going to play it by ear," he responded with a doubtful expression. "I want everyone to watch me as I might give you a cue at any time. If you see me start, all bets are off, and we are taking the perpetrators into custody immediately."

That seemed fair enough to me, and I thanked my friend for his consideration. He was going out on a limb for me and also the memory of a good friend of mine. I hoped it wouldn't come back to hurt him. I was going to help see that it didn't.

The ceremony went without a hitch, and I presented my eulogy in the order outlined in the small handout. The minister had a touching few comments, and then he asked if anyone would wish to comment. David and Evelyn Rogers proceeded me, and I was the only non-family member to speak. I said several things about her character, but I told them about our deep friendship and lost opportunities. Charles Rogers followed my appearance and then a receiving line was formed with the entire family standing at the casket. I never did view Judith that evening as I continually averted my eyes from that area.

Most of the people had exited the facility when I saw Freyer at the end of the line. I must admit that my attention became distracted by the intense feeling of the ceremony, and I fully became caught up and part of it. Freyer and his team had their priorities established somewhat differently, and they were now in action. His officers were positioned at the exits, so the Rogers' duo never had a chance. Franky and I stood at the door as they passed in handcuffs, but neither of them would give me the slightest glance. The elder Rogers had a surprised and confused expression as they exited and he stopped to ask if our firm would represent his children. I empathized with the kind old gentleman, but I respectfully declined. I did, however, offer to refer him to several other top criminal defense attorneys. He seemed further dismayed, but accepted and thanked me for my assistance. He was gracious to the end.

As Franky and I were standing beside his car in the parking lot, Freyer drove past with one officer sitting beside him and the Rogers sitting in the back. Evelyn gave me a strange empty stare as they passed, and I thought I was lucky to have kept my distance. Franky and I drove home discussing the merits of the evening. It had all gone well, and I was pleased to have it ended. Franky wanted to go to the club for a celebration, but I begged off. As he dropped me at the house, I bade him a good night and promised a later celebration.

I called Freyer after we returned. He had an attitude like I had blind-sided him, and I had to soothe his feelings without understanding what he was talking about.

"Why in the devil didn't you tell me about her!" he seemed to yell over the phone as I held the receiver away from my ear.

"What in the world are you yipping at me about?" I said with a great deal of confusion.

"You are always sandbagging me!" he continued his moaning. "And now I've sure got egg all over my trusting face. All you needed to do was give me a little warning and then maybe the D.C. Police Department wouldn't be raising all kinds of hell with me right now."

"If you would just be a little more coherent," I responded in defense.

"You're saying that you didn't know about that girl that you called Cassy tonight?"

"That's what I'm telling you," I came right back.

"Well, remember her telling us that she was sick when she turned around and went back to her car?"

"Right," I said as I was trying to think of something unusual about her appearance or activity. "I do remember her doing an about face fairly quickly outside of the chapel. Come to think of it, that was about the time that Franky talked somewhat loudly about the murder of Joseph Emory."

"I'm not sure what provoked her, but she tried to kill Ken Hobbs tonight at the hospital."

"What?" I heard myself yell into the phone.

"You heard me," Freyer growled at me.

"What happened at the hospital?" I said with my mouth still wide open. "Was anyone hurt?"

"She got past the cops on duty at the door by telling them that she was Hobbs' girlfriend," he related slowly at first. "The next thing that anyone knew, she had a pair of hospital shears that they cut tape and dressings with. She was stabbing that jerk, while he was squealing like a pig that just had its tail pulled. The cops at the door came rushing in as she was sticking those scissors right in his rear when he was trying to scramble out of bed."

"Was he hurt very badly?" I stammered.

"Only a couple superficial wounds, but nothing life threatening."

"What about her?" I asked with great

335

trepidation creeping into my thoughts. I hoped that I didn't contribute to any of her new troubles by a misstatement.

"She was taken into custody by the D.C. cops. I'm not sure about the charges yet."

"That's really wild," I told him. "Have they taken him into official custody like you did with the Rogers?"

"Yes, they did right after that incident with that woman," he responded. "We'll be working out the details later tonight and tomorrow. That protective custody status has officially changed, and he has been moved to the prisoner section of the hospital. He's just as safe there, but he can't decide to walk out anytime the notion occurs."

"Great!" I told him.

"You sure that you didn't know anything about this?" he asked again as if he didn't believe me the first time. "Positive and thanks for your help," I said as I hung up the phone.

I kept mulling over this incident that Freyer had just told me about at the hospital. Why would Cassy do such a thing, I wondered. It didn't make sense that she would attack Hobbs when she always defended him previously. I opened my diary and began to look at the beginning of the investigation. Something still was amiss as I continued to have that strange feeling somewhere on the back of my neck. I looked at the diary and then at the index cards.

Emory's great wealth was still not involved with the Rogers company. That was only a side diversion for a friend to help his son. He clearly had his beneficiaries named with a portion going to charity. The lion's share went to a Cassandra someone that no one ever heard of. It was supposed to be his illegitimate daughter. Cassandra could easily be a Cassy! Why not? I'll bet it was! Maybe that explained it all. But why would she be just a common clerk in the Accounting Department at Rogers and Emory? I clearly had some quick checking to do, and I surely needed to talk to pops about that Emory will that he was handling.

I shoved everything aside and picked up the phone. A couple seconds later, Kate McCain came on the line.

"Is that you love?" I said in my most upbeat charming voice that I hoped would transcend my absence.

"Prich?" she asked with a puzzled tone.

"Right love," I answered with an upbeat tone. "Sorry about calling so late, but I just returned from the memorial for Judith Rogers."

"And now you're lonely, right?" she groaned with a rueful tone.

"Hey, I'm always lonely for you," I told her, "and I was sure that you didn't want to go to something like that for a weekend date."

"Now that all of the grim things are over," she started, "what did you have in mind for the balance of the wrecked weekend?"

"That's why I was calling you," I responded with some growing hope. "I've been working so hard for more than a week, and finally I have some free time. I was hoping that you hadn't forgotten me by now. You can ask Suzie Q, kiddo, no fooling around at all by me. It's been all work, but I've been wanting to see you for so long now."

"Okay, quit whining, you big lug, and get yourself over here in about a half hour."

"You don't need to ask me twice, love!"

I was downstairs and about ready to leave when father called me aside. I quickly briefed him on the evening's occurrence and then my suspicions about Cassy's connection to the late Joseph Emory. He was very surprised and thanked me for all my efforts. He said that he would get the staff right on the possible connection to the missing heir to Emory's estate when the office reopened. He then told me that he was very happy that I had come out of the entire enigma without being hurt. It felt good to hear him say those kind words to me, and I thanked him as I was happily exiting the door.

I was outside Kate's door in record time as the old Mustang could perform well when the chips were down. Kate and I had a drink and talked about the possibility of an abbreviated time at the beach if the weather held out through the next day. That sounded extremely good for a change. It would be super to have the warm sun on my face while watching the breakers come in and someone I cared for next to me. That sounded great, but not nearly as wonderful as what Kate had planned for me that night. Wow! What a night, indeed!

Chapter 20

Epilogue

I can't begin to tell you what a wonderful time Kate and I had for the balance of the weekend, if you don't consider sunburns and sand ticks. Some of the romance did wane with complaining each time we applied the Aloe Vera cream to our baked faces and limbs.

When we returned for the new week, I was already involved with a grand domestic dispute between two very notable families in the social register who both had gay children who dated each other. Now, the kids had a super relationship, but the parents wanted to become grandparents. Both families were almost charter members of our firm after all those years and thought I could resolve the current problem as easily as we always had in the past. Some extraordinary new assignment, right? Go figure.

The Rogers family was even less fortunate than I. The two remaining children of Charles Rogers looked as if they were going down for the last time with all the evidence and bad press to add to their woes. Hobbs was copping a plea to testify against David and Evelyn Rogers. Freyer told me that Hobbs would probably end up with less than ten years after cutting his deal with the DA.

Cassy was another story entirely. At first I was completely bewildered by her and even more by what might be the outcome of her involvement with Ken Hobbs and the late Joseph Emory. Both, I'm happy to relate, are success stories. I can be proud, in some part, but it might be difficult to find a direct line to my front door. Some things in this world aren't as clear cut as we'd like them.

It seems that she was the illegitimate daughter mentioned in the Joseph Emory will, which meant she should inherit a vast sum of money. I brought her to our firm where she and pops worked through all the complicated aspects of the provisions of the will. It appeared that she had discovered her relationship to Joseph Emory several years before. She wanted to know something of the stranger before she'd ever commit to an open relationship. She found her opportunity with an opening at Rogers and Emory and hoped to learn more about the man while he wasn't aware of her. She could always walk away if she didn't find what she had hoped to discover. She was almost at the point where she would reveal herself when Joseph Emory was murdered. That event almost destroyed Cassy with guilt as she could've shown that gentle, loving man that he had a daughter cut from the same cloth.

Cassy was also the great beneficiary of the partnership agreement of the Rogers and Emory company. The previous attorney who constructed the partnership agreement had the standard right of survivorship clause in the agreement, but Emory's lawyer had been very skeptical of those blanket type clauses that often led to mischief with one of the parties. He also had a kick-out clause that stated the entire assets would become the property of the deceased side of heirs if anything illegal caused the dissolution of the partnership. Thus, Cassy received it all: lock, stock, and floppy disks.

Even more strange, the loan sharks didn't have any legal agreement with the company, so Cassy kept all the assets, while the Rogers family had to pony up the bucks or face the wrath of the bent nose crowd. That brought a wide smile to my face when I first heard it.

Father had several long discussions with the authorities about any criminal charges brought against Cassy. Those charges were dismissed after Hobbs failed to sign a complaint against the lady whose father he'd murdered. What's the big deal anyway? All she did was stab him in the rear several times before she was restrained. I count him darn lucky. He had been lying on his tummy at the time and then yelled like an insulted piglet. He could've been singing soprano had she arrived five minutes earlier. Darn lucky, indeed!

The last is for the fellow who started all that headache for me. Mr. John Evans, whom we all thought was a nerd and whom I told to leave the company, became the senior vice president working for the gal who was his subordinate a few months previously. Between Evans and Cassy, the firm had begun to show an honest profit with real new products. The last time I heard, he'd even been seen in a social setting with the same lady he'd been supervising. It seems Cassy decided a bright and faithful nerd was light-years better than any of those wild macho types.